"All right, Mr. Taylor. If I have any more questions, I know where to find you."

Mark Taylor started to ease himself out of the booth but then paused. He didn't want to leave.

Andi raised her eyebrows.

"You know, Sheriff," he said. "I'm a pretty good investigator. I spent a few years working the crime beat for the state paper before I came here." His skills might be a little rusty, but he thought offering to help might get him into the tight-lipped sheriff's good graces. Getting any details out of her was next to impossible. "I'd be happy to assist with your investigation. We could exchange information. Sure would make my job easier and the story better."

She nodded. "Thank you, Mr. Taylor. I'll let you know."

He shrugged one shoulder and stood. "I guess I'll just have to stick close to you, Sheriff Jackson. For my readers."

Dear Reader,

A Minute on the Lips began with a single scene that popped into my head as I was driving. I was taking a break from a local writer's contest and mulling over how I could write a beginning chapter with mystery elements.

I was also lost. This happens to me when I explore new places.

While driving in circles in the small town I'd chosen to explore for the day and searching for a fabric store, I passed a diner on the town square. The group of business-suited men gathered out front sparked an idea and became a collection of fun characters I'd never met. I enjoyed finding out their stories.

I hope that when you meet them, you'll smile, too.

Cheryl Harper

HARLEQUIN HEARTWARMING

Cheryl Harper

A Minute on the Lips

Recycling programs for this product may not exist in your area.

ISBN-13: 978-0-373-36666-8

A MINUTE ON THE LIPS

This edition published by arrangement with Harlequin Books S.A.

For questions and comments about the quality of this book, please contact us at CustomerService@Harlequin.com.

HARLEQUIN®
www.Harlequin.com

Printed in U.S.A.

CHERYL HARPER

discovered her love for books and words as a little girl, thanks to a mother who made countless library trips and an introduction to Laura Ingalls Wilder's Little House stories. Whether it's the prairie, the American West, Regency England or earth a hundred years in the future, Cheryl enjoys strong characters who make her laugh. Now Cheryl spends her days searching for the right words while she stares out the window and her dog Jack snoozes beside her. And she considers herself very lucky to do so.

For more information about Cheryl's books, visit her online at www.cherylharperbooks.com or follow her on Twitter: @cherylharperbks.

Deciding to call myself a writer has been a scary and amazing journey. I'm lucky enough to have great family and friends who never hesitated to encourage me, thought I could do it when I wasn't so sure, and always laughed in the right spots. And I owe a special thanks to my friend Susan, who took me to my first writing workshop and has supplied so many great titles like *A Minute on the Lips* through the years.

CHAPTER ONE

"OTHER DUTIES AS assigned" should be etched on Sheriff Andrea Jackson's office door. In fact, that could be the entire job description wrapped up in one neat phrase. As she drove into town, Andi had no idea what the day might bring—investigating, wild-animal wrangling, babysitting or some crazy-making combination of all three with an added wild-card adventure.

Andi made the full circle around the red-brick courthouse before she headed toward the office. As she pulled to a stop in front of the sign that read Reserved for Sheriff, Nettie, the part-time dispatcher, walked out to meet her.

"Morning, Sheriff, hon. Jackie over at the diner called to demand an investigation of his crime scene." She held up a cup of steaming black coffee. "I think you better head on over there first thing."

"Thanks, Nettie," Andi mumbled as she latched on to the cup and dragged it through the window. Caffeine didn't do much to wake her up after sleepless nights, but it did signal to her brain that it was time to get to work.

Campaigning and elections made it hard to sleep. Instead of getting up to do something productive that calmed her worries—like knitting or reading or eating half a gallon of ice cream—she'd stubbornly clung to her pillow and given herself the "go to sleep" lecture. That never worked. Neither did logically pointing out that she had only *this many* hours to sleep. One worry led to one regret, which led to a long guilt trip or a short visit to Anxiousville, population: one. The middle of the night could be rough. As the number of hours available to sleep shrank, so did her ability to do anything other than stare at the clock.

After a quick sip of coffee, Andi buckled her seat belt again and waved. "I'll head over there first, Nettie. If anything important comes up, use the radio."

"Sure thing, Sheriff, hon," Nettie answered. "Good luck!"

Andi nodded and pulled away. Nettie had

been a bingo buddy of Andi's grandmother since bingo was invented. Even though Andi was an adult member of the county's law enforcement team, Nettie had a hard time adjusting, so more times than not, she said "Sheriff, hon." It didn't bother Andi enough to try to change it, and she needed every good-luck wish she could get. This was not her first run-in with Jackie. He took his food very seriously, had the sheriff's office on speed dial and loved the threat of a good lawsuit.

As Andi rolled to a stop in front of the diner, she thought the town of Tall Pines might be at full capacity. It was going to be hot again, but cars lined both sides of the two-lane highway through the middle of town. October was the height of the season, and even though it was unusually warm, traffic had picked up accordingly. Arts-and-crafts fans meandered along the sidewalks. They might have wandered on into Jackie's Country Kitchen except he had the door barred and a small group blocked the entrance.

Andi could see Jackie's beady, excited eyes over the top of the crowd. He was standing on the bench he'd pulled over to block the door to the diner. Andi would need to get that fixed pretty darn quick or she and Jackie would both be on the mayor's hit list.

Andi glanced over the crowd as she asked, "Jackie, what seems to be the problem?"

Jackie wrinkled his brow in an ugly frown. "Sheriff, the problem is that I've got a crime scene here, and I don't want any of these suspects or looky-loos to muddy up the evidence."

Right. Andi nodded, hoping Jackie would think she cared as deeply as she had the first time she'd answered one of his calls. Or even the second or third. Then she hadn't realized how frequently she'd be giving Jackie the same nod. Now she knew better than to get her hopes up for a real case. "Why don't we go inside and have a look? And we can move that bench right back under the window, to get things back to normal."

Even before she got the second sentence out of her mouth, Jackie was shaking his head. The few red hairs that remained on top stirred in the weak breeze. "No, ma'am, first get statements from every one of these suspects. Then I'll let you in to look around, take your fingerprints and do any of that forensic investigation. You better hurry it up, though. I'm losing the breakfast crowd."

Andi stifled a heavy sigh as she looked at the crowd of "suspects" and decided it would be easier to go along with Jackie at this point. He wasn't going to like that her forensic investigation would be sorely lacking. She could take fingerprints and get some photos, but considering the crowd that went through the diner, unless she found something really out of the ordinary, she'd have a hard time calling anything she found evidence. Thanks to television, everyone expected her to have a crime lab, a source at Homeland Security and a psychic in her back pocket. In most cases, Andi's resources were limited to her powers of observation—which were pretty good. She was also lucky to work with talented deputies. For almost two years, they had been enough to stay on top of petty crime, not-so-friendly disputes, domestic violence calls, small drug busts and general safety concerns in Tall Pines. No laboratories needed.

Andi pulled out her pad to take down the names of Jackie's suspects. As Andi surveyed

Wanda Blankenship's tiny tank and long, lean legs exposed by very short shorts, she nearly convinced herself that Wanda was guilty of whatever had been perpetrated. Any woman who looked as good as she did with that much skin showing had to be up to no good. Feeling just a little guilty about judging Wanda's book by its cover, Andi straightened her shoulders in her neat, perfectly serviceable uniform, smoothed back any hairs that had escaped her no-nonsense ponytail, and asked, "Wanda, do you want to start?"

She shrugged. Andi figured she had to be innocent. There was no way she could hide a murder weapon or the crown jewels in that outfit. "Sheriff, I was jogging through town when Jackie grabbed me."

Jackie bent to point a bony finger in her face. "You were running away from the diner. If you didn't take it, you saw who did."

"Has something been stolen, Jackie?" Andi was surprised. And excited. Traffic tickets and accident reports kept them busy, but *this* was the kind of work she'd signed on to do.

He narrowed his eyes at Andi. "Yes, but I won't say what it is. One of these people knows and they'll confess." He turned to face the man lounging beside the door. "Or else."

Andi watched the stupid smirk cross the stupid face of the way-too-smart newspaper editor and suddenly felt hot under the collar of her uniform. There was always a gleam of mischief in his gray eyes, as if he could see right through her. Mark Taylor had moved into Tall Pines to take over the paper almost two years ago. And then he'd taught her a very valuable lesson: never trust a reporter. Following his leading questions, she'd been too helpful, too prominent, too speculative. Determined to show just how well she could do her job in the early days after her election, she'd given him way too much information on the county's domestic violence stats for an article he'd been working on, and she'd been paying the price with the local business and community leaders ever since. And instead of appearing only in the Tall Pines *Times,* the story had gone to the state paper, painting a stark picture of what really goes on behind closed doors even in quaint tourist towns.

Everything he'd printed had been true. He just hadn't told the whole story.

People had stopped her on the street to explain how stupid they thought she was. And she'd gotten one angry, vaguely threatening note in her mailbox at home. She wanted to hate him for it, but he'd been doing his job. He sold a lot of papers, and she should have been wiser. It had been an excellent lesson: a little truth could travel a very long way in the hands of someone determined to twist it. "No comment" was her favorite answer any time he called now. Since then, unless something was part of the public record or a feel-good piece for community outreach, she'd made up her mind to say as little as possible to anyone who might write it down and publish it for the world to see. She'd also stopped reports to the local radio station and had to think long and hard before she answered any emails to her office.

None of that kept him from calling, emailing or stopping her on the street to ask for updates or quotes. And sometimes she thought he did it just to annoy her. For him, it wasn't that hard.

Obviously she couldn't trust Mark Taylor. But he bothered her more than she'd care to admit. He was always rumpled, but it was hard to pinpoint the problem exactly. Maybe it was his hair. He knew his way around styling products. Hair that perfectly messy and adorable had to be worked at, didn't it? And it wasn't his height. As the girl who'd held down the middle of every back row of every class picture all the way through middle school, Andi knew a thing about height. And Mark Taylor was only average. He'd certainly never played center on the high school basketball team. As Andi studied the smirk on his face, she figured him for a fast, sneaky guard, the kind that would score before she even knew he was in the neighborhood. And that was likely the problem. Mark Taylor was smooth. And Andi distrusted both the eternally rumpled and the naturally smooth.

He'd moved to town and slipped right into the flow as if he'd always been here. Andi had heard plenty of stories about his Little League sponsorship, his volunteering to help the high school yearbook staff and his charming smile. The ladies of Tall Pines loved him and loved to talk about him. She'd been born and raised here. The only family she had was here, but Andi still felt so out of step some days.

As Mark's eyes met hers, his left eyebrow rose. And that one small gesture reminded her she was supposed to be investigating… something. "Sheriff, you have any questions for me? I'm completely at your service, but yesterday Joe Sales told me the fish are biting and Spring Lake is calling my name."

She shrugged and did her best not to blush at being caught off guard. The only solution was to cut to the chase. "What brought you to the diner, Taylor?" He'd rattled her with one question and a mobile eyebrow.

He pointed at Jackie. "This one called me before I even made it out the door and demanded I get over here. When I asked him why, he said I knew why and I better get to the diner or I'd be in serious trouble."

"And do you know why?"

He smiled slowly and shook his head. "Nope. No idea. But it might make for an entertaining story." He shoved his hands in the front pockets of his jeans. "Entertain me, Sheriff."

Jackie propped both hands on his hips.

"You were the first person I thought of, newspaper man. I know you're jealous of my recipes. I better not see any more turn up in that blessed newspaper or I'm gonna lawyer up, you see if I don't."

At last year's chili cook-off, Jackie won again, as he had every year since the contest started, but Mark, the new kid in the pot, won second place and published his recipe, minus one secret ingredient, in the paper. Jackie was convinced the recipe had been based on his. He'd never been able to explain how Taylor had gotten it or why he'd steal a recipe to alter it, but Taylor had produced a stained, handwritten recipe and a character witness in the form of his mother to prove his innocence. And he'd taken Jackie's accusations the same way he took everything: with a joke and a laugh. If Jackie was a man who took his cooking seriously, Mark Taylor seemed to be a man who took nothing seriously. Well, maybe nothing but the news and how well it sold, anyway.

Andi noticed Mark Taylor noticing Wanda and wished she could arrest him for something, anything, but that's not a game she wanted to play with the newspaper man, especially in an election year.

Before Andi could question the other man at the scene, Jackie's busboy, Oscar, Jackie motioned at him. "And Oscar didn't see anything."

Oscar nodded. Andi and Oscar looked at each other and waited. Apparently that was his best answer. One quick glance at Taylor showed he was politely refusing to laugh. Andi had no idea how long that would hold out or what would happen to her temper if he did laugh. It was definitely time to get to the bottom of this.

"Jackie, why don't you show me what's missing? And walk me through your arrival."

He hopped down from the bench and pushed open the door. The small group followed him in and froze in the doorway. Winning twelve chili championships means lots of trophies. A man like Jackie puts those trophies front and center so all who enter his restaurant may be astounded by his performance. And now Jackie had a big, empty trophy case with faint outlines of where the trophies used to live.

Andi waved her hand vaguely over the large case. "All right, so your trophies...they're missing?"

Jackie's glare was intense, but what bothered Andi was the sight of Taylor taking notes.

"Listen, Sheriff, the trophies are important, but they aren't nearly as valuable as the safe. This week's receipts, all my recipes—" Jackie rubbed his forehead and for the first time Andi noticed that he was worried "—and some important papers, things of mine and Mona's...they're all gone! Worse, somebody's got 'em!" He was more agitated than usual.

Andi wished she'd spent more time mainlining hot black coffee before attempting the day. "Show me the safe, Jackie."

The whole group followed him through the swinging door and crammed into his small office. The safe door was hanging open, and the safe was empty.

"I won't rest until I have everything back and whoever stole it is rotting in jail," Jackie said. Andi didn't doubt he meant what he said.

He turned to glare at Taylor. "If it's not the no-good newspaper man, then this girl here—" he motioned disdainfully at Wanda, who looked like she'd never been inside the Country Kitchen or any other establishment that served fried food in her life "—she knows who was here. She's got a guilty look about her."

In reality, she looked mildly revolted as she surveyed the diner and tried to make herself as small as possible, as if the fat in the air might attach itself to her thighs somehow. Taylor was amused. Oscar was bored. None of them seemed interested in trophies or recipes. It was hard to rule out an interest in money. "How much do you think was taken?" Andi had no idea how much business the Country Kitchen did, but any loss would be hard to absorb.

Jackie shrugged. "Have to check my ledger, but I think I had about eight hundred dollars and some change on hand." He shook his head and strangled the spotless white towel in his hands. "Those papers are priceless, Sheriff!" Jackie grabbed her wrist and waited for her eyes to meet his. "I mean it. Those papers… they're important."

Andi spent a lot of time being annoyed

at Jackie. It was an automatic reflex at this point, but the look on his face said he was worried and maybe a little…sad. She smiled with confidence, hoping to encourage him. "All right, Jackie. Let's find them then."

With a sigh, she settled down at the counter. "First, I'm going to need a big, steaming cup of black coffee, and keep it coming."

Jackie crossed his arms over his chest and shot her an evil glare. "Sheriff, I'm losing business until you secure this crime scene."

Andi silently counted to ten. Coffee was pretty much the only forensic aid she had at her disposal. "Of course you are, but coffee helps me think. While you get the coffee, I'll take some pictures and a closer look, maybe dust the trophy case for fingerprints. Then, after you get the next cup, I'll quickly interview everyone over there at that booth."

She turned to point at the booth she always sat in when she came to Jackie's. From there, she could see both the sidewalk and the kitchen, allowing her to time the arrival of her food and anticipate any unexpected visits from the mayor or Ray Evans, the former sheriff. He'd been forced to drop out of the last election after a heart attack, but he was back in fighting shape now, fifty pounds lighter and at least twice as mean—but only to Andi. Since she'd taken office, he liked to shoot her dismissive looks, make snide comments under his breath and generally act as a thorn in her side.

Jackie stormed off as Andi approached the trophy stand. He might be hard to please, but he kept a spotless place. Wanda didn't have much to worry about in the Country Kitchen. If fat left any residue, Jackie had ruthlessly eliminated it along with any other dust and dirt. The imitation wood grain of the six-foot-tall trophy case was almost spotless. The sliding glass doors that normally kept prying fingers away were open and moved to one side. There didn't appear to be any scratches on the wood or smudges on the glass. Figuring out how a person could manage that would be a gift to humanity.

"Sheriff, I gotta say it's an unexpected pleasure to run into you this morning. May I say you're looking lovely as always." Andi could see Mark Taylor's face reflected in the glass and did her best to appear perfectly unaffected yet slightly annoyed. Despite her best effort, Mark Taylor's husky voice that close to her ear sent a shiver down her spine. In a good way.

"Annoyed" was her number-one defense. If she spent too much time around him without it, she started to think about how handsome he was and how long it had been since she'd had dinner with a man, good-looking or otherwise. Thoughts like that distracted her from how dangerous he was, how easy he made it to trust him. And that was the last thing she needed. The only time she wanted to wind up on the front page was when she won this election.

She didn't turn to face him, but he stood close enough that she could smell clean clothes and warm man. It was a good smell. Andi licked her lips and said, "I am busy here, Mr. Taylor. We can chat momentarily."

When she braved a glance his direction, his lips twitched and he gave her a small salute. "I live to serve, Sheriff. Although I am going to enjoy having the shoe on the other foot."

"What do you mean?" Andi asked.

"I mean you'll be the one asking questions

this time. Maybe I'll be easier to work with than you are." He crossed his arms over his chest and waited for her answer.

She forced her shoulders back down to their normal spot and fought the urge to fidget with her shirt. "Of course, the fact that I wear a badge and gun will help you make a decision."

He whistled and went to sit at the counter.

Rolling her eyes at how easily he distracted her, Andi thanked her lucky stars Jackie'd been preoccupied.

Andi took out her phone and snapped a few pictures of the case and the sparkling glass before she walked over to check the door. There were no signs of forced entry on the inside. There were no scratches on the lock outside the door, either. No marks on the door. No broken glass. She went back to the office to snap pictures of the safe and Jackie's spotless desk. The safe had an electronic keypad, but it was just a good, basic burglar-and-fire safe. Whoever had broken in had spent the time to get it open instead of hauling it away. But why take the trophies? This didn't feel like a random theft.

Andi made a quick trip to her SUV to pull up the field kit. As she did her best to find clear, unique fingerprints on the door, the trophy case and the safe, she cataloged questions and what she knew. And just as she'd expected, she couldn't find a single print she'd call evidence.

She stepped back into the dining room and propped her hands on her hips, taking one last look to make sure she hadn't missed a thing. Every table in the restaurant looked to be perfectly placed, neat and set for the morning's service. The white counter and stools along the front of the room were absolutely spotless. The black-and-white linoleum looked clean enough to eat off of. A small crowd stood outside on the sidewalk. Andi opened the door and gestured for them to come inside.

As they entered, she handed each one a menu. "Morning, folks. You're welcome to sit anywhere. Someone will be over to get your breakfast order in just a minute."

Jackie didn't need to lose any business. And Mayor Jones didn't need to see distressed tourists loitering on the sidewalk. Andi contemplated darting out to move the bench back to where it belonged, but Jackie set her coffee on the counter.

"Jackie, you can open for business. I just want to ask a few quick questions for now."

He nodded curtly and marched over to her usual booth. He slid in and slammed his crossed arms on top of the table. As she picked up the coffee mug, Andi said in a low voice to the remaining suspects, "Thank you for your patience. I'll have you back on your way as soon as possible. Oscar, you can go ahead and get their orders. Jackie will be back in a second."

Oscar smoothly pulled out his pad and glided over to the table by the window where a family of four was perusing the menu. Their study shouldn't take long. At breakfast Jackie was big on the basics: pancakes, biscuits, sausage, bacon and eggs. The only real question was how much food they wanted piled up on the table at one time.

Andi slid in across from Jackie and pulled out her notebook and pen. She used to rely on her memory for all the pertinent details. Then Mark Taylor moved to town and Andi decided she might need her own little notebook.

"So, Jackie, is the diner exactly as you found it this morning when you came in?"

"You mean other than the lineup of criminals sitting at my counter? Yes. I didn't touch anything."

"Other than the door and the phone, you didn't touch anything, right?"

His bushy brows beetled over his nose. "Well, yeah, I had to touch the phone to call your office, didn't I?"

"And to call Mr. Taylor." Andi sipped her coffee and watched the color rise in Jackie's cheeks. He gritted his teeth and nodded curtly.

"What about the trophy case?" Andi asked. "Was it locked when you left last night?"

He stared over his shoulder as if the trophy case would tell him the answer. When he looked back, he was frowning, but he finally nodded. In her book, Andi noted that the case might have been unlocked. He didn't look certain.

"Was the safe locked? And where do you keep the combination?" Andi watched him think.

"Yes, the safe was locked. I didn't have the

combination written down anywhere I can think of." He sighed. "But I kept the override key in the top drawer of the desk. Probably wouldn't have been hard to find if he knew what he was looking for."

She made a note to check for prints on the key. A savvy robber might expect the key to be hidden in the desk, but it didn't change her mind that the thief was somebody who knew Jackie pretty well. He had a thing for organization and efficiency.

"And where was Wanda Blankenship when you stopped her?"

He huffed once. "She ran past me while I was unlocking the door. You know she makes laps. When she came by again, I grabbed her and told her to sit right down."

Andi pursed her lips. "And she did? She sat right down when you told her to?"

Jackie shrugged. "I might have threatened to tell a secret about her if she didn't stay put."

Andi paused, her pen ready to add whatever shocking secret Jackie had over Wanda Blankenship, but he picked that moment to clam up. "And what is that secret?"

He shook his head. "Nope. I won't tell."

"Listen, Jackie, it's honorable to keep secrets for people who've asked you to, but it might help me to know what Wanda's hiding. I'm pretty good at keeping secrets, too."

He frowned. "I might need that secret someday. It's already helped me once. I'm not giving it up."

Andi fought the urge to sigh. It was difficult but she managed, barely, to meet his eyes. "And it has nothing to do with this case?"

"Can't see how it does, Sheriff." He met her stare without flinching, and Andi decided to move on.

"Okay, does the restaurant have a back door, Jackie?" This strip of Main Street had been converted to smaller spaces from a large mercantile. Some of them had back entrances and some didn't.

Jackie shook his head. "No, Sheriff, we use the front door, have to carry trash around the end of the block to the Dumpsters out back." He pulled out his order pad as the door clanged shut behind new customers. Jackie glanced at them and back at Andi. "It's a real pain."

She jotted down his answer. "You mentioned important documents. Like deeds and legal papers…that sort of thing?"

"Yeah, stuff I wanted to keep safe, things that…well, it's all important but some of it's… it can't be replaced." He made the wrap-it-up gesture. "Just find my property, Sheriff. Fast. Mona's going to be real upset until you do, and I can't have that. The twelve gold trophies ought to be a real easy trail to follow." He pointed over at the new table of customers. "All right if I go now?"

She nodded. And made a note that Wanda wasn't the only one with some kind of secret. Jackie didn't want to talk about whatever was in the safe. Andi wrote down his wife's name and a big question mark.

Figuring she knew how it well it would go, Andi sucked up her frustration before calling over her shoulder, "Oscar, can I talk to you for a second?"

He silently glided over and hovered.

Andi pointed at the seat across from her. "Do you want to sit down?"

There was a minute adjustment of Oscar's head that might be a refusal. Apparently he preferred to stand.

"Jackie said you arrived after he did this morning. Is that right?" Another infinitesimal adjustment that might be construed as a nod. "What time did you leave yesterday?" Andi waited. This was going to be good.

"Four." She didn't know that she'd ever heard Oscar speak, but he had a nice, deep voice.

"Can anyone verify your whereabouts between four and when you arrived this morning?"

Her answer was a small tic that looked like a no but might also be a yes. She sighed. "All right, Oscar, go ahead and get back to work. I'll track you down if I have any more questions." *And a deep desire to ram my head against the wall.* Oscar would have known about the safe and the key, but he had to be smart enough to know he'd be the number-one suspect if something like this happened.

Andi glanced over to see Wanda Blankenship and Mark Taylor in what appeared to be a cozy conversation. Wanda was leaning against him. One tanned, leanly muscled shoulder rested against him. Andi took a deep breath. "Miss Blankenship, can I talk to you for a second? I know you need to be on your way."

Wanda looked at Andi impatiently before she patted Mark on the back. She leaned forward to whisper something in his ear, and they both laughed at whatever sparkling gem that might be before she slid off the stool. There's no other word for it. The woman was a slinker. She slunk across the diner toward the booth, and Mark Taylor seemed to appreciate every minute.

Wanda perched gingerly on the seat before she waved at him. Andi noisily flipped the page in her notebook to get Wanda's attention. "So, Wanda, I understand you were running on your normal circuit this morning when Jackie stopped you."

Wanda pouted. "Yes, Sheriff, I was running the block around the courthouse square like I do every day. I didn't notice anyone near this place as I ran, but it was dark when I started. The sun had come up when I saw Jackie unlocking the door."

Andi nodded. "Why'd you stop when he told you to?"

The question rattled Wanda, who was

clearly wondering whether Jackie had given away her secret, but she'd played this game before. She leaned back against the leather of the booth. "I am a *good citizen* and a *business owner* myself, of course. If I can help in any way to apprehend criminals who break into the businesses of our fair town, then I am *certainly* glad to do so. Besides, *I* didn't *steal anything*." She tilted her head forward. "Where in the world would I hide it?"

Wanda was laying it on pretty thick, which made Andi reconsider how juicy a secret it would be.

"Jackie says you've got a secret. He wouldn't share it. Would you like to? What makes an innocent woman follow Jackie's orders?"

She widened her doe eyes and fluttered her eyelashes. At this point it had to be natural instinct or just habit. It had no effect on Andi.

One delicate shoulder rose slowly. "Well, Sheriff, I—" she glanced around the diner and back at Mark Taylor before she leaned forward over the table "—depend on Jackie to keep certain habits secret."

Andi tried to process that as she asked,

"Like...?" She couldn't come up with a single possibility.

Wanda squeezed her eyes shut and then she mouthed, *Pie.*

Andi leaned back against the booth. "Did you just say pie?"

Wanda bit her lip. "I've got a real bad problem. Jackie's my supplier. The town's only fitness icon...and I'm addicted to pie." Her eyes filled with what seemed to be real tears, and Andi was stumped.

Finally she asked, "Where were you after the Country Kitchen closed last night?"

Wanda sniffed. "I left The Gym at my usual time, about six. I didn't leave the house until I started my run down here, and I think Jackie was the first person I ran into."

Wanda Blankenship owned the single health club in town. To be technically correct, her father owned it, but if anyone wanted a treadmill, an elliptical machine, a swimming pool or a tanning bed, then Wanda's place was the only game in town. She was a walking advertisement for good health and the benefits of regular exercise and short visits to tanning beds.

Wanda had plenty of time to break into the diner and no alibi, but from the mild look of dismay on her face, Andi was nearly certain Wanda would never want to. Unless she needed a way to counter Jackie knowing her secret, but what would she have been hoping to use as leverage?

Andi drew a line through her name on the list of suspects and quickly did the same with Mark Taylor. She just couldn't imagine what the motive might be.

Wanda looked down at her watch. "Am I free to go, Sheriff?" Andi nodded and picked up her steaming hot cup of coffee. As she sipped, Andi watched Wanda sashay across the diner to the counter where Mark Taylor sat checking his phone for whatever he checked…text messages from girlfriends, hot tips on no-news events in town, sports scores. When Wanda patted his back and bent down to say something, he laughed. Wanda turned to leave and amped up the seduction in her walk. All eyes, even those of the twelve-year-old boy in the booth by the window, followed her exit.

With a deep sigh, Mark Taylor turned to say, “Ready for me, Sheriff?”

Andi really didn’t think she was. She took another sip of coffee and put it carefully back on the table. “You bet.”

CHAPTER TWO

MARK TAYLOR SLID into the booth across from prickly Sheriff Andrea Jackson. Facing off against her was familiar but that didn't make it any less interesting. Or exciting. She was not a restful person. She was…motivated. Busy. Determined to prove herself. He ought to know. He was recovering from the same obsession himself. Burnout and watching his first wife walk away with a man who'd be home every night had convinced him to try a new life, one with free time and fishing.

Covering bake sales and school plays had taken some adjustment, but he'd embraced his new life wholeheartedly and had the lower blood pressure and friends in town to show for it.

When he settled against the booth, she crossed her arms defensively. As always, he watched the sheriff closely without letting her know he did. She wore her normal spotless uniform and had her hair pulled back so tightly he was surprised she could move her eyebrows. She looked like the type of person who'd build her own ammunition just for fun. He'd bet the fortune he didn't have that she wasn't wearing a speck of makeup. She was too tightly wound but pretty.

He braced his elbows on the table. The sheriff flipped a page in her notebook and did not meet his eyes. "So, Sheriff, how goes the investigation?" She was stubborn and uncommunicative on the best days. He wouldn't get much out of her without a poke.

"Fine. Want to tell me why you're here if you had nothing to do with this?"

He shrugged. "I knew there would be a good story. We put the paper out yesterday so it's time to start rounding up the news for next week."

He leaned forward like he had a secret. "That's sorta how the whole newspaper thing works, you know."

Andi picked up her full cup of coffee and stared at it for a second. As he'd chatted with pretty, obvious Wanda Blankenship, he'd watched the sheriff and the rest of the diners.

The sheriff was good at focus. She'd probably noticed every hair out of place on Jackie or Wanda, but she was bad on the periphery. He'd had experience in cataloging lots of tiny details all at once. Good stories depended on those. Oscar had refilled her cup at least once, and it was clear that this was the first time she realized it. He watched her watch Oscar and could almost see the lightbulb go on over her head.

"Do his ninjalike coffee skills make you wonder what else he might be capable of?" he asked as he reached over to ruffle the pages of her notebook. When she snapped her head back, stiffened in her seat and snatched her notebook out of his reach, he added a mental note to the list of things he wanted to know about the sheriff. *What's in the notebook?*

Curiosity had always been one of his best assets. It was also one of his biggest challenges. He'd never learned how to let a story go, something his ex-wife had shouted more than once.

When he pulled his hand back, Andi took a deep, calming breath. And then she went back on the offensive. "Oscar's skills aren't all that important right now, Mr. Taylor. Can anyone vouch for your whereabouts between the time the restaurant closed and when you arrived this morning?"

Something about that "Mr. Taylor" got to him. He wanted to ruffle her a bit. She wouldn't put up with it for long—she never had any time to waste. He'd better make it good.

He shook his head. "Nope, Sheriff. I spent last night at home." He leaned forward again and looked up at her through his eyelashes. "I was all alone."

Andi scribbled a note and met his stare again.

"Isn't that sad?"

"That no one can vouch for your whereabouts?"

He shook his head. "No, that I was all alone."

Andi snorted. Or tried to. It came out as a strangled snarf, but he gave her points for trying. With a huff, she retorted, "That is very sad. Hearts all over Tall Pines and the tri-county area would break if they heard such a sad story."

He did his best not to laugh. Andi Jackson was adorable when she was riled.

"All right, Mr. Taylor. If I have any more questions, I know where to find you." When he didn't move, Andi raised both eyebrows. "You can go." She made little encouraging gestures with both hands.

He started to ease out of the booth but paused on the edge. He didn't want to leave. "You know, Sheriff, I'm a pretty good investigator. I spent a few years working the crime beat for the state paper before I came here." His skills were a little rusty, but offering to help might get him into the tight-lipped sheriff's good graces. Getting any info out of her was next to impossible. "I'd be happy to assist with your investigation. We could exchange information. Sure would make my job easier and the story better."

She nodded once. "Thank you, Mr. Taylor. I will let you know if I have any questions."

He shrugged one shoulder and stood. "I guess I'll just have to stick close to you, Sheriff Jackson. For my readers."

Andi slapped her notebook closed and slid it into her pocket with authority. And meaning. What would she think if she knew he found that cute rather than authoritative? He should have his head examined. "We'll have to see about that, Mr. Taylor. I can't have you interfering with an investigation."

Of course not. She'd fight every step. That could be both frustrating and fun. He wanted to know what her problem was, why she fought him so hard. Some cops were glory hounds, anxious to get their names on the first page. Not Sheriff Jackson, not even in an election year. It was weird.

"I'm not sure you're seeing the big picture, Sheriff. A newspaper editor spends a lot of time tracking down the real story and in this town, there's a whole lot more than meets the eye. I know a few things that might surprise you." He thumped the table with two fingers and smiled at her over his shoulder as he left the diner.

ANDI WATCHED HIM leave. She couldn't help it. Jeans and a polo were his normal summer uniform, but it worked for him.

As she slid out of the booth, Mark stepped outside and maneuvered the heavy bench back into place under the window. When it was situated in the perfect spot, he stood up and put both hands on his hips. Their eyes met through the window and he ducked his head as if to say, *See what I did there?*

Andi rolled her eyes and fought back a smile. She mouthed, *Thank you.* He nodded once, then turned around to take a seat. Sitting on a bench and watching the world go by might actually be part of a newspaper editor's job. The boredom would probably kill her. Andi looked around the diner. Since the breakfast crowd didn't appear to be too hectic, she walked over to the counter. "Jackie, I'm just going to take another quick look in the back."

He waved a hand as if to say, *Sure, don't bother me,* as he went to help a customer at the cash register.

Oscar was washing dishes as she walked through the swinging door. Jackie could stand to have extra help. Andi wandered back to Jackie's office and made note of the window over the freezer in the back. The window was small and pretty high off the ground, but someone Oscar's size could fit through it.

She stretched, but the freezer kept her from reaching the latch.

"Hey, Jackie?" Andi called out. He stuck his head through the order window. "Is this window locked?"

Jackie glanced from her to the window. "Well, yes, why wouldn't it be?"

Andi silently counted to ten. "Are you sure it's locked?"

Jackie's lips moved without sound before he said, "Oscar, grab a chair and check the window."

They both waited while Oscar floated across the kitchen to Jackie's office. He came back with what appeared to be the first metal chair ever made. Rust dotted the legs, and Andi wondered if metal ever got dry rot. When he climbed on top, she moved behind to catch him in case the metal gave up the ghost.

Oscar yanked on the handle, and the window rose soundlessly.

"Why is that window unlocked?" Jackie's face was a brilliant red, and Andi wondered if the three hairs he had left were going to run away in fear.

Oscar shrugged. Andi did, too. "Well, I'm going to take a look outside. I'll let you know if I find anything new, Jackie."

MARK DID HIS best to contain a grin when Andi turned the corner into the crazily clean alley behind the diner, saw him leaning against the wall and cursed silently. He'd have to give Sheriff Jackson credit. No matter how often he caught her off guard, she recovered quickly. This time she straightened her shoulders and resumed a precise march.

"What are you doing back here, Mr. Taylor?" She didn't meet his stare but obviously looked to his left and right in what she'd call "searching for clues." There were none. He knew that very well.

"Just waiting on you, Sheriff."

Andi pulled out her phone to take pictures of the alley. "You didn't touch anything, did you?" There was a scowl on her face. Mark figured it was an automatic reaction at this point. He decided then and there to change it. Automatic smiles were so much better, made for easier working conditions. And her smiles were really nice, probably because they were rare.

He shook his head. "No, ma'am. I used to work with the police a lot. I only invaded one crime scene without permission, but I learned quickly not to do it again. The detective had a good six inches and a hundred pounds on me."

"Did you destroy any evidence that time?" Andi glanced back to watch him.

"Nah. I got lucky. My guardian angel kept me out of trouble that time or maybe it was dumb luck. Either way, I'm pretty sure the only reason I'm standing here today is because Detective Wright yanked me back by the scruff of my neck just as I was about to make a fatal error."

Andi was curious. He could tell by the way she turned her head in his direction without really looking at him. She was also determined not to ask. "Okay, do you want to tell me what you're doing back here? Other than standing right beside the scene I'm investigating?" He was cramping her style. Good. That would make him impossible to ignore.

She'd already given him more than her normal blank-faced "no comment."

"Just want to make sure I've got enough details for my story, Sheriff." He glanced around the alley. "I don't see much of interest back here."

Andi shot him a peeved glare.

He held up both hands. "Don't shoot the messenger. Tall Pines may be the only place in the world where even the back alleys are litter free."

He ticked off his observations on the fingers of one hand. "Pavement means no footprints or tire tracks. Window's got no scrapes or scratches. Traffic on a weeknight is almost nonexistent so the thief had the opportunity to come in through that window, even with a stepladder, but there's nothing here to say he did."

Andi propped her hands on her hips. "There's no proof that he or she did, but the window was unlocked so I can't rule it out."

"Not much to go on, is it?"

Andi shook her head. "On the bright side, no one murdered the mayor or robbed a bank, either."

They walked back toward the end of the alley.

"Still, you know Jackie's going to make your life difficult until he has someone to point fingers at." He shrugged. "And, of course, there's the fact that you don't like loose ends."

Andi frowned at him. "How do you know my feelings on loose ends?"

"Good guess." He surveyed her neat uniform, tidy hair, polished boots and precise steps. "Let me help."

Andi raised both eyebrows, communicating her surprise and disbelief. "Why would you want to help me? What's in it for you?"

"I know it's not easy to deal with an unhappy Jackie. Plus, it's good for me, too. People read the *Times* for news and stuff. This would be the news. Most of the time, I've just got a whole lot of the stuff." He thrust both hands in his jeans pockets. After what felt like a full minute of contemplating his arms, Andi locked both eyes back on his face. He moved closer as if he was about to tell an important secret. Andi started to lean back but managed to hold her ground. "And, if helping you out with this case means that from now on you'll be a little more open to sharing information, I consider it worth the effort."

When he stepped back, Andi inhaled deeply and blinked before she said, "Mr. Taylor, you and I both know why I won't be accepting your offer. Besides, I'm really good at this. You just go ahead and toss your lure in the lake, okay? I'll let you know how it all turns out."

Mark whistled. "Hmm, a low blow." He reached down and grabbed her hand to slow her forceful retreat. "Sheriff, no matter how hard you work today, there's going to be twice as much tomorrow. Twice as many crooks. Twice as many questions with no answers. You should learn to enjoy each day anyway. The work will always be there. Don't forget about life." He trailed his thumb over her pulse and the smooth, warm skin of her wrist before he let her hand slide out of his.

REFUSING TO RUB away the odd warmth lingering on her wrist, Andi turned and walked over to her SUV. The sun had risen, so instead of a nice, shaded truck, it was a metal box set on broil. Add that to the fact that she'd probably had her weekly intake of caffeine between the ride over to the diner and Oscar's ninja coffee skills and the close proximity to the newspaper editor and Andi was starting to feel a bit steamed and a whole lot jittery. She needed air-conditioning, a gallon of water and some distance. It was no wonder her fingers were tingling like that. It probably had nothing to do with Mark Taylor.

Taking a deep breath, Andi yanked open the door and managed not to take two steps back from the heat blast. Leather seats were such a bad idea.

Still, she was satisfied that she'd managed to stand her ground with Mark Taylor even if she hadn't actually gained any. Andi dropped down in the driver's seat with a wince at the heat baking through her uniform pants, started the car and pulled away from the curb. As she reached down to crank up the air conditioner, she looked in the rearview mirror. Mark Taylor was standing at the edge of the curb watching her drive away with that smirk on his face. Andi was suddenly less sure whether she was holding her ground or losing the battle and she just didn't know it yet.

CHAPTER THREE

THE SHORT TRIP back to the office was lengthened by multiple stops for nervous tourists who were darting into the streets outside the designated crosswalks. If the pavement hadn't been hotter than the sun, Andi might have pulled over and issued some stern warnings. Jaywalking was illegal—it was a safety issue. Scaring people straight was part of the sheriff's job, but the mayor didn't appreciate that.

When she finally pulled into her designated parking spot, Andi turned off the ignition. She might have rested for a bit except she was afraid of baking her brain. She slid out quickly and slammed the door. Her palms still had a slight tingle going on, the effect of a massive amount of caffeine. Obviously.

"Morning, Sheriff." Lori had taken Nettie's spot at the dispatch desk. Nettie worked early mornings, when things were a bit slower and she didn't have to deal with as many citizens. Andi envied her the right to choose.

Lori and Andi had gone to school together, but Lori stayed in Tall Pines to marry, divorce and remarry. Every greeting she issued might come with a smile, but there was also the edge of sharp teeth and the hint of a grimace. She'd worked for the old sheriff and might resent Andi taking his spot. He was her father, after all. Still, a job was a job and in Tall Pines, no one quit a good job on the principle of the thing. They were just too hard to come by. So Lori performed right on the edge, well enough to keep coming in every day but not so well that it could be misconstrued as approval or anything other than a deep-seated wish to inflict nonfelonious harm.

Lori and Andi had a history anyway. Lori had been homecoming queen and head cheerleader. Andi had been president of the math club, a desperate overachiever intent on winning a college scholarship. She'd snatched valedictorian out of Lori's pom-pom-waving paws at the last minute and still congratulated herself on that now and then. Lori probably didn't think about it much. She had two beautiful little boys to show off. Pictures lined the wall beside the dispatch desk. The towheaded twins had to be about eight years old. Their names were Alexander and Andrew and they were perfectly identical. When they came in, Andi had no idea which was which and settled for a jovial and nonspecific "boys" whenever she had to address them directly.

Andi's small pangs of jealousy hadn't driven her to put up pictures of her cat, Mojo, on the same wall. Not yet.

"Morning, Lori. Is there anything urgent?"

"Nope. Dan's headed out to check on the one call we've got. Mrs. Haley thinks there's been someone prowling around her garage at night."

Andi nodded. This prowler would probably be just like the last, a deer knocking over the chairs on Mrs. Haley's porch, but the woman had a shotgun and an active imagination. It would be a good thing to check out.

Andi waved at Dan as he stood up from one of the four desks crammed into the large room. It was time for the patrols to change over, so both Dan Jones and Jimmy Monroe were there. Jimmy was writing a report, and

Dan had just finished checking any notes left from the previous shift. It was a small office. There were six full-time deputies for the entire county and reserves who helped out as needed.

Jimmy looked up. “Anything we need to know about the incident over at Jackie’s?”

Andi scratched her forehead as she tried to figure out how to answer. “Well, his trophies and the money and everything else in his safe were stolen. He’d corralled Oscar, his busboy, Wanda Blankenship and Mark Taylor when I got there. I couldn’t see any signs of a break-in, and Jackie swears the door was locked when he got there.”

Dan crossed his arms over his chest and Jimmy leaned back in his chair. Andi could smell Lori hovering behind her. She had a thing for strawberry bubble gum.

“So it’s somebody with a key,” Dan said. “Should be easy enough to figure out.”

Andi agreed. Mostly. “Unless it’s a random thief who’s good with locks and safes.”

They both shook their heads. “Doesn’t seem likely.”

“Except…I can’t rule it out, either,” Andi said.

Dan held up three fingers. “C’mon, boss. Motive. Means. Opportunity.”

“It’s hard to come up with a reason for stealing trophies, but money’s always a motivator.”

Lori popped a bubble dangerously close to Andi’s ponytail. She couldn’t help but think it would be even more difficult to prove criminal intent for gum in her hair.

Dan picked up his radio and walked around the desk. “Sounds personal, boss. You should definitely find out if Jackie has any enemies.”

All three of them were quiet for a minute before Andi snorted. “Right. This is Jackie we’re talking about. If he wasn’t the best chili cook in this part of the state, he probably would’ve been chased out of town after his second lawsuit.”

Both Dan and Jimmy nodded. They had strict instructions to stay away from Jackie. One of the deputies in the former administration had gotten too close for comfort, and Jackie had taken him all the way to court for harassment. He hadn’t won, but the court of public opinion was harder to argue with than the men in black robes.

Jimmy slapped Andi on the shoulder. “Well, there’s always the traffic camera.” Another heavy silence filled the room before all four of them burst out into guffaws. The traffic camera was suggested at least once a season, most often by a tourist who’d seen years of police dramas and wanted to find out whether something had been taken from his car or hotel room.

Tall Pines had a single stoplight on the two-lane highway that ran through town. And there was no camera on it. Everywhere else, traffic was controlled by well-placed stop signs and law-abiding citizens. Most of the time everyone was happy to live in a place where the only security they might need was the lock their car or house was already equipped with.

“I will certainly get right on that, Deputy. That is a fabulous suggestion.”

Dan waved as he walked out into the bright sunshine. Lori wiped the smudged mascara from underneath her eyes and wandered back to the dispatch desk. Jimmy shuffled the paperwork on his desk into a folder and handed it to Andi. “Let me know if I can give you any help with that investigation, boss.”

She nodded and slid the folder under her arm as she headed for her office. “Sure thing. You guys might want to avoid the Country Kitchen for a bit. Jackie will make any visit miserable until I can get some information for him.”

“Got it,” Jimmy said. “See you tomorrow.”

Andi made a detour to the small kitchenette for a glass of ice-cold water. As she perched on the edge of her chair and did her best to ignore the squawk it made as she leaned back, Andi set the glass down and pulled out her notebook.

She opened a new incident report and transcribed the few details she’d managed to pick up from her interrogation of the “suspects.” She also tried to brush aside the memory of Mark Taylor’s hand wrapped around hers.

Her gut said this was an inside job. Someone with a key had waited until the diner was closed to take the money Jackie had on hand. Surely everything else was an afterthought. Why take trophies?

Knowing Jackie and his suspicious nature,

the list of people with keys would be short. Maybe only Jackie, in fact. Maybe his wife, Mona. Possibly Oscar. But the back window was unlocked, so all three of the people she'd interviewed had means and opportunity, as well. Maybe Jackie had accidentally left it that way. Maybe Oscar had opened it for himself or someone else. She didn't figure Jackie drank his coffee out of a World's Best Boss mug.

As far as an action plan, she had only two options. First, Andi would have to ask Jackie what his list of enemies looked like. She'd need to take a much larger notebook on that day. And second, she needed to get her hair done. Luckily, it had been almost two months since her last visit, and she had an appointment already scheduled. She could take care of both tomorrow.

AFTER A BLISSFUL afternoon spent at her desk pushing paper around and detoxing from a caffeine high, Andi decided to relax at the Smokehouse—Tall Pines's answer to finer dining. Jackie's business was a breakfast, lunch and snack proposition except when the fall color hit. For the Fall Festival, he spruced up his dinner menu with chili any way and every way he could imagine it. Otherwise, the Smokehouse was the place to go for an evening meal.

When she walked into the shadowy coolness of the restaurant, Andi sighed with relief. It was a bit early for dinner but that would be a good thing. She could avoid the mayor and enjoy her meal in peace and quiet.

A steady flip-flop approached, and Andi turned and smiled at Sarah Wilson. The Wilsons had been her neighbors growing up. Sarah's parents still lived in Tall Pines but Andi did her absolute best to avoid that neighborhood now. It was too painful.

"Afternoon, Sheriff. Want your usual spot?" If she'd thought about it for a minute, it might have bothered Andi that she was so predictable. She had usual drinks, usual meals and usual spots. That constituted a rut.

"That'd be great." Andi followed her to the table, biting back the advice that wanted to tumble out regarding proper restaurant footwear. It wasn't her place. And so what if *flip-flop, flip-flop* was annoying? If it didn't bother Amanda in her own restaurant, then it shouldn't bother Andi. Clearly, she needed to concentrate on what was important here: dessert.

Andi decided to take the seat facing the kitchen, with her back toward the door. The place was deserted now but it was only a matter of time until someone came in, spotted her and tried to pump her for information on what had happened at Jackie's. She had no illusions about the spread of the story. At this time of day, Andi could call somebody two counties away and get some distorted version of what had happened, what she said and where the body was hidden.

"Can I get you something to drink?" Sarah asked.

"Sweet tea, please," Andi responded, as always. Sarah flip-flopped her way to the kitchen to get Andi's drink.

Even though she'd be having her usual, Andi perused the menu because that was the right thing to do in restaurants. A small breeze stirred over her shoulder and, thinking it was Sarah returning with the tea, Andi looked up with a smile on her face.

Mark Taylor smiled back. "Well, Sheriff, I have to say I didn't expect such a warm welcome." He pulled out the seat across from her and sat down before he rested both elbows on the table. "What are we having?"

Andi snapped the menu closed and got ready to blast him. She did not want her dinner interrupted by Jackie's case.

Sarah intervened with a sweaty glass of iced tea. "Well, Mark, I didn't know you were joining the sheriff. What can I get you to drink?"

Andi opened her mouth to say that his drink should be delivered to another table, any other table, but she could tell with one quick look that Sarah would have trouble remembering anything she might say. Her large blue eyes were locked on Mark Taylor like he was the second coming of Tom Cruise right here in Tall Pines.

He didn't see her worshipping gaze. When Andi looked at Mark to give him the stunning glare of death, he was smiling back at her. "And that's more like it." He shot a glance up at beautiful young Sarah and said, "Make it tea."

She nodded distractedly. Andi wondered if Sarah heard his answer but then realized it didn't matter. She would have his choice memorized.

"Are y'all ready to order?" Sarah asked them both, but she was looking at Mark.

Clearing her throat, Andi said loudly, "I'll have the chef salad with vinaigrette on the side, Sarah."

Sarah nodded again but didn't take out her notepad. She had probably already put in Andi's usual order.

"A salad? In a rib joint?" Mark looked at Andi. Both eyebrows were raised and his mouth hung open. He was clearly offended. He glanced up at Sarah. "Can she do that?"

Sarah answered with a maniacal giggle. "Well, I guess so, Mark. She does it almost every time she comes in."

He shook his head as if he couldn't quite believe it but he'd allow it anyway and handed over the menu. "I think I'll have the special tonight, Sarah. And make sure it has the sweet sauce instead of the mild, okay?"

She stacked the menus and put extra swish in her exit, glancing back over her shoulder to see if she had an audience. When she saw that Andi was the only one watching, she straightened her shoulders, slammed the menus back in the basket next to the phone and pushed through the swinging doors.

"So, Sheriff, a salad? Here? In the home of the best ribs in the northeast part of the state?" His lips twitched as he pointed to the sign hanging over the front door that listed that exact honor. The Smokehouse had been voted number one in the newspaper's annual poll.

Andi nodded. "Yes, but you'll wish you'd gone a different route when Sarah brings me a slice of cheesecake bigger than my head."

"Ah, I get it. You store up a few karmic calories so that you splurge on dessert." Mark shrugged. "Whereas I live by the philosophy that there's absolutely no reason I can't have both if I want to."

Andi tapped her finger to her lip before she said, "You know, that doesn't surprise me a bit." She opened her napkin with a snap and spread it over her legs. "And if I lived by that philosophy, I'd definitely have to buy a bigger uniform."

"Sheriff, I'm beginning to think you don't know me at all." Mark made a show of glancing over her tan uniform. "But this uniform looks pretty good on you, so your philosophy must be working."

Andi couldn't help it. She rolled her eyes.

He laughed. "What? You don't think my flattery is sincere?"

"Honestly, I'm not sure anything about you is sincere." It was a good thing the restaurant went for mood lighting. If they'd been anywhere with lightbulbs stronger than forty watts, he'd be able to see how flustered he made her. Sarah brought out their drinks, a basket of rolls and pats of butter. She didn't say a word but retreated to the front door to greet any new visitors that might come in.

"Now, Sheriff. That sorta hurts my feelings." Andi couldn't see it in this lighting but he might have slapped on a halo before he answered. "I believe you have me pegged as some sort of city slicker out to pull the wool over your eyes for some nefarious reason."

Andi shook her head. "No. I have you pegged as some city clicker who's out to pull the wool over my eyes because it keeps you entertained. And if you get a juicy story, too, so much the better. It sells papers." She snorted. "Am I wrong? You did move here from the city. You do seem to take extreme pleasure in poking at me. And now you're trying to convince me that you find my uniform attractive. And the truth is you could crook your finger and have any number of women lined up, so there's no reason to tease me."

As he buttered a roll, he considered Andi's answer. He took a big bite and offered the rest to her. She gave him a repressive frown but knew it was a waste of time.

After a quick swig of tea, he said, "Yes, I moved here from the city but maybe that's an example of my sound judgment. Did you ever figure that?" Without waiting for her answer, he added, "And I enjoy teasing you, that part's true. If you could see your face, you'd have a hard time always doing the right thing, too."

He leaned forward. "And as far as that uniform goes, I never meant to say I found it attractive." Andi shook her head and managed to meet his gaze. "I find you attractive. And that's nothing but the truth."

He sat back with a satisfied smirk on his

face. Andi needed a gulp of air but she didn't want to appear undignified. To buy some time, she picked up her glass and managed to snort tea straight up her nose. As she coughed and sputtered, Mark calmly devoured his roll.

After she wiped her face and managed to catch her breath, Andi croaked, "You can't say things like that to me. Are you trying to kill me?"

He laughed softly and shook his head.

"Listen, I don't know anything new about Jackie's robbery yet. When I do, I'll pass it along, okay? I promise. You don't have to follow me around to eavesdrop."

"Okay. Glad to hear it." He picked up another roll and an amazing glop of butter and introduced them.

"Don't you have someplace else to be?"

He looked confused. "Uh, no. I've ordered dinner. It'll be here momentarily…" He paused dramatically and Sarah's flip-flops sounded from the kitchen as she entered the dining room with a tray on her shoulder.

He leaned back to let Sarah place an overflowing plate of ribs right in front of him, with sides of slaw and potato salad. She set down

Andi's meal—iceberg lettuce with chopped vegetables and a few strips each of ham, turkey and grilled chicken—then reached back to get the dressing. When she'd cleared the tray, Sarah tonelessly said, "Enjoy."

As she watched him pick up the ribs and start eating, Andi scratched her forehead. "You've ruined her day, you know? You could pay her a little bit of attention."

He looked up quickly. His mouth had a small smear of barbecue sauce on it. Andi wanted barbecue sauce in that minute more than she'd ever wanted it. She glanced back down at her uninspiring plate of rabbit food.

"Who? Sarah? I'm a pretty good tipper."

"No, she wants you to *notice* her."

He looked in the direction Sarah had disappeared and shrugged before he returned to the ribs. He muttered, "She's just a baby," before taking a big bite.

Andi watched him chew for a minute and picked through her salad for the choicest, meatiest bits. "It must be nice to have all that attention."

He mumbled something like "from babies" but didn't look up from his meal.

Andi still wanted that barbecue sauce. "Wanda Blankenship's no baby."

He glanced up before he hooted. Andi looked around the nearly empty dining room and tried to *shh* him, but the hoots turned to guffaws and he dropped his ribs back onto the plate. When he finally managed to get control of himself, he took a long drink of his tea, then leaned across the table. He looked left and right, then he whispered, "You're jealous!" Andi shook her head furiously as he sat back and clapped his hands twice. "Jealous! I love it! And I'm honestly relieved, Sheriff. I mean, I managed to charm my way into most of this town's good graces, but you…you've been a real challenge."

Andi tried to pretend she didn't know him. She would have pretended not to know herself if she could figure out how. It was one thing for him to be right and a whole different thing for him to *know* he was right.

Andi tried to act calm. She took measured bites of her tasteless yet perfectly suitable salad and sipped her inoffensive iced tea. When Sarah came over with a refill, Andi thanked her politely.

And she waited.

After his celebration ended, he picked up his ribs again and proceeded to demolish them. When he leaned back with a sigh, he said, “All right, Sheriff. Clearly you have the hots for me but you don’t trust me. I can understand that, as I am a newcomer in a town filled with people who sprang up here when the earth was formed.” He shook a finger at her. “What I don’t understand is why you won’t work with me. In my experience, there are two kinds of cops.”

Andi sighed. “Oh, really.”

He nodded. “There’s the grandstander, who considers publicity a perk and a duty. Most places, I find a few of those and I’m set. And then there’s the strong, silent type. Apparently you’re one of those, even though some publicity would help a woman running for reelection. I mean, it was one story, Sheriff. I quoted you directly. How did we go from that to ‘no comment’ on each and every question?” The look on his face said he was mystified and maybe a little…hurt? And that made her mad.

She dropped her fork on her plate with a

loud clatter, picked up her tea and tried to convince herself to let it go, just let this moment pass without telling him exactly what she thought. She didn't need bad press now. But when she put the glass back down with a thump, he'd sat back in his chair and for the first time, he looked serious.

So she took a deep breath. "Yeah, okay. Let's think back to that story, why don't we? Domestic violence. You asked for a solid definition, statistics and tips on what to look for and what to do."

"Yeah, and that's what I put in the article. Word for word. Just the facts. None of that seems like a reason for the cold shoulder."

Andi shook her head. "Honestly, I can't even… Don't you know what that story did?"

He tugged on his earlobe and considered the question. "Well, it reported on the problem of domestic violence in small communities and provided tips on how to help." He frowned. "I'd expect you to be happy about that, Sheriff. I know it's an issue you're really interested in." He tapped his finger on the table. "I *called* you because that was something you spoke about in your campaign. What's the deal? Did you want more credit?"

Andi realized her tense shoulders were creeping up and forced herself to relax. "What I would have liked was for you to report the story, the whole story, not pick and choose and make me look like some…"

Mark glanced around to see if anyone was listening, and Andi realized she'd raised her voice. The kitchen was probably enjoying the show.

"Like some what?" Mark asked. "I reported the facts, and they weren't just for this town or this county. I had other sources, too."

Andi rubbed the crease between her brows. "What you did was pick and choose. You didn't include my comments on how well the people in Tall Pines support their neighbors, how lucky we are to have a close-knit community, how the incidents of abuse have been in a steady decline over the past five years, or how the previous sheriff contributed to that with his own programs. You didn't even compare our statistics to rates in larger cities. So what you did report made it sound like we were this cute little town with a big problem, and that I was convinced I could ride to the rescue." She picked up her fork and shuffled lettuce around on her plate. "And maybe I even believed the last part, but I would never have said it."

When Mark didn't answer, Andi chanced a look up and saw that he'd braced both elbows on the table and covered his face with his hands. Telling him the rest was easier that way. "People stopped me in the street to tell me just what they thought of my point of view and my taking credit. I got a few threats. And I've been…wading through public opinion since, doing my best to protect the people who elected me even though they don't think much of me."

His shoulders slumped. If she believed his face, he was surprised, miserable and maybe a little bit sick. "Sheriff, I had no idea. I just… I think I've spent so much time going after public figures that…" Mark wiped his mouth with his napkin. "How come no one in this town came after me, the new guy? You're a native. Seems like they'd be ready to tar and feather me instead of you."

Andi sighed. "That's a long story."

"One you sure don't want to tell me because of how I'll report it, right?" He shook his head. "I'm really sorry."

She almost believed him. Instead of charming or teasing, his face was dead serious, the smile absent. "I just wish more journalists—" she shook her head "—no, more people, would stop to consider that there's a lot more to truth than just the facts."

He leaned forward again. "More to truth..." He looked like he wanted to understand but had no idea what she meant.

Andi wished she'd decided to have a microwave dinner. "Truth is..." She sat back. "In Mandarin, you'd say *shí huà*. The first character means real or solid and the second is more like talk or conversation or words. Mandarin's an analytical language so you have to study the context, the order of the words, to understand the meaning."

"So, you speak Mandarin." He looked as if he didn't really know what to do with that.

Andi got the same reaction from everyone in town anytime it came up. "I worked for the FBI translating, monitoring persons of interest."

"In Chinese?"

"And Persian, although I read that better than I speak or hear it." She felt like such an idiot for bringing it up. Possibly because he was looking at her as though she had two heads. "My point is this...in linguistics, you get a real good understanding of what words can do and what they can't do. No matter that we're both speaking English, truth means different things to you than it does to me. Because of context."

Mark studied the ceiling while he thought about her answer. Finally he nodded. "I've got it...but to me, that's semantics."

Andi laughed. "Actually, that's called pragmatics and it's a case of six of one and a half a dozen of the other."

Mark wrinkled his brow. "Isn't that what I just said?"

"It's close. You think facts are truth."

He shook his head. "Aren't they?"

"Not always, no. Facts are black-and-white. Truth...it has more depth."

"Are you actually speaking Mandarin now? Because I'm afraid the conversation has gotten away from me. And that never happens. I'm a writer. I live on words, you know?"

"It's like...the facts might be that someone broke into the Country Kitchen. You can put in the time and the amount that was stolen. You might even be able to put in the name of the thief and a confession, but that's not the truth of the story. Or not all of it anyway. You'd be missing the context. I want to know the why. And I can't help but look for it. That makes me good at my job. I don't think most reporters spend a lot of time thinking about that context." Andi shook her head. "Just let me eat my salad in peace, please."

He reached across the table to squeeze her hand. "I'm not sure I agree, Sheriff, but I think I understand." He shook his head. "What I don't get is why in the world you're still here. If you win this election, you've got two more years of the town's scrutiny to look forward to. Why not head out for greener, more crime-ridden pastures? FBI experience would probably open most any door you wanted around here, wouldn't it?"

Andi bit her lip as she tried to figure out a way to shunt him out of the Smokehouse. She'd get up herself but not without her cheesecake. "I can't leave Tall Pines, not yet. My grandmother's still…she needs me." Two years ago, when she'd heard about her grandmother's fall, Andi was frantic to get home. Her career hadn't meant much then. Gram wouldn't move to Atlanta, so Andi had to make her way in Tall Pines. Unfortunately, that meant old history, elections and politics.

Mark wadded up his napkin as Sarah returned to take his empty plate. He smiled up at her, then smiled at Andi. "You're ready for your dessert now."

Andi had cleared a bald spot in the middle of the forest of her salad. He was right. She was ready for her reward.

Before Andi could give Sarah her usual order, he said, "She'll have her usual and I'll have what she's having." Sarah smiled and marched back to the kitchen. Mark and Andi both watched her go, then Mark turned back to look at Andi. "I do appreciate your jealousy but I'm not sure you know what you're talking about. She seems fine to me."

Andi pointed to the table with a single twentysomething man near the window. "I think she's got someone else to attract at this point."

He heaved a troubled sigh. "Well, all right. At least I've still got you." The corner of his mouth tilted up, but he didn't say another thing about jealousy. "I'm surprised I hadn't heard about your FBI experience. The first thing some people did when I moved to town is trot over to tell me all about Tall Pines's most famous citizen."

Andi was ready to blast out a defense. Her father had quit his job at the radio station, divorced her mother and left town to pursue his dream. He'd landed in Nashville where he hosted a popular country music talk show, and every Christmas he sent her a card with a check. Until she was eighteen, she'd lived with the morbid curiosity and sometimes pity of the people in town who knew he hardly called and never visited his daughter. She didn't want to talk about her father, either his successes or his monumental failure.

Sometimes she had to face the bitter truth that she could place a big part of her drive to be the best and build a successful law-enforcement career at her father's feet. She was determined to prove herself better than him, better than anyone who'd pursue their own selfish goals like that, through serving the public and excelling at all she did. But now was not the time to get into that.

Mark held up both hands in a gesture of surrender. "But I don't want to talk about that. It's nice to know more about you. Why don't you ask me whatever burning questions you have? You might start to see me for the fine, upstanding citizen I really am. Then maybe we could work together."

"That's one idea." Sarah placed a towering slice of cheesecake complete with strawberry drizzle on the table. After she'd left both plates, Andi added, "Or you could sit there and be quiet so I can enjoy this piece of cheesecake."

"I don't get you, Sheriff. People generally like me. Everybody except you. And Jackie, but him I can live with." Andi didn't say anything, because that was exactly the problem: people always liked him. He could get away with murder because he was charming. Her father had been the same way. Everything was fun and games until he lost interest, found a better option and moved along, leaving other people to pick up the pieces. And she'd tried to do the very best job she could, but it wasn't enough here.

He tapped his cheesecake with a fork and shook his head sadly. "You seriously do not get how this date thing goes, do you? We're supposed to trade our favorite colors, movies, songs and end with a rousing display of our five-year plans."

Andi tilted her head to the side. "I'm not sure I'm the one with the problem in understanding, Mr. Taylor. I'm pretty sure you could ask ten people and they'd all say a date should start with an invitation. And I'm also pretty sure we can both agree there was absolutely no invitation involved in this little dinner."

Andi picked up her fork and took her first bite of the sinful satisfaction that was cheesecake at the Smokehouse.

"Ooh, that was a burn. I think you got me." He watched Andi take her second bite. "If I had asked, what would you have said?"

"No. Of course the answer would be no."

Andi rolled her eyes. "You just want to talk about Jackie's case."

"What if I promised the case wouldn't even come up?" Mark tilted his head to the side.

"My answer would be a louder no." Andi sighed. "And I don't believe you. You've already proven the story is king."

He shrugged. "I'm a really good investigative reporter, and my stories are fair. You can trust me. My mother will vouch for me, of course, as a fine young man. What's the harm in a dinner or two, just to ease relations between the paper and the sheriff's office?"

Andi shook her head. "I don't see the need. I won't give you the inside scoop."

Both of his eyebrows shot up. "You don't see the need? For the sheriff's office to work with the newspaper? For the woman running for reelection to get some positive press? I don't believe it. You're smarter than that."

He had a point. She did her best to fight back the smile that threatened when he rolled his eyes. He forked the last bit of dessert into his mouth before he wiped it with the cloth napkin.

"Maybe you're right about that, but is having a better working relationship with the sheriff's office worth following me, invading my space and playing the getting-to-know-you game?" She had no idea where the question came from. Possibly the sugar rush.

Mark blew out a gusty sigh. "Yes, my job would be easier if you could see me as a good guy, one who only wants to serve Tall Pines… with the facts *and* your truth, if I can wrap my head around it." He arched an eyebrow to make sure she caught his drift. Andi nodded. "And there's something about you, Sheriff. I want to help you even when you make me crazy. As a sincere apology and proof of my good intentions, let me help with Jackie's case."

He motioned Sarah over and asked for coffee, then rested his elbows on the table. "Or I can keep following you around, jump out when you least expect it and ruin other desserts."

The steady pressure of his stare got to her. She wanted to enjoy her last bites, and she couldn't do that with him watching so closely.

He shrugged. "I used to be just like you, Sheriff. Worked harder, longer hours than anybody else because I believed in what I was doing. I wanted to save the world one news story at a time. All that got me was an angry ex-wife who didn't believe a man could be working all those nights—so there must be another woman—an ulcer and trouble sleeping at night. But I want to help you and I'm very good at asking the right questions. Let's work together."

Then he waited. When Sarah returned with the coffee, Andi huffed a put-upon sigh. "Why are you even here in Tall Pines? It's not exactly a hotbed of news or social life."

He licked his lips, then smiled. "Okay, since I don't think you're going to play the game correctly because you have a decided ornery streak, I'm going to give you the long, convoluted answer."

And Andi was hooked. That one sentence told her that he understood a whole lot more than she'd given him credit for. And she wanted to know more.

He stirred cream and sugar into his cup and placed the spoon on the saucer. "I love news but more than anything I love newspapers. I worked for my high school paper, my college paper and I studied journalism. I love the words and how they look on the page. I like how newspaper smells and I even enjoy the black smudges ink leaves behind." With a sigh, he said, "And since you won't ask me, I'll tell you that I love them because my father and I would read the paper together every day. When I was little, he'd hold me in his lap and ask for my considered opinion of the headlines, but when I got older, we would talk about sports or current events at the breakfast table. He's been gone since I was a senior in college, but newspapers remind me of those times."

So his entire life hadn't been charmed. It was clear he still missed his dad a lot. Uncomfortable with her discovery, she pushed away the plate that once held a lovely tower of cheesecake and asked, "But why Tall Pines?"

Andi could tell he was pleased. He believed he was reeling her in—and he just might be—but she wasn't going to let him know.

"Burnout. It's as simple and complicated as that. My whole life was about the job. I pursued the biggest stories I could, tried to make a name while fighting a kind of crusade. And I was very good, but everything else fell apart. Here, I love what I do again. The *Times* might be stories of elementary school spelling bees, histories of old farmsteads and the occasional unsolved mystery, but I like the pace. Advertising is easy to sell. There's not much of a crime beat, thank God. I can breathe, sleep through the night and fish very badly." He smiled at Andi. "I have a life here, not just a job."

"Right. So were you looking for small-town papers for sale and stumbled upon the *Times?*"

"Nah, I actually knew the editor from way back. When he decided to sell, he sent me an email to see if I'd be interested."

"Wasn't it hard to pack up and move hours away to a place where you don't know anybody? I can't imagine trying to wedge myself into a town like this where everybody knows everybody from way back and most of them are related somehow."

He shrugged. "It wasn't hard. I think Jackie's accusations helped make me a sympathetic figure, and I've made a real effort to fit in. If you'd told me five years ago I'd be entering cooking contests and running recipes under my column, I'd have asked what planet you were from."

He squeezed his eyes shut, then opened them and rolled his head on his shoulders. "You aren't going to ask about my personal life, either. I can tell. I was divorced about six months before I moved to town. She's remarried to a corporate lawyer who makes very good money and spends every night with her. And I'm here, living the good life."

Andi snorted and he laughed. She wondered if this might be what a really good date was like. She'd had so few of those that she wasn't sure.

"Sounds like you might be too unbusy to help." Andi shrugged. "And I can handle Jackie's case on my own. Besides, how would it look if I needed your help to solve this case? Ray Evans would have a field day."

Mark glanced around the shadowy restaurant, and Andi noticed the crowd had gotten a little larger. When she saw Sarah and

Amanda with their heads together, whispering in the corner, she realized how this might look to the people in the restaurant.

"There's an easy enough way to handle that. We'll pretend. We'll go out to dinner again and just like that, we're dating. No one would suspect that I was your secret weapon then." He reached across the table and picked up her hand. "How am I doing?"

Andi wasn't sure if she gasped or not. His hand was hot and the tingling in her fingers was back and spreading.

"What, like a *working* date or something?" She jerked back her hand and straightened in her seat.

Sarah chose that minute to deliver the check. Mark snatched it out of Andi's numb fingers, took a couple of crisp bills from his wallet and handed it back to Sarah with a smile. "Keep the change."

She flushed before she flip-flopped back to the kitchen.

When he looked back at her, Andi wiped one sweaty palm over her brow and tried to take calm, even breaths.

For once in his life he did the right thing.

He didn't say a word. He didn't smirk. He didn't tap or jiggle or jostle or in any way appear impatient. When Andi managed to look at him, he just looked certain. And that scared her more than anything else.

"I don't get you. I've made your job really difficult. On purpose. And now, all of a sudden, you want to help. Why?"

He shrugged. "Honestly, this is the first chance I've had to smooth things over. This is the first time you've done anything other than silently murder me with your eyes. Let me help. Think of how much better the story will be if I have all the facts…truth." He tilted his head.

Andi looked down at her missing watch and pretended to know what time it was. She needed out and she needed him to have his head examined before the next time they met. Business, working together, that was one thing. A date, even a pretend one where they were really working, was something else entirely.

"I just don't think it's a good idea, not even a *working* date. So…I need to go check on Gram." She patted the table with both hands.

"This was… Thanks for buying dinner, Mr. Taylor." And she wanted to smack her head against the table. Mr. Taylor? That was just stupid at this point.

"Mr. Taylor?" He didn't add on the "that's just stupid" comment, but she could read it on his face.

Andi's shoulders slumped and she couldn't resist hiding her face in her hands. She finally mumbled, "Yeah, you're right. I think we're past that." She was nothing if not brave. She lowered her hands and said, "Thank you, Mark, for buying my dinner."

There were the beginnings of a smile on his face as he nodded. "You are very welcome, Sheriff. Please just think about it. Maybe when I ask again, you'll say yes."

Andi shrugged and put one hand over her stomach. She was afraid if she didn't reach a calmer state soon her cheesecake was going to make a return appearance. "Change my mind? I guess maybe you don't know me as well as you think."

His smile grew as he scooted his chair back. Andi did the same and was hyperaware of him following her out of the Smokehouse.

She wanted to fidget with her uniform but managed to fight off the impulse. When they made it back onto the sidewalk, they stopped. The heat had subsided to a heavy blanket instead of a frying sizzle.

Suddenly Andi couldn't figure out what to do with her hands. She finally settled for crossing her arms over her chest.

Mark pushed his into the front pockets of his jeans. Maybe his hands didn't know how to act right, either.

He rocked back on his heels. "Sheriff, can you forgive me for that first story? I guess I didn't understand how things work here. After talking with you…well, maybe I'm starting to see your point."

With a sharp nod, Andi glanced up and down the street. Jackie was looking out the window of the diner. If she didn't get out of there pretty soon, he'd be headed her direction to demand some progress. "You made a mistake. I understand that. I've made a few. But…that doesn't make it easy to forget, M-Mark."

He nodded. "Fine, but maybe now…maybe

we can work together. How about you let me call you Andi like a friend?"

She thought about it for a minute. Her friends called her Andi, that part was true. He wasn't really a friend at this point, but she didn't figure it would hurt anything. Andi forced her clenched fists and tight arms down by her side and gave each hand a shake to loosen things up. She took two quick steps toward him, held her hand out and shook his twice when he finally responded. Then she was shuffling back toward the SUV. She laughed at his disgruntled expression before she waved. "You can call me Andi, Mark. Thank you for dinner."

She hopped in the truck and forced herself to calmly buckle the seat belt and check oncoming traffic before she pulled out. Her stomach was a knot of nerves, and she felt this stupid smile trembling along the edges of her lips. This didn't feel like her rut anymore. Mark Taylor was dangerous.

She waved at him again. He was motionless on the sidewalk. Andi wanted to burn rubber but acted in the absolutely appropriate, speed-limit-obeying manner befitting an officer of the law and drove sedately away. She looked in the rearview mirror again and for the second time that day, Mark Taylor was watching her drive away.

CHAPTER FOUR

ANDI WAS STILL rattled when she came to a stop in front of her grandmother's unit at the assisted living facility. Shady Pines had opened just as they needed it. Gram was now recovered from the fall that brought Andi home to Tall Pines, but she wasn't well enough to live alone. They argued on a pretty regular basis about her living arrangements. Andi wanted her to come back home. She wanted to take care of Gram the same way Gram took care of her when Andi's mom had lost her battle with cancer.

Gram was happy in Shady Pines and had no desire to return home where she'd have to cook and clean and entertain herself. At Shady Pines, she had shoppers and cooks and a constant stream of card games whenever she wanted. That was her story. She never deviated from it.

As stubborn as Gram was, there was no way Andi was leaving. Not yet.

As long as she won the election. When she'd first come home, she'd applied more than once for the sheriff's office. She would have been content as a deputy, maybe even in dispatch, but Ray Evans held a mean grudge. When she'd first come back, desperate to make a good impression, she'd swanned into the sheriff's office and proceeded to tell Ray just how much she could improve the workings of the sheriff's office with her advanced training.

Obviously she'd been gone so long she'd forgotten some key factors about living in Tall Pines. Natives were pretty sure the way they had done things for decades or centuries was the right way. No newcomer would tell them any different. The fact that she'd made her little speech in front of the mayor, the president of the bank and richest man in town, and other assorted head men in charge had pretty much sealed her fate. Ray would hold a grudge. He might even deserve to. If she could figure out the kind of apology it would take to set things right, she would make it. When…if she lost this election, Ray would have the last laugh.

Andi loitered outside until the heat and the flutter of the living room curtains signaled it was time to go in. Dealing with her grandmother was tough on the best of days. She was sharp. Nobody pushed her around, not even for her own good. She might need a walker to get around and a little help keeping the floors scrubbed, but she had eagle eyes and a mean intellect. Andi didn't think it would do any good to pretend everything was normal, but she wanted to try.

"Hey, Gram!" Andi called as she opened the door. She'd lectured Gram over and over about keeping the door locked even during the day, but those words had fallen on selectively deaf ears. Andi thought she remembered to lock it at night and tried to content herself with that. She also told herself not to check because the knowledge that Gram might forget would make her crazy.

"Well, Andi, I was beginning to wonder if you were going to sit in the car all evening." Gram's voice was low and soothing. Unless she was mad. Then it could reach decibels that might register in the next county.

"Just checking in with dispatch, Gram."

As Andi bent to kiss her cheek, Gram reached up for a hug. She smelled of clean laundry and vanilla; it was comforting. And sometimes it brought tears to Andi's eyes, but not tonight. She was too nervous to be sentimental.

"And were you thinking you'd have two big stories in one day?" Gram leaned back in her recliner and watched Andi closely. She froze for a second, certain that Sarah had called Gram before she'd even delivered Mark's ribs. Finally she took a deep breath and looked out the window to stall before realizing she was just talking about Jackie. Gram obviously hadn't heard the possibility of a second hot story.

Andi shook her head as she dropped down on the cushiony sofa and asked, "Have you had dinner, Gram?"

She nodded serenely. "And have you?"

There was just something about the look. Andi wanted to blithely acknowledge her salad and cheesecake and gloss over anything else. Two things stopped her. First, Gram knew something was up. Andi could tell from the look on her face. And second, if someone else told her about the dinner with Mark Taylor, and someone would—they always did—she'd be livid. Gram didn't expect Andi to keep any secrets from her. And Andi understood that. Gram knew her better than she knew herself sometimes.

Andi stretched out her legs and plumped a pillow behind her head. She crossed her arms over her face and managed to mumble, "Yes, ma'am."

"And what did you have?" Her sweet tone voice wasn't fooling Andi. She was pretending to be patient. Gram wasn't patient. Never had been, obviously never would be.

"I had a salad, a slice of cheesecake, and…a dinner companion. At the Smokehouse." There was silence. It was a long, uncomfortable silence. Finally, Andi moved her arms down and looked over at Gram. She was staring down at her hands. Just waiting. She had always done that. And Andi had always hated it.

"Mark Taylor." When she didn't say anything, Andi added, "The newspaper editor."

Gram nodded slowly. When she had nothing to say, Andi continued, "He didn't ask me out. He just showed up, sat at my table, forced me to talk to him and paid for my dinner."

"Funny sort of date."

"This wasn't a date, and he's a funny sort of man."

"Hmm, did he ask you out again?" Gram sounded as if she didn't believe she was getting the whole story.

Andi held up one finger. "Let's be clear. He never asked me out the first time." One corner of Gram's mouth quirked up, but she didn't answer. "He offered his help with Jackie's case."

"And I hope you were at least polite when you turned him down." Gram picked up her crochet hook and yarn and started working on the dishcloth in her lap. She'd always crocheted, but her projects had gotten smaller to match her space. On the bright side, every church yard sale made a nice chunk of change from her donations. Gram had to have a project going at all times.

"So you think I was right to tell him no?"

That surprised her a little. Gram made no secret of her wish for Andi to go out more, live a little.

Gram arched a single eyebrow and tilted her head. "Well, now, I never said that. I just know how you feel about him." She returned her attention to her dishcloth with a little sniff. "Seems a shame to turn away help, even from the newspaper man."

"But, Gram…" Andi huffed. They'd been through this before.

"Andrea, he was doing his job. I said it then. I'll say it now. Maybe you don't like the way he did it, but not everyone has the same…attitude you do."

"So I'm wrong to be upset over the angry calls I got?"

Gram's mouth tightened before she dropped her crochet hook. "You're wrong to take everything so personally. The only way you can avoid angry phone calls is to perform absolutely perfectly or do nothing at all. And we both know what you've chosen."

Andi rolled her head on the pillow. This was an old conversation, too. Gram had never understood her goals, her ambition. As she closed her eyes, Andi realized that wasn't exactly true. Gram understood better than anyone why Andi was driven to be the best. She just thought Andi ought to take it a little easier.

Andi was starting to wonder if she was right.

She rubbed her forehead. Of course she was right. Gram was always right.

"Well, this might surprise you. I'm thinking of taking him up on his offer. Being on better terms with the newspaper editor during an election couldn't hurt."

Gram nodded. "And he's very popular in this town. Could help you with voters."

That stung just a little bit. "I'm thinking of agreeing to his offer of a date, a sort of working dinner where we talk about the case but it looks like something more to everyone else.

"This time listen to me." Gram shook her finger. "Maybe you try a *real* dinner and *normal* conversation. Forget the job for two seconds and enjoy yourself with the town's most eligible bachelor. And if you can't, you've got to go, Andi. You have to get back to Atlanta or wherever it is that you can enjoy life a little. That's what you should be doing, not campaigning to win a job you don't really love."

Andi sighed. This was how it went between them. And as she usually did, she ignored Gram's orders to go. "Fine. So you think a date would do that? And I should just forget that he runs a newspaper and is firmly attached to Tall Pines and I'm…"

The silence stretched out as they both considered how to fill in the blank. Andi wanted to go. Gram wanted her to. But it wasn't the right time. Not yet.

Andi waited.

Finally, Gram pursed her lips. "It wouldn't hurt to go for dinner once or twice. Let your hair down a little. And maybe try a smile or two."

This was familiar territory. Any social difficulty Andi encountered was because she didn't smile enough. She'd need to have a smile surgically implanted to keep up with Gram's demands. So she was serious. She always had been. Was that a crime?

As the town's sheriff, Andi was uniquely qualified to affirm that being serious, logical and dependable was not against the law. In some places, those characteristics would even be celebrated. In fact, being serious had made her very successful in her FBI field office. Maybe she'd been out of step there, too, but at least she recognized the music. Tall Pines had a completely different song.

Clearly a subject change was required. Gram agreed. "There was a bit of a bother over at Jackie's this morning."

Happily, Andi nodded. This she could talk about easily. "Yeah, before I even made it to the office, Nettie had me turned back around and headed over there. Someone broke into his safe and took money and some important papers, along with all of his cook-off trophies. He had a group gathered, but I can't see any of them being involved.

"Mark was there this morning," Andi continued, "and he might be the type to play a joke on someone…" The lightbulb went off over her head because this was exactly what she was afraid of. It was easy enough to rule him out as a suspect because he wasn't the kind of guy who'd intentionally harm someone. At least she thought so now. And something inside loosened up a little. She believed him. None of that meant he wouldn't take advantage to get the inside scoop—all in the name of the "truth"—and let the chips fall where they would.

"And?" Gram was watching Andi closely again.

"And I don't think he'd try to hurt Jackie on purpose. And Oscar's an employee. Jackie might be hard to work with, but would he risk his job for what little money Jackie kept on hand?"

Gram worked a few double crochets before she answered. "I don't know if you can rule it out. What does he say?"

"Absolutely nothing. He manages a yes or a no and every once in a while a single-word answer."

"Who are his people?"

Andi smiled. She should have known that question was coming. Gram would never hold it against him, being born away from Tall Pines, but she still asked. "His mother teaches at the school. They seem to be a real nice family. Awful quiet though."

"And was that everyone?"

"No, Wanda Blankenship was there, too."

Gram glanced at Andi over the top of her glasses. "Have you interviewed her?"

"Just for a minute. Of course, she was the perfect example of cooperation. After she flirted with Mark Taylor."

In a dry voice, Gram said, "I think she must be guilty, then." Andi laughed as she sat up straight on the couch.

"Gram, I absolutely wouldn't mind if she were, but I somehow don't think life is going to work out that neatly. It never does."

Gram put her crochet hook on top of the dishcloth in her lap. She reached out to take one of Andi's hands. "Well, it hasn't always been easy, that's for sure. That's why I don't understand why you stay here."

Andi shrugged. "I stay here because you stay here."

Gram closed her eyes for a minute. "You know I'm not always going to be here. Then what?"

Andi smiled at her. "I'm pretty sure I'm headed to Vegas right after the funeral, Gram.

I've always wanted to be a showgirl. Without you holding me back, I'm going to be a star."

Gram tilted her head and squeezed Andi's hand. "How did you get to be so hard-headed?"

Andi bugged her eyes out and gave her head a wiggle. "Why, I do declare I have no idea." The truth was they both knew that as soon as Andi had the chance, she'd leave Tall Pines. No matter how well she did as sheriff, Ray Evans would continue to oppose her while he was able and every election would be a battle.

Gram picked up her crochet hook. "You probably ought to get on home. It's getting dark out there."

She seemed to forget that Andi was an officer of the law, licensed to carry a gun and use it when necessary. And that they lived in a small town where a business robbery was the biggest news in a while. To Gram, no one should be out after dark. Nothing good happened after dark.

The sleepless night and long day were wearing on Andi so she decided to take Gram up on this piece of wisdom. "Okay, night,

Gram. When I stop by tomorrow night, I'm going to have a new hairdo. Got any advice?"

She pretended to study Andi and her long brown curls. "I think you should go blond." She laughed as she said it so there was no possibility that Andi would take her seriously.

Andi shook her head. "Okay. Don't be surprised if I show up with a blond buzz cut tomorrow. You had your chance. Maybe it's time to shake things up around here."

Gram waited for Andi to kiss her cheek. "Baby, I think you might be right. You go ahead and shake some things up. Try smiling at that handsome young man."

Andi pulled back and gave Gram her best lawman's gimlet-eyed stare. "How do you know he's handsome?"

She shook her head. "Some lawman you are. His picture's in the paper, dear." Her tone was mild but Andi could hear the unspoken *duh* in it.

"Right." Andi walked over to the door, opened it and made a theatrical show of turning the lock on the knob for her.

When Gram said, "Good night, Andi," she waved and walked out to her car.

On her way home, the streetlights illuminated empty roads. Jackie's Country Kitchen was closed for the evening. A lamp in the back sent weak shafts of light through the dining room. Andi stopped and tested the door. It was locked. She got back in and drove around behind to check the alley. It was well lit as far as alleys go, and it was deserted. On the way home, she passed the newspaper office. Mark Taylor had an apartment on the second floor of the building. Lights were on up there but the newspaper office was dark. Apparently the news did sleep, maybe right after the weekly paper went out.

Andi turned onto the two-lane highway that led out of town then made a quick right down the lane to her house. It was a well-loved place. That was clear even in the bright moonlight. It was neat. There were healthy bushes and well-kept outbuildings. And someone was waiting for Andi. Her cat, Mojo, sat in the living room window as she pulled to a stop in front of the house. Sometimes she thought about getting a dog. After years of living in an apartment, she was lucky enough to have plenty of space now and the Tall Pines shelter was always crowded. If she were sure this was going to be home, she might. The only problem was Mojo. He had a bad attitude and lightning-quick reflexes. They'd ironed out a tenuous peace over eight years, and he'd almost forgiven her for packing him up and driving him more than two hundred miles. That had taken more than two years. She had no idea how long the recovery period might be for bringing home a dog. Plus, she liked the routine she and Mojo had established. She tried to get him to talk to her in the morning and evening with a can opener, and he tried to ignore her the rest of the day.

As she dropped her keys on the kitchen counter, Andi sighed with relief. It was good to be home. And no matter how hard things might be in town, when she was here, Andi felt safe. She could remember family dinners here, back when she was sure she'd never be happier than she was at Gram's kitchen table. Mojo meowed loudly at her feet.

"All right, cat. Here comes the chow." As she pulled down a tin of expensive cat food, Andi smiled and hoped for a good night's sleep. Her campaign was going to kick into high gear tomorrow. It might be the last night of good sleep until she made her acceptance speech.

CHAPTER FIVE

THERE WERE A few things Andi could not compromise on. Black coffee was one. It was the only proper way to drink coffee, and it had not escaped her notice that Mark Taylor drank his the wrong way.

Another thing that was nonnegotiable for Andi was having nice hair. Sure, she kept it tamed in a ponytail for almost all her waking hours, but it was nice to know that she could let loose her crowning glory if she wanted to. Crowning glories didn't come cheap or easy. For Andi, it required a morning in the chair over at the Hair Port under the very capable hands of Lynn Davis. Lynn was the only person Andi trusted to get her color the right shade of "better than the original but not quite noticeable enough to cause talk."

Lynn looked like she'd just moved up to the eighth grade, but she'd actually been doing hair in Tall Pines for about five years. And there was not a single secret in the county that she didn't know. There's a power in being a hairdresser. She had a captive audience.

Going to see Lynn was a double-edged sword. Even after growing up as the subject of more than a few conversations, Andi had to fight the temptation of trading information with the ladies in the Hair Port to fit in. So she'd just listen. And keep her mouth shut. All the time. Because any details Andi let slip would travel across town before she made it back to the office two blocks away. If Andi could do that and pick up anything about Jackie's case or the suspects, the hundred-dollar check she was going to leave behind would be money well spent.

When Andi went to see Lynn, they always had the same conversation. As the bells rang over the door to the Hair Port, that conversation started as it always did.

"Morning, Sheriff. It's good to see you."

Andi nodded.

"Are we gonna make any changes this time?" Lynn asked.

Andi could understand Lynn's total lack of hope when she asked that question. Today,

Andi glanced around the shop to assess the crowd. It was a pretty light day so far, but things changed quickly at the Hair Port. As the only shop on the courthouse square, Lynn and the other three stylists got a lot of walk-in traffic. Normally that made Andi happy. Good business meant that Lynn would stay here and keep notes on her color mix. Now Andi wanted the smallest crowd she could get as she said, "Let's do something different today, Lynn."

Crickets aren't a normal sound in the middle of town, but if there'd been any around, they would have had a nice little concert. There was absolute silence in the Hair Port, as though all the humans in the room were collectively holding their breath and the air-conditioning was waiting for the okay to run. Andi glanced around self-consciously.

The Hair Port went for a minimalistic style. Everything was white. White walls, white floors, white furniture, white uniforms and white drapes on the customers might make a person wonder if this was what beauty shops in heaven look like.

Lynn shot a quick look at the other stylists

and held out her hand. "Well, now. That I did not expect." She patted her chair. "Just what did you have in mind, Sheriff?"

Andi cleared her throat and slunk across the floor to hunker down in the seat. Her shoulders rose protectively to hover around her ears, but she'd already started this. "Well, I don't want to change the color."

Lynn nodded. "Yeah, I can see that. It's a pretty good color for you, maybe just a bit redder than your normal brown but not enough so people think you're channeling Lucille Ball." She pulled the rubber band out of Andi's hair, and the heavy weight spread across her shoulders and down the middle of her back.

Lynn turned Andi to look into the mirror as she ran her fingers through her hair. "Lots of curl. We could go short and get some really pretty ringlets going, Sheriff."

Andi shook her head slightly. "I don't want to lose the ability to pull it back. I can imagine the trouble I'd have with the old codgers on the square if I looked like a fluffy girl."

She looked at the curls balanced precariously and beautifully on Lynn's head and wondered what it would be like to have that much control over her hair. Lynn smiled and said, "Sometimes it's good to be a fluffy girl, Sheriff."

Any sign of softness would be seen as weakness by Ray Evans. And even in Atlanta, far from this town and before elections, Andi had difficulty with softness. She'd spent a lot of time pretending she was in control. She had kept most relationships perfectly cordial and businesslike and performed every task she was given well enough to leave no room for criticism. Both really helped her in the FBI, an organization that appreciated no-nonsense hair. Andi sighed. "Yeah, I think I might like it, too, but let's go somewhere in the middle. Can you do that?"

Lynn nodded. "Yes, ma'am, I can do that. We'll cut some of the length off, maybe put in some long layers so that when you want it to curl, it has nice body, and...what do you think about bangs this time around?"

It was only hair, right? Lynn had asked about bangs every two months since they'd started working together. Maybe it was time to embrace the bangs. "All right. Let's go for bangs."

Lynn and her stylists whooped as if she'd said, *Remember the Alamo*. Andi started to worry right then and there.

A drape floated across her lap, and Lynn snapped it shut. She patted Andi on the shoulder as she said, "I'm going to go mix up your color. Want something to drink?"

"Do you have tequila?" Andi muttered under her breath, but it wasn't low enough.

Lynn laughed and answered, "How about a bottle of water? Will that do instead?"

As she returned with the hair color and the water, the bell over the door rang and two ladies entered. When Andi saw Miss Margaret, a retired sixth-grade teacher, and her best friend, Edna, who'd been secretary at the First Baptist Church since Noah built the ark, she sighed in relief. Edna was the biggest gossip in town and didn't need much to prime the pump. Normally Gram caught up with them at Purl's Place, the town's one-stop craft shop, which was run by Andi's best friend, Tammy, and her mother. With a few well-placed questions, Andi could sit back and soak up the news. They were both decked out in the latest in grandma chic: blinged-out velour sweat suits.

"Well, good morning there, Sheriff!" Miss Margaret still used her perky, let's-all-get-ready-to-learn voice when she spoke to anyone under forty. That made sense. She'd been the first person to tell Andi she needed good grades to get into college. Andi probably hadn't even thought about college at eleven, but it had been good advice and it stuck with her.

Miss Margaret had helped her get out of Tall Pines the first time. She might not have recommended a double major in Mandarin and Persian Studies, but it's hard to tell where life's twisting paths will take a tween. They'd been highly sought after fields for FBI work. For retail jobs in Tall Pines? Not so much.

"Hi, Miss Margaret." Andi would have nodded also, but Lynn was slowly moving over her head with a smelly, frothy paintbrush. Every now and then one sprig of hair would flop over her eye. She tried not to think about how ridiculous she might look to anyone who glanced in the window. And she pasted on a smile of greeting for Edna. When the two ladies were settled in chairs with Sue and Rhonda, two stylists in the shop, Lynn threw out the first volley. "Did you hear about the fight Amanda and her husband got into last weekend at the Smokehouse?"

Everybody knew someone who'd been there at the time, which might or might not have been true but it was a popular place. Apparently George had been spending too much time out on the lake instead of manning the smoker and Amanda'd had enough. Andi squirmed through that conversation, certain her date with the newspaper man would be the next hot topic. She told herself she was hanging on every word because a good sheriff knew clues could come from the most unlikely places. Lynn finished up the hair color and had Andi move over to one of the more comfortable chairs in the waiting area. She took a long drink of water while she listened to the conversation swirling around the shop. When they'd finished enumerating the long list of people who were fighting, going on vacation and coming home from the hospital,

Andi cleared her throat. "Uh, Lynn, are we almost done with the first round?"

Lynn nodded. "Yes, ma'am. Let me go set up for the highlights and it'll be time."

Margaret and Edna continued to flutter and flit through all the juicy stories. Andi watched the hand on the clock. At some point, someone would ask her about Jackie. And if she was lucky, no one would ask her about Mark Taylor. And then it happened.

"Why, Sheriff," Miss Margaret said, "I meant to ask you this when we came in, but can you tell us about what happened at the diner?"

Andi heaved a mental sigh. The best course was to stick with the facts. Any time Andi gave her opinion, it came back through the grapevine as gospel. "Yesterday morning Jackie called me over to the Country Kitchen because someone broke in and took the contents of his safe and his trophies. I don't have any new developments at this point, but I'll be interviewing people today. I hope to have some more information for Jackie tomorrow."

"The newspaper man was a suspect," Edna said.

Miss Margaret tsked. "Some people will

try to pin every bad thing on the newest person in town. I just can't see that nice young man doing something so terrible."

Andi bit her tongue. It was nice to hear her giving a newcomer the benefit of the doubt. Andi's burgeoning hope for mankind was dashed when Margaret added, "He's too handsome for something like that."

Edna snorted. "Handsome doesn't mean innocent, Margaret. You ought to know that by now." Much as Andi hated to agree with Edna, this time she was right.

Margaret flapped her hands as Sue walked her over to sit under the dryer next to Andi. "Of course I do. But it certainly doesn't hurt, does it?"

She had a good point there.

"All right, Sheriff. Come on back, and we'll rinse that out of your hair so I can add the highlights."

Warm water nearly always made Andi sleepy. Despite her certainty that she'd lie awake contemplating every single thing she'd said to Mark Taylor and pondering every one of his smirks, she'd slept much better than the night before. But she kept waking up from weird dreams.

All of them had featured Mark in some form or fashion, but her favorite had been seeing him launched to the moon with a monkey companion. She *had* watched a show about the space program before bed. That had to be it. She didn't even want to think about the symbolism.

After she rinsed the color out, Lynn led Andi back to her chair and gave her hair a quick rough cut and dry. As Andi watched her work through newly cut bangs, she listened. Margaret, Edna and the rest of the ladies were on a juicy topic.

Edna took the lead. Sue was removing the rollers she'd used to set her hair so clearly time was winding down. A few fluffs and Edna would run out of prime beauty shop time.

Edna casually studied her nails to ratchet up the suspense. "Well, I don't know whether or not y'all have heard this, but I got the news from Rosa down at the grocery store. She saw it all herself so it's the honest truth."

There was that word again. *Truth*.

If those crickets had miraculously shown up in the Hair Port, they would have been able to hear a pin drop right then. Lynn had lifted the dryer to check again or Andi would never have heard Edna's intro.

Into the tense and expectant silence, Lynn said, "All right, Sheriff, let's go get you a rinse."

Andi hoped she'd be fast. The shampoo was usually her favorite part, but she wanted to hear Edna's hot lead. Andi made a mental note to start spending more time in the grocery store and monitoring Facebook. For work purposes, of course. It would be sort of like listening to the police scanner but in reverse.

When Andi thought about it, her growing interest in the sources of all this "information" worried her. Growing up as the focus of the stories that spread through town, she'd been certain other places were different. They weren't really, mainly because Andi was the same. Whether Andi was in Tall Pines or Atlanta, she wanted to know what was going on. And even worse, she wanted to drop something juicy just to watch eyes light up. There was power in knowing something no one else did. She imagined Edna felt the same and squirmed in her seat. If she stayed here where she knew everyone and everyone knew her, someday she might be sitting in this same chair, wearing a blinged-out tracksuit, happy to share the latest thing she'd overheard. She might be Edna someday. And eighteen-year-old Andi, the one who'd hated being the focus of that interest, would be gone.

Secrets, Andi. You wanted to know them. Pay attention.

When Lynn finished rinsing her hair, all the ladies in the shop were discussing who had the best source of up-to-date news. The Hair Port was the undisputed winner.

Miss Margaret cut through the chatter. "All right, so everybody's got a different source, but I want to know what the story is, Edna."

Oh, me, too. Thank you, Miss Margaret.

"Well," Edna said, and paused dramatically. "I hate to be the one to spread the news, but there's been a truck parked over at Maylene's house."

Andi suppressed a shrug, but there were titters all around. Lynn's steady scissoring paused for a second then she asked, "Whose truck is it, Edna?"

Andi could see Edna's face in the mirror.

She looked very, very happy and alive in a way that she hadn't when she walked in. The pink tint to her fluffy curls might have helped with that a bit.

"It's Jimmy Monroe's truck, ladies." And Andi would swear every head in the place swiveled in her direction. They probably expected her to have known somehow, but she didn't track the movements of her deputies after they left work. Besides that, he was single. And Maylene's divorce had been final for at least a year. They were both in their late twenties, old enough to know exactly what they wanted and smart enough to understand the consequences at this point. Unless they were growing an illegal crop or plotting a treasonous rebellion, Andi didn't care. And she was ready to set an example—a nice, indifferent example.

At the growing silence, Andi decided she had to say something. She looked up at Lynn. "Are you done?"

There was a silent but collective sigh. The windows of the Hair Port didn't fog up at the heated disappointment, but it was a close call.

Lynn said, "Yes, ma'am, let me dry this out so we see what we've got."

Andi nodded. When hair started flying, she closed her eyes and pondered what she should say. Lynn worked quickly and soon Andi could feel a fluffy cloud of curls touching her shoulders. When she turned the dryer off, Andi kept her eyes closed. She'd once received a direct shot to the eye from a can of hairspray. Without protective gear to fall back on, she used her eyelids.

After Miss Margaret and Edna paid, they paused at the door and Edna, possibly burned at how little reaction Andi had given her news, said, "Well, Sheriff, I do hope you'll tell Jimmy that his activities with Maylene have not gone unnoticed."

Andi risked opening her eyes to meet Edna's glare directly. "He's a grown man. She's a grown woman. They're both single. There is nothing illegal in their activities, and as such, I do not consider it any of my business." Andi watched Edna narrow her eyes and said calmly, "He does an excellent job of serving this town. Until it affects me directly, I'm not going to spread this story around, much less hurt my friend Jimmy by repeating gossip."

Edna made herself as tall as she could. Andi wasn't impressed. At best she was the center of the front row. She'd never be back-row material. "Gossip? I would never repeat gossip." Andi squeezed her eyes shut and bit her tongue, silently willing Edna to move along. "Rosa saw it herself. I'd think as sheriff you'd be interested in the goings-on of your deputies."

Andi shook her head. "And maybe you ought to take a little trip to the dictionary for the definition of gossip." She couldn't help it. She had to go there. "The fact is that there's been a truck parked in front of Maylene's house. Big deal. You've made that into some kind of…who knows what you imagine they're doing. But it's not your business or mine. And spreading it while implying something…else about it, that's gossip, Edna."

Edna sneered, and Andi knew she was in for it. "A girl like *you,* somebody who could turn her back on her own grandmother, forget this town and her family just like her father did, might not understand the importance of good laws and good morals, but we value both here in Tall Pines," Edna said. "A good sheriff would understand that."

Andi heard the emphasis on *you*. The rest of the shop heard it, too, and there was a gasp from one of the other stylists. Things were about to get real in the Hair Port. There was no way she could let that pass, but she had no idea what to say that wouldn't set Edna's newly pink and fluffy hair on fire.

Before Andi could gather her breath and her wits to let Edna know what she thought about her viciousness, she heard a masculine drawl from behind her. "Now, Edna, there's no call for that. The sheriff doesn't love a good story like the rest of us, but she's also loyal, something we like in our sheriffs, am I right?"

When Andi spun around, she found Mark Taylor in Sue's chair. He must have come in while she was deep in the blow-dry stage because she wouldn't have missed his entrance for any other reason. Sue was trimming his hair, and he was clearly on his way to shorter but still rumpled. And he looked pleased with himself. Maybe he'd managed to avert verbal

Armageddon with his cleverness, but Andi wanted to unleash on Edna. She wanted to say the magic thing that would convince people in this town to leave Jimmy and Maylene alone, to realize that what they said could hurt people, not smooth over choppy waters.

Mark smiled at Andi in the mirror. Miss Margaret seized her chance to usher a calmer Edna out the door. "Well, ladies, it's been a real nice visit." The clang of the bells over the door was a welcome sound. And simultaneously all the women in the shop took a deep breath.

Lynn whipped off the cape and said, "Sheriff, why don't you take a peek and let me know what you think?"

Andi managed to tear her eyes away from Mark's to see what Lynn had wrought. She had to give the girl credit. Even if she didn't look old enough to operate a motor vehicle, Lynn was a magician with scissors. Andi had appeared tired and frumpy but businesslike when she walked in. Lynn wiped all that business away and now Andi had bombshell hair that fell in nice fluffy waves to her shoulders. Bangs softened her look and she might even seem younger. Around here, that could be a problem. But she'd worry about that later.

Andi spun the chair around, stood and walked over to Sue's station.

Mark Taylor smiled up at her and then whistled long and loud. "Howdy, Sheriff. That's a real nice look for you."

"How long have you been here? Are you following me?"

He tried to seem innocent. "I did warn you, Sheriff. We could do dinner or I could continue to show up when you least expect it. But I've had this appointment for a month. You can ask Sue." Sue pursed her lips but didn't make eye contact. He might have been telling the truth but it didn't look good.

"And I got here just as Edna dropped her bombshell."

Andi thought back and tried to remember how incriminating the evidence might have been at that point. The remnants of her rage made her snap, "I did not need your help. There was no call to defend me, Mark Taylor. I am perfectly capable of telling Edna just exactly what I think." And the words still burned on her tongue. Maybe if she could remember the rage brought on by having her past thrown in her face, she could fight the temptation to soak up hearsay like a sponge. It would be good for her, just as soon as she got her blood pressure under control again.

He held up both hands. “Believe me, I get it. I wasn’t protecting you. You looked ready to murder. Still do, and it might even be justifiable homicide. I was protecting her. And maybe the decor. Bloodstains are hard to get out, I hear.” He didn’t smile, but the corner of his mouth quirked and his eyes were…warm. Understanding.

And no matter what he said, he’d probably saved her from herself.

She gave a silent sigh. It might have been audible, however. His eyes took on a wicked glint as he added, “I was sorry to have missed all the fun at first. When I walked past the window, you were under a dryer with enough foil on your head to protect you from an alien probe.”

Andi wanted to kick his chair. He brought out her hard-to-find violent tendencies, so she wanted to kick something. She didn’t. In fact, she realized where she was just in time. The whole salon was silent, no doubt listening to their exchange carefully, the better to dissect it after they left and spread mostly true bits like rice at a wedding.

Andi cleared her throat. “Okay, then. I guess we’re on a completely unrelated yet coincidental schedule.”

“I think I’m beginning to see what you mean by the difference between facts and truth, the importance of context. Such a deep thinker. Edna’s probably still trying to figure out what happened.” He reached out to take her hand and she froze. Andi could almost hear the chortles of glee sounding in the brains of every woman in the room. He smiled. “Your hair looks really nice, Andi.” And then imaginary jackpots went off. No one said a thing, but Andi could feel the weight of their stares. She knew he could see the distress on her face. Astronauts on the International Space Station could see the distress on her face. But she couldn’t move. He finally squeezed her hand and let go. “How about dinner later?” He glanced around at the other women.

And here it was. He was the most diabolically clever man in the world. Andi was surrounded. She couldn't retreat gracefully. And she'd gotten nowhere on finding out who stole from Jackie's diner. Mona and Jackie were probably worried sick, and it was her job to solve this theft quickly. Maybe Mark Taylor didn't completely understand her, but he was trying and that was…refreshing. She'd wanted to annihilate Edna on her own, but she'd really like to have some help with Jackie's case. She couldn't for the life of her figure out how to say yes. Plus, the longer she stood there, staring into his warm eyes, the harder it was to breathe. If she didn't answer—and quickly—the whole town would forget about Jimmy and Maylene to talk about the ambulance rushing over to the Hair Port to resuscitate the sheriff.

Finally Andi managed to clear her throat of the obstruction blocking both air flow and words. "Can I have a rain check, M-Mark?" She hated that stutter. But it had to be done. "I'd like to do some work on Jackie's case tonight. Everybody's going to expect some progress soon."

He leaned back in the chair and studied

her for a minute, happy surprise on his face, and he finally nodded. “All right. How about Saturday, then?”

That gave her time to figure out what in the world she wanted to do about Mark Taylor, so she agreed. Maybe she could stumble on a suspect and solve the whole thing before that. Then she could spend her Saturday night like she usually did: in front of the television, knitting. *Please save me from this rut.* “That sounds great.”

Andi avoided everyone’s eyes as she backed away toward the cash register. She could feel them all watching her, but only one of them mattered. She handed Lynn her check, told her to make another appointment in exactly two months, and made her escape.

WHEN THE SHERIFF passed in front of the window, Mark started a silent countdown. And in three, two…

The place erupted in chatter and Lynn raced over to pat him on the back. “You dog! After the sheriff! I love it!”

As Sue unsnapped the cape, he reached up

to give his hair a ruffle. He'd had it trimmed a week ago. "Thanks for playing along, Sue."

The petite brunette snorted. "You didn't give me much of a choice, Mark. You were in my chair with the cape on before I heard the bells over the door. I didn't even know you could move that fast."

He shrugged. "Sometimes a man's gotta do what a man's gotta do."

He slid out of the chair and inspected his hair carefully in the mirror. "Y'all don't know anything of interest about the break-in, do you?"

Lynn wagged her finger at him. "You don't think we'd tell you instead of the sheriff, do you?"

In a slow drawl, Mark said, "Well, now, you might." He winked at Lynn and laughed when she rolled her eyes.

"You can't charm me, Mark Taylor."

He raised an eyebrow at her.

Lynn said, "I mean, we could exchange information, maybe."

"I don't have anything to exchange, Lynn. Maybe you ought to tell me what you know."

She pursed her lips. "Well, now, I'm not

sure about that." She waved her hand airily as she walked over to pick up the broom and start sweeping up the less-than-heavenly floor. "Seems you might know about your upcoming date. And how long you and the sheriff have been seeing each other. And maybe what your plans are, even."

Mark laughed. "I might. But if I told you, the sheriff would kill me. Dead. I'd be dead and you'd all be sorry. Is that what you want?"

She swept up small piles of Andi's curls and sighed. "I guess not. She might get into trouble and I really like Andi."

He nodded. "You know, one good way to help her is to give me any info you might have to solve this case. If she doesn't get it taken care of quickly, Ray Evans is going to have a pretty strong platform for reelection."

Lynn and Sue traded speaking looks before Sue hesitantly said, "Well, now, I don't want to get anybody in trouble, Mark. I didn't see enough to tell you who broke into Jackie's. And I would have told the sheriff but I… got distracted by the show." She shrugged. "Never mind. I'll just head on over to her office to talk to her instead."

Mark pulled out his wallet and said, "You could do that…or I could tell her for you. I need all the help I can get with the sheriff, ladies."

Sue sighed. "Well, I closed up that night. I had a perm run long, and I was the only one left in the shop. When I drove home, there was a pickup truck parked on the curb, but no one was in it. I didn't think to get a license or anything. I didn't think I was witnessing a crime, you know?"

Mark put down enough to cover his impromptu trim. "Sure. Can you guess on color or what kind of truck? Was it old or new?"

Sue shook her head. "I think it was dark, maybe black. And it was an older model, but I can't for the life of me figure out who drives it. I've been watching the street but nothing seems to fit."

"Well, there's probably one pickup truck for every person in this town so it's a pretty big selection." He smiled. "But thanks for telling me. I'll pass it along to the sheriff. Maybe that will help narrow things down."

"You be a gentleman with my friend, Mark Taylor," Lynn said. "She deserves a nice guy.

I'm not sure you are one, but I know for certain you can help her shake things up. Those bangs were only the start, I bet."

Mark waved and opened the door. "Thank you, ladies, for all your help."

As he stepped back out on the sidewalk and looked in through the window, Mark could see all the ladies huddled together, no doubt cussing and discussing everything that had happened that morning. The Hair Port did a nice business. They were talented stylists, sure. But the real attraction came from skillful investigation and reporting techniques. Maybe he ought to put them on the payroll.

He rubbed his chin and stared down toward the sheriff's office.

Even though he'd lectured himself about leaving her alone since she'd driven away the night before, when he'd seen her standing up to the town gossip and looking so, so pretty and good and just…noble, he'd had to go for it. And he'd caught her at a weak moment, so now they had a *working* date. She hadn't been able to say that, but he'd read the qualification in her eyes.

He couldn't ignore the crazy flutter that

was either excitement or fear or both at the idea. When he realized he already missed her and wanted to run down to see her with this new excuse, he had to ignore a shiver of dread. She could be bad news of the forever kind. He couldn't remember missing someone five minutes after they'd walked out. So he decided to wait and pretend he wasn't headed for lovesick at a high rate of speed. This information could help Andi. And the honest fact was he couldn't depend on having the bargaining power for long. Lynn, Sue and the other Hair Port ladies would dole it out as they saw fit, and then it would spread through town in a wave. He'd lose his advantage. He needed that.

With her, he needed every advantage he could get. He could see the desire to bolt in her eyes. She had been half a second from turning down his request in the beauty shop. If he left her alone too long, she'd talk herself out of having dinner with him.

Mark shook his head. He ought to have it examined. She was rigid, prickly and desperate to be anywhere but here. The dating pool was pretty shallow in Tall Pines, but she wasn't the only pretty girl in town. Why was he ready to sign on to her particular brand of frustration? It didn't help that she was so cute when she got mad. Or that she was mad all the time. Or that he admired her strength and smarts. He wanted her cooperation, just to make his job easier, but maybe he also wanted to take her out, get to know her, shake her up. Now he had a nice reason to surprise her when she least expected it. He'd gamble and hold on to it for a little longer.

CHAPTER SIX

ANDI MANAGED TO walk briskly down the sidewalk in front of the Hair Port without looking in the window to see either Mark Taylor or the banked uproar that would no doubt erupt as the bells jingled on Mark's exit. She made it back to the station, where Lori greeted her with a grim smile. "Sheriff, Tammy's in your office."

Andi nodded and skirted her desk and the crowded room behind it. When she opened the door to her office and saw Tammy's Post-it-noted strategic plan leaning against her desk in full neon glory, she wanted to close the door quietly and tiptoe back out to the sidewalk.

Tammy's hoot stopped Andi dead in her tracks. "Woo, girl, look at that new hairdo!" She clapped her hands and danced around Andi to get the full effect. Andi had known Tammy since first grade. She was about six inches shorter than Andi, athletically perfect with straight fine blond hair, and looked as if she'd never been in a bad mood. She had. She just never looked it.

Andi walked around her desk to collapse in her chair, which promptly let out a loud screech. In this instance, it was a comforting sound. It matched Andi's mood perfectly.

Tammy perched on the edge of her own seat and said, "You oughta get that looked at."

"My hair or my chair?"

Tammy laughed. "I meant the chair. The hair's pretty fabulous. If you were wearing anything other than that uniform, I'd think you'd come from one of those makeover shows."

Andi nodded. "Right. So, Mrs. Campaign Manager, what have you come up with?"

Tammy waved a hand dismissively at the poster she'd clearly spent some time on and said, "We'll get to that. Let's talk about the hair some more. I want details. And how soon can we get a new campaign photo taken?" She pulled out her phone and said, "You know what...you and I both know it'll never look this way again. I'm going to call Peter and see if he has time to come over and shoot you right now."

Andi nodded. Some days she felt as if she'd pay someone to shoot her…literally. Yesterday had been one of those days. Today was starting to look the same. Peter was Tammy's husband. He worked at the bank, but his hobby was photography.

"Hey, baby, Andi's gone and gotten herself a really nice hairdo. Can you come over and take some photos at lunchtime?"

The answer must have been yes because Tammy's previously perfectly happy face lit up and she said, "Love you, baby." When Tammy smiled and nodded at her, Andi did her best to smother the jealous twinge that kicked in whenever Tammy and Peter were together.

Tammy dropped her phone back in her purse and said, "He'll be here in fifteen minutes. Now, dish."

Andi shook her head. "Don't you think a bit of makeup would be a good thing if I'm about to have my picture taken?"

She held out her hand. "Pass me your bag

and we'll see what we can do. And then you better talk."

Andi pulled out the small bag she kept in a drawer for campaign emergencies. She never spent much time worrying about anything more than mascara on most days. Plain sheriffs seemed a whole lot easier to support than glamorous ones.

Tammy walked around the desk and sat on the edge of it as she dug around in the bag. She pulled out powder and blush and quickly applied those before she started working on Andi's eyes. "I want to know everything. What brought on the bangs?"

Andi closed her eyes. "Maybe I'm getting tired of the way things are, doing the same thing day in and day out. Maybe I'm thinking about making some changes."

Tammy hummed. "That doesn't sound like you. What prompted this adventure?"

Andi smiled. Then she braced herself. "I think that would be Mark Taylor's fault. Unless you count Jackie's robbery as the real beginning, Mark is the source."

Tammy paused and Andi blinked her eyes open. She closed them again when Tammy headed back toward her with a small brush. "We ran into each other at dinner last night and he said some things.... I finally told him what I thought about his news reporting, he apologized and offered his help with the case. Today I couldn't figure out how to say no to his dinner invitation so I said yes, and now I think we have a *working* date on Saturday."

Andi expected to be blinded by brilliant rays of sunshine from Tammy's huge smile. Instead, Tammy bit her lip. She worked carefully with the mascara then leaned back. "Andi, that's great. He's seriously cute."

"That wasn't quite the reaction I expected. Aren't you the same girl who signed me up for an internet dating service?"

Tammy sighed. "If I thought this was going to be an actual date, I'd be dancing on the desk. The fact that you can take anything and turn it into work worries me—you know that."

"I have to prove myself. As my campaign manager, you ought to understand that. Besides, it's dinner. Out. At night. That's a date, right?" Andi told herself it didn't matter what Tammy thought. But it did.

Tammy shook her head, worry clear in the tiny frown on her forehead.

A knock rattled the window in Andi's office door and Tammy opened it to let Peter into the tiny room. "Girl, there's more to life than work, even in Tall Pines."

Peter raised an eyebrow as he kissed his wife but he didn't ask. He had a lot of experience walking into the middle of their conversations.

"Hey, Peter, thanks so much for taking the time to seize this chance." Andi picked up the single lipstick out of the bag and carefully applied it. When she looked up, Tammy and Peter were communicating with their eyes. Andi couldn't hear a single word, but she knew she was the subject of the conversation. Again. And she heaved a quiet sigh.

Tammy worried about her. To her, the keys to happiness were a strong marriage and lots of time for her family. She just didn't understand Andi's need to prove herself. Why should she? She'd never been the town's favorite subject of discussion, she ran one of the most popular businesses in town and she had a husband who'd love her until the end of time. Tammy didn't need to prove anything to anyone.

"All right. Where do you want to do this?" Andi asked.

Tammy looked around the office and went to open the blinds for more light. "Let's try for one shot in here then head outside to get one by the sign and maybe one or two with your car if the heat doesn't kill us."

Peter saluted and started giving direction. Andi did her best to follow all of his instructions, but something about having a picture taken made her more uncoordinated than normal. She lost count of how many times Peter had to say, "No, your other left."

After roughly one thousand photos, Tammy was satisfied, and Peter was on his way back to work. They'd escaped the heat as quickly as they could. Andi and Tammy were reviewing her "strategy board" in the nice, cool office. Andi wanted to make air quotes every time Tammy mentioned the strategy board, but she would not have appreciated that. As she was Andi's one and only full-time campaign worker, Andi needed to keep her happy.

"I'm not sure a debate's a good idea, Tammy. Besides, how would we get people to turn out?"

Andi desperately wanted a big, tall glass of sweet tea. Her caffeine levels were running dangerously low after a morning in the beauty shop and the unplanned photo shoot. She carefully sneaked a look at her watch. Jackie's lunch crowd would be long gone by now. Andi would have to put up with his questions, but she could also get a nice, cool drink and something for lunch. And she would happily buy Tammy's lunch. If she'd only let Andi get the invitation out.

"Listen, I've got a plan. We're going to get one of the groups from town to play in front of the courthouse to draw a crowd. Your boyfriend, Mark, can moderate and also do some advance promotion. We'll set up podiums on the stage and spend thirty minutes talking about the issues."

Andi still didn't think it was a good idea. Public speaking didn't terrify her but it didn't please her, either. Tammy had no doubts. Finally, Andi wrapped one arm around her grumbling stomach and said, "All right. You set it up with Mark and Ray, and I'll be there."

Tammy clapped her hands. "I can do it. We'll go through a little practice beforehand to be sure you're ready."

"Maybe," Andi replied. She was quiet and they both laughed when her stomach rumbled loudly enough to get attention. "If I don't eat soon, I'm going to lose my laid-back personality."

Tammy snorted. "Right. Well, we wouldn't want that."

They had done enough for one day. Tammy had outlined the basics of the "media plan," and since it consisted of yard signs, a billboard, a few postcards and several ads in the newspaper, Andi couldn't see much to change. They'd done practically the same thing for the last election. And Tammy had everything ready to go because they were on a deadline. The new photo was an unexpected bonus that made Tammy's eyes sparkle when she talked about it. The billboard was a new idea and Andi wasn't sure how she'd feel seeing her name that big, but she trusted Tammy's instincts.

"Let's walk over to the Country Kitchen. I'll drop the strategy board in my car on the way." Tammy picked it up but paused in the doorway. "I guess Jackie'll eventually let you eat in peace?"

Andi shrugged. "We've got to give it a try."

Jackie made a beeline for Andi as soon as her right foot cleared his threshold. He dropped two menus on the table and yelled over his shoulder, "Two sweet teas, Oscar." Then he turned his laser focus back to Andi and said, "Any news, Sheriff?" His eyes narrowed as he studied her face, as if he knew something was different but he couldn't quite put his finger on it.

Andi shook her head, enjoying the swish of her now-shorter ponytail, and sighed with happiness as Oscar magically appeared and set the glasses down on the table. Before they left her office, Andi had pulled her curls back up into a ponytail as required by both the heat and her need for authority. "Not yet, Jackie, but a list of anyone who might have a personal reason to steal from you—something other than taking the cash you have on hand—could help. Also, can you tell me who else has a key to the restaurant?"

"Only people with a key are me and Mona,

but I can make you a list. What'll you have for lunch?" Jackie asked. He looked a little anxious and a little ticked off.

Andi didn't open the menu. She didn't need to. "Club sandwich and chips, please."

"Make it two, Jackie," Tammy added.

"How's Mona doing?" Andi asked.

"As good as anybody can be with a burglar on the loose. Sure hope you'll fix that quick." He snatched both menus and went back into the kitchen to make up the sandwiches. Andi thought about asking again just what kind of papers were in the safe, but she figured her chances of finding out were even worse with an audience.

While they waited, Tammy said, "So…you and Mark. What's the plan for this *working* date?" When Andi didn't immediately launch into a heartfelt confession, she waggled both eyebrows.

Andi snorted a little of the sweet tea she was methodically draining from the glass, but she had no worries. Oscar would have it refilled before she knew it was empty.

When she caught her breath, Andi said, "There's not much to say. He asked me out. I said yes. We're going out on Saturday. We'll share information on the case, try to come up with some new direction. Right now, that's all I know."

Tammy tilted her head and waited.

"Really, that's it, my whole plan." She shook her head. "And if you don't believe me, just wait a bit. You'll hear the tale of how he asked me out over at the Hair Port. Also, that I nearly verbally murdered Edna for comparing me to my father, but Mark saved the day."

Tammy's eyebrows rose and she tore her napkin into small pieces before she answered. "Wow, all that with an audience. That's not the Sheriff Jackson I know." The concern on her face brought on an old familiar lump in Andi's throat. Tammy had been there through it all, and her care was enough to burn past the rage to the hurt that lingered and resurfaced anytime her father came up. "Sheriff Jackson's usually firmly in control." She rolled her eyes. "And she'd never let someone else come to her defense."

Andi opened her mouth to argue because Tammy looked a little hurt as she said it, but it was the truth. She'd practiced long and hard to pretend her past no longer got to her. The idea that she'd need anyone else to protect her was silly.

"But...Mark Taylor. He's the kind of guy you should go for. I mean, if you lived for anything other than work." This was an old argument. Andi had explained how important serving this town flawlessly was, and it had been enough to get her on board for the first campaign. "Wouldn't it be nice to have someone who would fight for you, even if you don't really need it?"

"Tammy, it wasn't a fight. It was a clever remark that...deflated the tension." Which was better than the smoke and ash she'd have left behind. She might owe him a grudging thank-you for that. "And I said yes to his working date because I want to solve Jackie's case quickly and I want to be reelected sheriff. Getting along better with him will help, but this isn't a love match."

Saying it out loud seemed to lift a heavy load off Andi's shoulders. "You know I'm only here for a little bit, Tammy. I'll win this election, do a very good job, and by then, Gram should be settled." Maybe. She hoped.

"I want to take advantage of Mark and his connections. That's all. I'm not settling down here."

Tammy sighed and looked resigned. Maybe even disappointed. "I'm just saying he's pretty cute…has his own business. He's a catch. Maybe you should…you know, try to catch him. Most men—a lot of men—stay, Andi. They don't leave their wives or kids. And I think you'd be happier if you took a chance on a good one sometime."

Andi shook her head. Tammy had never put any direct pressure on her to come home, but Andi had the feeling she'd be over the moon if Andi settled down right here with the newspaper man and a white picket fence. She watched Tammy smile determinedly and tried to ignore the pang brought on by the thought of leaving again, missing these lunches, relying on weekly phone calls to know what was happening with her best friend. Following right behind that was the burning guilt that filtered in anytime she thought about leaving her Gram or Tammy behind in Tall Pines again.

Maybe Tammy was right about taking a

chance, but she didn't understand that Andi's work with the FBI was important. She couldn't give up forever the satisfaction it gave her, not even for her best friend.

Jackie came back with the sandwiches and deposited them wordlessly. And Andi's tea glass was full again. She was really coming to appreciate Oscar's abilities. She took a more-aggressive-than-strictly-necessary bite of her own sandwich and chewed forcefully.

"Did you hear anything else over at the beauty shop? Any news?" Tammy took a bite of her own sandwich.

"Edna couldn't wait to tell us about Jimmy and Maylene." Andi shook her head. "And I wasn't going to repeat it. What's wrong with me?"

Tammy laughed. "That's not news to anyone who knows Maylene, Andi. She's been smiling ear to ear like a lunatic. *She* knows how important a good man is. They've been dating for four months. Edna must be slipping."

Andi leaned back in her seat. "Really?" She picked up a potato chip and crumbled it into pieces. "Everybody seemed surprised."

Tammy waved her hand. "I'll guarantee you that most of them already knew it. Half the fun of getting your hair done is seeing who can tell the best story. They don't really have to be breaking news."

Uncomfortable at the reminder that there was so much going on that she didn't know about, Andi asked, "When do you think you'll get the debate set up?" Back to business. It was easier.

Tammy shrugged. "It would be nice to wait until it's cooler."

It was the beginning of October now. Clearly there was no guarantee it would ever get much better. "Mayor Jones won't be happy to lose a night of singing on the square for a debate when the tourists are flocking to town."

She nodded. "You're right. I'll aim for three weeks and see how that works with everyone's schedule. Maybe we can squeeze into one of the nights already booked."

Jackie marched back to the table to deposit the check. Andi used her own developing ninjalike quickness to snatch it up before Tammy even knew there was a contest. Jackie also had three pages stapled together. It looked like a list of everyone in Tall Pines with a few names Andi didn't recognize. She didn't know if those were tourists who'd come through town once or maybe people he'd met the few times he'd stepped foot outside the county lines, but she was pretty sure she could cross Willie Nelson off the list of suspects. One down and about eleventy million to go. He'd helpfully written numbers beside each name and short descriptions of why they were after him.

Andi tried to ignore the sinking feeling she got about how long it would take to read the list, much less work through everyone on it, and she smiled up at him. "This is good, Jackie. Are the numbers a ranking system? Maybe I should start with number one and work down the list?" Just like his spotless restaurant, Jackie made a ruthlessly organized list.

He nodded once sharply. "Exactly. I don't expect most of 'em have the ambition or pure want-to to accomplish this, but it's hard to tell about people sometimes."

"Is Mona around? I'd really like to talk to both of you."

Jackie snapped to attention and shook his head. "Not right now. She'll be back about four to help out after Oscar's shift. We're shorthanded until I can get somebody hired." His eyes tightened suspiciously as he handed her change. "Maybe you can leave her out of this. I don't want her more upset than she already is."

Telling him that she wanted to check with his wife about her whereabouts and, more importantly, find out what exactly was taken from the safe would send Jackie into a full-on fit. Instead, Andi said, "Oh, I want to check with her to see if she's noticed anything around here that needs to be investigated."

She wasn't certain he believed her. He finally nodded. "Come on back after four, then."

Andi left a generous tip and followed Tammy back out to the sidewalk. From the corner of her mouth Tammy asked, "You want to get Mona's take on the whole thing, right?"

Andi smiled and said, "You bet."

Tammy hugged Andi and thanked her for lunch. "Come on by the store when you have a minute. We got some new sock yarn in, and I picked the most obnoxious color combination just for you." She said the last bit in a singsong voice because she knew it was a temptation. No matter how much sock yarn she had, Andi could be counted on to buy more. Knitting was therapy.

She acted uninterested. "Yeah, but I've already got enough yarn to make everyone in town a pair."

Tammy pretended to think it over. "Wonder if that would work as a campaign promise. Vote for Andi, and she'll give you a pair of ugly socks."

Tammy didn't get it. Sock knitting was the perfect kind of knitting: small, quick and precise—just the way Andi liked her projects. She shook her head sadly. "While it might work for me, it would definitely not work as a slogan for Purl's Place."

Tammy snorted. "You're right. Forget I mentioned it. Besides, you'd make me knit a pair or eight hundred and that would ruin my life."

As she opened the door to her shop, Tammy stopped and pointed at Andi. "Swear you'll call me with any new developments."

Andi was confused but she nodded uncertainly. "Okay, sure. If I find out anything concrete about Jackie's robbery, I'll give you a call."

Perky Tammy stomped her foot. "That's not what I meant." She looked up and down the street, then said in a stage whisper, "I was talking about Mark Taylor, girl."

Andi should have known. Tammy didn't think twice about crime in this town except to consider whether or not it would get Andi elected. She'd known Andi a long time. Except for the years she'd spent in Atlanta, she and Tammy had talked almost every day and just about every day they talked about boys. They'd mainly been Tammy's boys, not Andi's, because Tammy had gone a much saner accounting route while Andi had done a double major. Thanks to the scholarship that sent her to college, Andi didn't have much choice except to concentrate more on books than boys. Thank goodness she'd always been able to live vicariously through Tammy.

Andi gave her a thumbs-up and Tammy waved before stepping inside the shop. She looked at the clock on the tower above city hall. She had less than an hour before Mona would be over at the diner. Andi walked back to the SUV and decided to try Oscar's house.

After introducing herself to Oscar's mother only to learn they'd already met at the school's field day, Andi verified that Oscar had been home on the night of the break-in. As she was getting ready to leave, she said, "One more question. You mentioned he liked working at the diner. How does he feel about his boss?" Andi expected to get some good dirt with this question.

Mrs. Martinez shrugged. "Jackie gives him forty hours or more a week and pays on time every time. He understands that I sometimes need Oscar's help with the children and has always been flexible." She nodded once. "And yes, Jackie has a temper. But it takes quite a lot to ruffle my Oscar."

She was probably right about that. Andi sighed. Logically, it was possible that Oscar might have another reason to unlock the window, but she remembered watching him drag over that metal chair, clamber on top of it and struggle to reach the handle. Eagle-eyed Jackie would have noticed. Andi mentally drew a black line through his name.

She'd thanked Oscar's mother and headed back to the diner. With no other suspects, Andi decided to take a closer look at Jackie's list. She needed to widen her net. Maybe Mona could help with that.

CHAPTER SEVEN

MONA WAS ALREADY behind the counter when Andi walked into the diner. After she took a deep breath of the nice, cool air, Andi slid onto a stool in front of her.

"Howdy, Sheriff. How's your day going? Any news?" Jackie's wife looked tired, and maybe older. Her eyes were puffy, as if she'd been crying, and when she smiled it didn't reach her eyes. Andi rolled her shoulders as she smiled at Mona. "Well, I've had better, but I'm hoping you can help me with that."

Mona filled a glass with ice and set it in front of Andi before she filled it with sweet tea from a nice, sweaty pitcher. She put the pitcher on the counter and one eyebrow rose higher and higher as she watched Andi drain half the glass. When Andi noticed her fascination, she carefully set the glass down. Mona refilled it, and Andi forced herself not to touch it.

Andi had known Mona a long time. She hated to see her upset. As a Sunday-school teacher, Mona had been one of the first people to try to teach Andi that patience was a virtue, along with the Golden Rule and the stories of all the Bible greats. When Jackie and Mona opened the restaurant and Mona had taken over the church youth group, she'd looked like she might have known the Bible heroes firsthand—she was all sweet smiles and never-ending good humor. Now a halo would perch comfortably right on top of her fluffy white curls.

She and Jackie might be the opposite sides of a coin. She was all goodness and he was ornery cussedness. Jackie kept people stirred up and talking, but Andi had never heard a bad word about Mona. In one way she and Jackie matched: height. Mona couldn't stand any taller than five feet even. Today she somehow seemed even smaller. She was one of those people who made Andi understand Godzilla's dilemma when confronted with Tokyo. One wrong step could flatten something important, but a giant lizard's gotta do what a giant lizard's gotta do. And so did sheriffs.

"I've talked to Jackie's group from yesterday morning." Andi looked at the tea glass. Condensation slid down the side and her fingers inched a little bit closer.

Mona shook her head. "I don't know what he's thinking sometimes."

Andi knew exactly what she meant. "He's determined to find what was taken from the safe." Andi watched Mona's face closely enough to see her small frown come and go. "But I can't come up with a good reason for Mark or Wanda, or even Oscar, to steal the recipes."

"Oscar?" Mona asked, with her eyebrows raised high enough to merge with her hair.

Andi shrugged. "It would've been easy for him to actually steal the stuff, but he likes his job. He's too smart to mess that up, surely."

Mona shook her head and wiped down the spotless counter. "He's the best employee Jackie's ever had. He thinks the world of Oscar. If we could find another one like him, I might convince Jackie to retire or at least cut back some. He's always wanted to see the

Grand Canyon, but at this rate we're running out of time."

It was hard to imagine either Jackie or Mona aging. Maybe there was something magical about the atmosphere of the Country Kitchen. Neither one seemed to have changed much over the years. Of course, Andi was getting older, too. Maybe her memory was the magical part of the equation.

She pulled out the list and ran her finger down the first page as she read quickly, and she realized that Oscar's name wasn't there. Jackie hadn't thought his employee had a motive, either. And that was saying something. Jackie probably stayed up all night on Christmas Eve just in case Santa did try to come down his chimney. Only instead of milk and cookies, he'd offer a loaded shotgun and a sour expression.

Andi handed the list to Mona. "These are the names Jackie gave me of people who might have something against him." The paper crinkled as she laid it flat on the counter. As Mona put on her glasses, Andi asked, "If you had to narrow it down, which ones would you question first?"

Mona was as thorough as she had been when she drilled teenagers on their memory verses each Sunday. Andi lost count of the snorts and tsks Mona issued as she read, but her hopes were building, as Mona went on, that she'd help weed out the frivolous names and get to the real suspects. While Mona was distracted, Andi drank her tea. Yes, all of it.

"Honestly, Sheriff, I don't think there's a person on this list who'd break in to steal what little money Jackie kept here." She slid it back to Andi and picked up her towel again. "It's got to be a prank of some sort. Maybe the principal over at the high school could give you some names of kids who might be interested in something like that."

Andi wondered how that conversation might go. *Mr. Brown, could you narrow down the high school population to two or three kids who might have nothing better to do on a school night than rob a local business?* The principal would probably think she'd lost her mind. And at this point, the last thing she needed was more possible thieves. Scratch that. The last thing she needed was another wild-goose chase. She was in desperate need of a legitimate suspect.

Andi was refolding the list to stash it in her pocket when Jackie hustled in. “Hey, Jackie, I’m glad you’re here.”

He slipped behind the counter and lurched to a stop. He quickly assessed the empty diner and then did a survey of his wife’s face. Mona smiled at him, but he didn’t look relieved. “Got some results?”

“Not yet. I’m still looking for a solid lead.”

“Well, Sheriff, I already made you a list. You want me to do the rest of your job, too?” His face was turning red, but he hadn’t reached full steam yet. He wrapped an arm around Mona’s shoulders and squeezed her close.

“I was hoping to have the chance to speak with both of you privately.” When neither of them said anything, Andi added, “About what was stolen from the safe.”

Jackie pointed at Andi. Aggressively. “I told you, it’s important stuff.”

Andi nodded. “What I’m wondering is whether that might have been the real target. Can’t you tell me more?”

Mona started to answer, but Jackie shushed her. She frowned but didn't interrupt.

"Papers. All my recipes. Things that mean a lot, Sheriff." Jackie shook his head. "I couldn't sleep last night, thinking about my recipes out in the world, particularly this close to the cook-off."

Andi believed he couldn't sleep. She just didn't buy that it had to do with recipes. He had everything committed to memory. That's who he was.

She fiddled with her tea glass while she tried to figure out how to ask the question. "So, Jackie, the part about this that puzzles me is the trophies. No random thief would steal them. Other than bragging rights, they don't have any value. That seems to indicate someone with a real personal motive, maybe even revenge."

Jackie propped his hands on his hips. "Yeah, Sheriff. Exactly. And now he's got my…recipes and stuff."

Andi glanced at Mona to see her staring intently at the floor.

"Here's the thing. Remember when I asked about Wanda and you didn't want to talk about her?" He nodded. "Well, I get the feeling that wasn't the only secret I'm working around. You know more about who broke in or what they were after, but you don't want to tell me."

Jackie pursed his lips and pulled Mona closer.

"And I can see you want everything back. I get that. I want to find out who did this, too, but I think I need to know..."

Mona sighed. "Honestly, Jackie, if we can't trust the sheriff, who can we trust? Besides, it's not like we can keep it a secret now that... well, the cat's out of the safe."

Jackie frowned ferociously, but he didn't disagree.

Andi rolled her shoulders and did her best to look honest, trustworthy and quiet.

"No one knows this, Sheriff. Before Jackie and I moved to Tall Pines...I had a son. He died in an accident when he was ten. That safe held all his photos, his birth certificate, the newspaper clippings...his death certificate. Important stuff."

Andi reached across to squeeze Mona's hand. Mona looked miserable, and she could feel the sympathetic tears rising to the surface. Crying into her tea glass would probably not be reassuring. "I'm really sorry to hear that, Mona. I always wondered if you and Jackie… Well, you must have been a great mother."

Mona sniffed and smiled at Jackie. "We would have been great parents."

"Why not tell me this in the very beginning?" Andi had no idea why anyone would take such personal stuff, but now she was even more determined to find out who had stolen it.

Mona shrugged. "Well, I'm guessing Jackie didn't tell you… He wasn't the father. I got pregnant and had the baby all on my own before Jackie came along."

And now Andi understood the secret. She did her best not to gape in shock. An illegitimate son, even so many years before the town knew them, would cause talk thanks to Mona's previous spotlessness. Having to relive the loss all over again for curious friends and neighbors could be devastating. Andi was uneasy as she considered who might have access to Mona's secrets.

"It's okay that the secret's out, but I want those photos, Sheriff. I need them." She blinked away tears. Jackie wrapped his arms around her and rested his forehead against hers. Andi felt a pang in the general area of her heart while she watched Jackie melt under his wife's tears. She had to bite her lip.

He'd been doing his best to protect Mona's secret. Andi had to admire him for that.

"We're going to find them, Mona. I promise. Before I go, I have to ask…did anyone else know what you were keeping in that safe?"

Jackie thought for a second. "Can't see how they would, Sheriff. But I'm guessing they know what they've got by now."

He was a guy who collected feuds like baseball cards. The answer had to be on his list.

Since most of the town's population was on there, the possibilities were mind-boggling. Andi shook her head as she folded the wad of paper and put it back in her pocket. To steel her nerves, Andi picked up her tea glass and emptied it. As she thumped it back down on the counter, she slid off the stool. "I'll let you know as soon as I find something, Jackie."

Andi met Tammy on the sidewalk in front of the diner. And following on the heels of her best friend were the two people she least wanted to see: Mayor Jones and Ray Evans.

"Hey, Sheriff, I was hoping you might still be here. I ran into these two and wanted to see if I could get everybody together for a quick minute to talk about a debate." Tammy was wearing her best perky smile. Andi could feel the gray cloud forming over her head.

When she'd agreed to the debate, Andi had thought Tammy would have a hard time pinning down one or the other of these men. The fact that she'd managed to do so—and Andi along with them—in less than three hours shouldn't have surprised anyone, least of all Andi. She dropped down on the bench outside of Jackie's Country Kitchen. A huge, gusty sigh rattled around in her brain for long seconds but did not come out of her mouth.

Andi was pretty sure it showed on her face.

Mayor Jones might not patrol the sidewalks, picking up litter, measuring all grass and flower heights, and making sure the benches were placed precisely at equidistant intervals, but he seemed the type. He was a real politician who loved his job and knew that it depended on tourism. Tourists want tidy towns. And convenient benches. He was a ruthless enforcer of both.

The mayor always seemed to be wound a bit too tight, and today was no different. It had to be the bow tie. Not the winding, but the appearance. Although the two could be related.

Under a brilliant white cowboy hat, Ray Evans had a satisfied smirk on his face as he gestured for Tammy to take the other half of the bench. He propped his hands on his leather belt and rocked back and forth on his cowboy boots. Ray Evans looked exactly like a sheriff should look, especially if there were ever a showdown at high noon in the middle of Main Street. In the face of his picture-perfect cowboy persona, Andi was aware of her own inadequate tough-guyness. She straightened up her sprawl to make room for Tammy, and Tammy perched delicately beside her on the bench.

Tammy lobbed the first volley. "Well, gentlemen, I wanted to talk to you about setting up a debate before the election."

The mayor was already shaking his head. "We aren't going to take away any time from the music on the square right in the thick of the season. You ought to know better than that, Sheriff."

Andi opened her mouth to defend herself, but Tammy's sugary sweetness interrupted the oncoming rant. That was probably a good thing. Andi wasn't feeling very conciliatory to any of them at this point. Tammy knew good and well that the major portion of her unpaid job was to handle this stuff without involving Andi and here she was, right in the middle of it. And Ray, well…the whole darn thing was his fault. Andi could be happily working her shift and driving home at the end of it instead of politicking. He deserved some heavy, heavy blame.

"Of course we wouldn't interrupt the most important business the town does, Mayor. Andi and I had already discussed that carefully." Tammy blinked innocently up at both men.

The mayor looked thoughtful. Ray Evans

could not care less about a debate. Andi knew he was already the favorite.

Finally, Mayor Jones crossed his tweed-covered arms over his chest and nodded once, sharply. The calendar might read October, but the bank sign still said "86 degrees" this late in the afternoon. Tweed jackets were an overkill of catastrophic proportions. But that was Mayor Jones to a T.

Finally he said, "All right. We'll do it. In three weeks. Darla can carve us out some time in the program. What do you think, half an hour?"

When he looked at Ray Evans for confirmation, Andi had a sinking feeling that she knew exactly how well the debate was going to go.

Andi opened her mouth to let him have it, but she was interrupted. Again.

MARK COULD SEE the displeasure building on Andi's face from across the street. He'd been working on a fluff piece about Melba Simmons's one-hundredth birthday when he'd noticed the unholy gathering in front of the

Country Kitchen. All it would take to complete the set would be Jackie.

He was sorry that Andi had pulled her hair back into her standard ponytail. But there was nothing she could do about the bangs. She fidgeted with them every now and then as if she couldn't really believe they were there.

He'd known that Andi didn't need rescuing and she certainly wouldn't thank him for it, and then he'd headed out into the heat to do just that.

He slowed his jog before any of them looked up, and he pasted on a false, friendly smile. "Well, now, this is a very important meeting of the movers and shakers of Tall Pines."

Instead of a pleased smile, Andi flashed him a disgruntled frown before she leaned around the mayor to survey the window of the newspaper office. After a quick glance from that window to the diner, she nodded at him. Her lips twitched. Finally, she was getting the picture.

He shook hands with both men and waved at Tammy before he rested against the wall next to Andi and put his hand on her shoulder. Right there in front of the mayor, her opponent and her best friend. Andi stared at his hand. And then she looked up at him. He watched her face closely, ready to jerk his hand to safety if needed, but she just tilted her head and looked back at the mayor. There might have been a slight pink to her cheeks but he liked it. A lot.

There was silence before he brightly said, "So what's the scoop on this nice afternoon? Y'all solved the robbery yet?"

Mayor Jones shot Andi a distinctly peevish look. "Of course not. Although I'm sure the sheriff is doing the best she can." Everyone there could hear the unsaid portion: *But that's not very good, and if we had a different sheriff, this might not have happened in the first place.*

"So glad you're here, Mark," Tammy said. "I wanted to speak with you about the debate we're planning. Andi and Ray are going to talk over the issues in front of the town." When she added, "And we thought you'd make the perfect moderator. Would you be interested?" both Ray and the mayor did double takes. That might have been the brightest spot of the whole day.

"Really?" Mark squeezed Andi's shoulder as he spoke. She looked a little miserable at the suggestion, but she wanted to win this election. He wouldn't mind helping her if he were sure that winning was what she needed, no matter his own vow to stay as far away from politics as possible. Might be another way to make up for any unintentional stress he'd caused with the domestic violence article. "I'd be happy to moderate the debate. I think I can put together some questions that people in town would like answered."

Ray Evans crossed his arms over his chest. He might not have been aware he was doing it, but the whole time Mark spoke, he shook his head. "Now, hold on a minute. We didn't talk about the moderator." He jabbed a finger in Andi's direction. "And it doesn't look like he can be 'unbiased.'"

Mark scratched his forehead with his free hand. He didn't take the right hand off Andi's shoulder. "You might be right about that, Ray. I have asked Sheriff Jackson out to dinner." He paused to shoot a look at her. And then with a nice smile that showed all of his teeth but little warmth, he said, "And she finally said yes, so that's something to think about. I'll do my best to ask fair questions, though."

Ray looked at him for a second. Mark could see the *yeah, right,* but he never said it out loud. He should get points for that. He finally motioned at Mayor Jones. "I think Tim oughta do it. As mayor, he's an impartial party."

Yeah, right. He was in no way impartial, but he tried to keep everyone working toward the same goal. Mark admired that commitment to the good of the town even if he privately thought the mayor tried to run Tall Pines like his own little island. Term limits were unheard-of, and after pulling all the strings for more than a decade, the mayor had taken a proprietary view of the town and the people in it. Since most everybody seemed happy, Mark absolutely did not feel the need to challenge to status quo. No, he didn't. He was a small-town newspaper man now and if his inner journalist, the one who thrived on investigating politics and power, ever sniffed the air like he might be after a story, Mark did his best to ignore it. He'd nearly killed himself following that urge. And moving to Tall Pines was supposed to be the cure.

Tammy smiled sweetly. "What a fabulous idea, Ray! I agree. Let's go with both of them, and we'll be sure everything is covered." She patted Andi's leg as she stood. "I think this is going to be good for Tall Pines and the sheriff's race, don't y'all?" As she headed down the sidewalk, she called over her shoulder, "Mayor, I'll check in Monday to make sure everything is scheduled."

When Tammy was safely away and the ex-sheriff and mayor looked confused about what had happened, Andi stood and smoothed the legs of her uniform. She held out her hand. "Ray, I'll be happy to debate the issues with you."

Mark wasn't sure he was going to accept the gesture, but Ray eventually wrapped his hand around hers and gave it one firm shake. "I guess Tammy will let me know the time and everything."

"You bet. She'll give you a call and let Mark know so he can get the details out in the paper this week and next." Andi looked at him with a question in her eyes. He nodded. "And so we're set!"

Andi's own attempt at perky optimism met mixed results. Ray and Tim seemed to think the heat might be getting to her. Mark thought it was cute. And when she did the awkward dance where she tried to figure out what to do with her hands, he wanted to hug her close.

"Fine," Mayor Jones said. "I'll get with Tammy, and we'll let everybody know what we set up."

When he and Ray wandered on into the Country Kitchen and slid into a booth in front of the window, Mark had a feeling he knew exactly what the hot topic in the diner would be.

Andi glanced in the window and then turned to face him. "I agreed to a *working* date."

"Yeah, I'm surprised you didn't spell out your terms right there in the Hair Port. I guess our plan to work the case undercover was more important, huh?" She had that small wrinkle on her brow. He wanted to smooth it away. Really, he had the strangest urge to kiss her forehead. Mark would never have guessed someone as prickly as the sheriff would bring out his protective instincts or his softer side. Unable to help himself, he took both of her hands in his and squeezed. "The debate wasn't your idea, right?"

Andi rolled her eyes. "Well, no. Tammy makes all the strategy suggestions, but when we talked about it over lunch, I decided it might be a good idea to go ahead and get all the mud flung at one time instead of having little bits and pieces tossed at me when I least expect it."

He nodded. "Good plan. Did it work out like you hoped?"

"We had decided we might need both of you to moderate if that's what you mean. I wish there was more time to prepare, but the Fall Festival can't be stopped. I guess the timing's still good."

His thumbs traced circles on the backs of her hands, and he asked, "Well, you know you've given yourself a deadline, right?"

Andi was watching his hands. Mark managed to contain a wild grin. She was distracted. By his hands on hers. He wasn't sure she even heard his question.

He pulled one hand away and waved it in front of her face. "For solving Jackie's case? You'll have to find the thief by then or Ray's got a pretty powerful way to discredit you in front of the town." He shrugged. "Not that anybody has a lot of love for Jackie, but they will want to know who broke into his place."

"Oh, man. You're right." Andi groaned. "And I've made it exactly nowhere today."

He clutched one hand to his chest. "As soon as I recover from the astonishment of hearing you agree with me, I'm going to offer my help again. You need it now more than ever." He held up one finger and looked at the sky. Andi swatted his hand away.

"Ow, ow! Okay. Fine. Tomorrow I'll pick you up at six. We'll eat at Fat John's and then we can figure out what to do from there. Pretend it's just a regular date and we don't tell anybody we're working on Jackie's case. What do you think about that?"

Andi stepped close to him, near enough that he could feel the drag of her buttons on his shirt. This time she looked left and right like she had a secret to share. And then she smiled. She put every bit of winsome sweetness she could manage into it. That smile was like the first sunny spring day after a long, cold winter. Warm. Exciting. New. Beautiful. And a little unlike her. That made him nervous. She looked pretty pleased with herself.

He should expect some payback for laying his hand on Andi as though he could do that anytime he wanted. Waiting for that shoe to drop would have him nervous.

When they were this close together, Mark could see the shadows in her dark blue eyes and crazy-long eyelashes. And she smelled like starch and hair spray and warm woman. On her, it worked. She licked her lips and said, "I think that sounds fine. Over dinner we can talk about ways you can help me solve Jackie's case?"

He swallowed and nodded.

"And you aren't going to turn this into anything other than a *working* dinner, right? Because I know better defensive moves than I've shown you so far."

He shook his head slowly.

Finally Andi smiled again. She stepped back and took a deep breath. And he started to breathe, too. "This is going to be fun, then." Andi took two steps back. "You know where to find me?"

A smile flirted on his lips when he raised his eyes up to the awning over the Country Kitchen. Then he obviously looked over his shoulder at the Smokehouse. Finally, he made a show of leaning over to peer around Andi at the Hair Port behind her. He'd had zero trouble tracking her down in the past two days. He had skills.

Reluctantly Andi laughed. "Oh, yeah. Got it. I'll see you at six then."

She backed up a few steps, then spun around and pretended she didn't care whether he was watching her walk away. As she opened the door to her SUV, Mark called, "Hey, Sheriff!"

Instead of her normally hard-to-read expression, Andi had a slightly goofy grin on her face. She put her hand over her eyes so she could see him better in the glare of the late-afternoon sun. He propped his hands on his hips. And this time he couldn't contain the smirk. He was getting to her.

He held up two fingers in what might

have been construed as a victory sign. "Two things."

Andi raised her eyebrows. "All right. Go ahead."

"First, after you left the Hair Port, the ladies told me they might have seen a dark, older-model pickup truck outside the Country Kitchen on the night of the break-in."

Andi took out her notebook to jot down the information. They both knew that having that description was akin to narrowing down the hay field to the haystack. It was still going to be nearly impossible to find the needle.

After she made a note, she looked up at Mark. "All right. Thank you for passing that along. What's the second thing?"

"Wear your hair down." In front of all the people in the Tall Pines downtown, that's what he said.

Andi shot him her best *do not mess with me, buster* glare. She slapped her notebook closed, got in the SUV and drove away. Mark watched her turn the corner and head out of town, and he did his best not to do a victory dance in front of the Country Kitchen. He was making progress.

CHAPTER EIGHT

As soon as Andi got back to the office, she called her grandmother to tell her about the date and ask if she'd like to go shopping. Once Gram got over the shock, she was up for a trip, even though Gram would have to make a number of changes to her busy Saturday schedule.

After working late to catch up on reports and update her notes on Jackie's case, Andi drove home just before dark fell to meet a jubilant Mojo. Most of the time, Mojo kept his emotions well hidden, but Andi could tell by the faster-than-normal flip of his tail that he was happy to see her. She *was* the only one who could reach the cat food.

The next morning Andi stumbled out of bed early and drove Gram's car to Shady Pines. Every Saturday, Andi took Gram grocery shopping and over for a visit with the group that assembled at Purl's Place. Andi was sorry to miss the normal Saturday stitch-in, but she had every intention of demanding to see the new sock yarn later in the week. After she solved Jackie's case and smiled all the way through the preparations for Fall Fest, she would reward herself with a new skein.

Every week, after Andi got her grandmother settled in the passenger seat, Gram told her to sell the car, but it was nice to be out of the sheriff's SUV for a while. Plus, if she didn't win reelection, Andi was going to need as many paid-for necessities as she could hold on to.

"Morning, Gram!" Andi tried to pretend she was chipper. Her grandmother looked at her as if she'd lost her mind.

"This is not a good hour, Andrea. Please do not pretend that it is."

Gram wasn't a morning person, either. It had made getting ready for school rough during Andi's senior year. Well, that had been a drop in the bucket of rough things that year, but it sure didn't help.

Andi shut the door to Gram's apartment, locked it and helped her get situated in the front seat before she stored her chair in the trunk. In the early days, Gram had been convinced she wouldn't go anywhere if she couldn't walk under her own power. People would talk. And she wasn't that kind of person. In time, Andi's steady dripping onto her rocky stubbornness actually wore her down. Her grandmother had decided she didn't give a good gosh darn about it. Gram didn't cuss, either, but it was the rare person who failed to get the message from her eyes.

They didn't say a word for the hour-long drive. When Andi pulled up in front of her favorite boutique shops, her grandmother turned to face her. There was a small smile on her face when she said, "Good morning."

Andi laughed. "Good morning, Gram."

"I see you decided against blond." Gram opened her car door, and Andi grabbed her chair to help her out. "But I like the bangs."

"I thought it was time for a change."

Gram arched an eyebrow but withheld her comments.

They made it to the store just as the salesperson flipped the sign to Open. Andi started pulling things down and stacking them in Gram's lap. And when she didn't like Andi's choices, her "shopping cart" would not accept the clothing. Gram politely handed every single reject to the woman following them around. Andi couldn't blame her for keeping a close eye on the two of them. The things that came out of Gram's mouth would be pretty entertaining unless she was aiming them too close for comfort. Andi cringed a few times but laughed more often than not at Gram's succinct judgments.

After a frustrating hour and a half, Andi walked out with twice as many clothes as she needed. Shopping with Gram was a fun but expensive proposition. If Andi was ever in doubt about getting something, Gram's answer was always yes.

Her grandmother also had some firm ideas about what was appropriate date wear, and all of them required showing more skin than Andi was strictly comfortable with. When Andi showed her the first outfit she'd picked out, a long broomstick skirt and a cotton button-up with three-quarter sleeves, Gram had asked if she was getting ready to move west in a wagon. That had entertained the entire store.

They stopped for a quick lunch, then Gram insisted they both get manicures. She was having a great time, but Andi was starting to wear down. Before long, Gram was ready to head back home, too.

When she loaded her grandmother into the car, Andi asked, "So do you think I'm ready for this?"

Gram looked over at Andi with one eyebrow raised.

Andi snorted. "You know what I mean. Will we convince people we're just two people out for dinner?"

"Well, aren't you?" Gram patted her leg. "You know my answer. Try smiling." She shrugged as she looked out the side window. "And just in case, wear the short skirt."

As Andi started the car and pulled out of the parking spot, she said, "If you'd made it to Purl's Place, you'd have heard about Jimmy and Maylene spending time together and how I told Edna it was none of her business."

She glanced over at Gram to see how she took the news. She and Edna had been friends for a very long time.

Gram folded her hands together and then

flicked her fingers to watch the light shine off the red nail polish. Gram had always been colorful. "Probably didn't hurt her any."

Andi smiled. "That's it? No shock over the news?"

"Well, now…which news? If you're talking about making Edna mad, no way. She gets a lot of mileage out of being mad. You probably made her day. And if you're talking about Jimmy and Maylene, I don't see how that's a big surprise. I wish them luck and happiness." Gram tilted her head. "You could take a page out of their book, Andi."

Stumped on how to answer that, Andi concentrated on the traffic. But Gram wasn't ready to let it go. "You have two people doing what makes them happy. They've been here long enough to know the consequences, but a little talk isn't going to keep them from going after what they want." Then Gram turned to look at the passing scenery. "In fact, Edna's got nearly the same philosophy if you really think about it."

And apparently that's all she had to say. The lack of response was a little deflating.

The drive back took longer thanks to the

weekend tourist traffic. Andi didn't mind. She loved driving the curving roads and was happy to spend time with her grandmother. She decided to get Gram's opinion on the rest of Jackie's list. She pulled the folded papers off the dashboard and showed them to Gram. "Do these names ring any bells? Like maybe I ought to investigate them?"

Gram read the list quickly before she pursed her lips. "No, honey, I can't say they do. I mean, it seems I remember a few small arguments between Jackie and some of these folks, but I think you're looking for a special someone who'll go to the trouble of stealing something for revenge."

She held the paper out and Andi folded it up and put it back on the dashboard. "Yeah, you're probably right. I think I'm out of options."

Andi huffed as she wiggled around in the seat to stretch her legs. "And now, thanks to Tammy, I've got a deadline. If I don't have the answer by the debate, Ray's going to nail me to the stage."

Gram shook her head. "It's too bad that he's running against you. As I recall, he always was a big-man-on-campus kinda guy. I think he was the same year as your daddy in high school."

"Were they friends? I thought Daddy would have been the big man." Andi looked over at her. "I used to wonder what he saw in Mama. She was so quiet. Reserved."

Gram patted her hand. "And she was so very beautiful. Just like you, Andi. That's what he saw." Gram chuckled. "And yes, he was very much a big fish in a little pond even in high school. You can imagine how many times he and Ray butted heads."

"What about Jackie and Ray? Can you remember any trouble between the two of them?"

While Gram thought about her question, Andi waved her fingers on the steering wheel to admire the sheen of the French manicure her grandmother had talked her into. Normally Andi was completely low maintenance. If her fingernails were clean, she was happy, but now she knew she could be happier. It was amazing what primping had done for her spirit and general outlook on life. It was a little humbling, too. In the big scheme of things, a manicure was a small luxury, but it put a smile on her face and that was a pretty big thing.

Finally, Gram said, "I can't think of any big blowups, but you know that Jackie hasn't changed a bit, and if he keeps you running back and forth, he'd have done the same with Ray." She looked over at Andi and shook her head. "And I have my doubts that Ray was as polite about it as you."

They passed Jackie's diner, and Andi was pleased to see he had a good crowd. Maybe he was difficult, but he had a nice menu, and she wanted every business around the courthouse square to take full advantage of the season. It wasn't always easy to make a living in Tall Pines. Good tourist traffic made all the difference.

As Andi pulled to a stop in front of Gram's unit, she thought about her answer. Ray Evans hadn't been on Jackie's long list of suspects, so they'd either ironed things out to his satisfaction or he'd forgotten to add the ex-sheriff. Considering the length of the list, it was also possible he'd run out of ink.

"Now you get on home and start primping.

If I don't hear about the scandalous way the sheriff was dressed by the end of the church service tomorrow, I'm going to be demanding some answers." She shook her finger. "And don't you work all night, Andrea Louise Jackson. It's a night out with a handsome man. Live a little."

Gram's eyes sparkled as she laughed and suddenly the whole day made Andi happy. She still had a case to solve with an annoying lack of suspects and if she thought too long about going on a date with Mark, her stomach tied itself in a knot, but it didn't matter. Gram was happy. It was a beautiful day. Business was good. She had some time to figure out everything else.

After she helped her grandmother inside, Andi kissed her cheek and said, "I'll call you when I get in tonight, okay?"

She shook her head. "Tomorrow is soon enough. You stay out too late and have too much fun."

Andi snorted. Too late for her was after ten. Andi was a real wild child. She opened the door and made a theatrical show of locking it before she said, "I love you, Gram."

Gram made a shooing motion with both hands before she reached over to answer her ringing phone. "Love you, too, Andi. Now get to work."

When she caught a glimpse of her hair in the rearview mirror, Andi knew her grandmother was right. It was going to take some work. Andi had about two hours to create a new, better Andi. She didn't think it was going to be enough time.

Mojo was waiting as Andi staggered into the house under the load of her purchases. He might have been a smidge concerned, but after Andi put out some food, he gobbled it up and went back to his spot in the window. Clearly, she was on her own.

Getting ready for this adventure took every bit of that two hours. In fact, Andi would have taken two more if she'd figured out a way to turn back time. She showered, shaved, loofahed, lotioned, dried, straightened, curled and straightened again. Her hair went up, then down, then back up, and finally she left it loose around her shoulders. The curls were tamed when she surrendered, but they had a funny way of sneaking back when she stepped away from the mirror.

Andi applied a very little bit of makeup then tried on everything in her closet and the new clothes she'd brought home…twice. And she hated all of it. Since Mojo refused to offer an opinion, she decided to go with Gram's favorite outfit of the day. It was casual, but she liked that message. Andi just wished it had more fabric. The scrappy cotton skirt ended in a flare just above her knee and the magenta button-up was sleeveless.

As Andi stood in front of the full-length mirror doing her version of positive affirmation, she heard the doorbell ring. A panicked glance at the digital alarm clock showed that he was right on time.

She strapped on the woven leather belt—Gram had insisted it would define her waist—and slid her feet into the sandals she'd picked out. Then she scooped up her watch and earrings.

Andi was sliding the second hoop into her left ear when she opened the door. She could hear Gram's repeated advice and pasted on a nervous smile.

Mark had done a little extra prep for tonight's date. This might be the first time Andi had seen him wearing anything other than running shoes. Instead, he wore loafers that worked well with his dark jeans and crisp button-up. The sleeves were rolled up to show off his really nice forearms.

When he didn't say anything, Andi forced herself to look away from those arms and saw that he was stuck, too. "You have legs."

The smile slid off her face. She had imagined a hundred different opening lines. This was not one of them. Finally she rolled her eyes. He didn't see that, either. She grabbed her purse and called, "Mojo, be good," as she pulled the door shut behind her. He was still frozen in place so she brushed past him, bumping his shoulder in her haste to get things moving.

"Hey, wait, where's the fire?" Mark propped his hands on his hips.

"Just... Can we go?" Andi stopped at the bottom of the steps and watched him shake his head before he followed her down.

Andi would have stormed off. She meant to.

Instead, she froze in place when he grabbed her hand.

He looked embarrassed when he said, “I’m sorry. That wasn’t the way I meant to greet you tonight. I must be out of practice or something. Let’s start again.” He raised both eyebrows and waited for her answer.

She nodded once.

He pulled her back up the steps to the porch and stopped in front of her door. And he waited.

She raised one hand to fidget with her hair. “What?”

He pulled her hand down. “Let’s do this from the beginning. And this time, I want you to introduce me to Mojo, whatever a Mojo is.”

Andi sighed as she yanked open her purse, snatched out her keys and jammed the key into the lock. She stomped over the threshold and slammed the door in his face.

MARK COUNTED TO ten and then rolled his head on his shoulders as he tried to put his reaction into perspective. He laughed at himself standing in front of her closed door like a teenager on his first date. *Get it together, man.* He punched the doorbell again.

When she yanked the door open, she wore a slightly bedraggled smile. Then she raised both eyebrows and waited.

"You look really…" He was changing his mind about what he meant to say. Soft. Gorgeous. Feminine. Right. Good. And he finished with "Pretty. You look really pretty, Andi."

One corner of her mouth quirked up. "Thank you. You look nice, too, but I'd like to know what you were going to say instead of pretty."

He rubbed his forehead before he put both arms up in a defensive stance. "I was going to say you looked really soft."

"But you remembered I normally carry a gun?" Andi's lips twitched.

Mark frowned as he pretended to consider his answer. "No, and I really should have thought of that much sooner."

Andi laughed. "All right. I'm sorry, too. It's just…hard to figure out how to be normal with you, not mad."

He snorted. "I think I know what you mean.

I'm usually a lot better with opening lines. Not gonna lie, the skirt threw me for a minute. I think it's because I've only seen you in the uniform. And it's clear that you do have legs, but it's not obvious how amazing you look in a skirt. The surprise sent me right back to junior high."

Andi opened her mouth and shut it. She looked as if she were stumped. Then Andi crossed her arms over her chest defensively. "My grandmother said it was a nice outfit." She slapped her own forehead. "And of course, grandmothers are usually such fashionistas."

He wiggled his hand under hers and managed to unravel her arms before he stepped inside. "Well, yours was right. It's a good look for you."

Andi tried to tug her fingers out of his grip as she said, "My choice was a prairie dress that would have been modest two centuries ago."

That did not surprise him one bit. He'd half expected her to wear her uniform. Mark walked over to greet Mojo. "I'll have to pass along my thanks to Gram the next time I see her."

She held out a hand and said, "Wait, he hates men." To prove her wrong, Mojo rubbed his head against Mark's palm as he scratched behind the cat's ears.

One corner of Mark's mouth tilted up. "Oh, he's a friendly fella, isn't he?" When the words came out in the tone of voice one normally uses to speak to a newborn, Mark coughed and tried to look tougher. But it was too late. He was a cat person. And Mojo wasn't a typical cat. He was large, had a perpetual frown and looked down on the world from his lofty perch. "Where'd you find this guy?"

"I pulled him out of a rain gutter when he was just a kitten," Andi said.

As a true-blue, dyed-in-the-wool animal person and a lover of near-lost causes, Mark liked her answer. His already good opinion of Andi ticked up another notch.

"He still hasn't forgiven me for moving him here, but he hasn't killed me in my sleep, either. When he learns to open his own food, I'll have to sleep with one eye open."

"Oh, I don't believe it." Mark ran his hand down Mojo's back and escaped the maneuver without a single extra stripe. "Nice to meet you, Mojo."

Mojo responded with a dignified mew.

"What do we have here?" He picked up an obnoxiously colored skein of yarn that was dangerously overneedled. He held it toward Mojo, and Andi quickly snatched it from his hand.

"That is a sock. And if you drop one of those needles, you and I will both be sorry." Andi carefully wound the yarn around the needles and sock in progress.

Mark shook his head. "No, I've seen socks. They don't come in that color, and you buy them in the store."

Andi sniffed. "I might have guessed you'd not understand the sock as art form."

"Art form, is it?" He laughed. This was an amazing revelation. He loved it! She was a knitter, of all things. "In a million years, if I'd had to guess what your hobbies would be, I would never have put sock knitting on the list."

Andi crossed her arms again. "And why is

that? Because you don't know a thing about sock knitting maybe?"

"Possibly. And also because knitting makes you seem…"

"Are you about to say *soft* again?" Her lips twitched as she fought a smile.

"Of course not." He scratched Mojo behind the ears again and crossed to stand in front of the door. He held out his hand, but she held her ground.

"Not until you tell me what you were going to say." She tilted her head and waited.

He shrugged. "Colorful. I was going to say that sock right there makes you seem more colorful." They both looked at the garish self-striping yarn. Neon-green mixed with orange and rust in a pattern that suggested a weird science project gone horribly wrong.

She laughed. "Okay, I can see that."

As she put the sock in progress—with all the dangerous double-pointed needles and crazy-colored yarn—in a basket by Mojo's couch, he asked, "Will you knit me a pair of socks?"

Andi rolled her eyes. "Right. And you'd wear them if I did."

He wasn't really sure he would, but if she ever knit him a pair of socks, life as he knew it would've changed forever. He shrugged one shoulder. "You wear them."

"Do you know the legend of the boyfriend sweater?" she asked. The skeptical look on her face said she was pretty sure he had no idea what she was talking about.

"Let's see. The boyfriend sweater. That's got to be the one about the…" Mark shook his head. "Uh, no. Of course I don't."

She tried to look serious as she said, "Oh, well, we better talk about socks and what they might mean later. After we know each other better."

After we know each other better? That was promising. "Fine. I'll hold you to that. We can pick up this conversation on our second date."

"Well, if we don't solve Jackie's case tonight, you mean." She tilted her head down. "With your help, I expect to have this taken care of quickly. Then we can both get back to our normal lives. Right?"

Finding the thief would mean no more "working" dates. He wasn't sure how she did it, but all of a sudden work was the last thing on his mind.

"Why don't we make it through tonight before we decide the rest of our lives?" He raised his hand and waited to see if she'd take it.

After a moment, she walked over to put her hand in his.

"MOJO, BE GOOD for real this time."

Mark waited for Andi to relock the door and then he helped her into his truck. They were quiet on the short drive over to Fat John's, and when they arrived, the noise of the crowded restaurant was shocking. Andi was happy to have the chance to catch her breath.

Mark looked around and leaned close to ask, "Want to try eating outside tonight? It's awfully loud in here."

They wound their way through the dining room. Mark waved at people who called out to him and shook hands as they went while Andi tried to blend in with the crowd. The sparsely populated deck overlooked the lake. Andi might have polka-dot skin by the time the mosquitos were through feasting on her, but she was glad it was less crowded out there. When Mark suggested Fat John's special supreme, Andi nodded gratefully. Little Reanne Butler took their order and returned quickly with two sweet teas. Andi had gone to school with Reanne's mother before she'd had to drop out because Reanne was on the way. And Andi suddenly felt very old.

To get the conversation started, she said, "Nice night."

"Yeah," he replied. "I think it's starting to cool off."

And then they could hear crickets and the clink of silverware and snippets of conversation and nothing else.

Finally, he cleared his throat and leaned forward to put his elbows on the table. "And this is awkward."

Andi smiled at him. "Finally, we're normal. All first dates are awkward, right?" She glanced around to see if anyone had heard her say "date" and then relaxed. That was the whole plan: sell this as a regular, run-of-the-mill date. No one was paying the least bit of attention to them. That was unexpected and a bit of a letdown.

He nodded. “I guess you’re right.”

“So maybe we should start with the one item on the agenda—how you can help me solve this case. Now that I have a deadline and no suspects, I’m willing to solicit your help.”

The corners of his mouth twitched. “Well, okay, so let’s look at what you’ve got.” They were both silent. Finally, he shook his head. “You’ve got nothing.”

It was the truth. Andi hated it, but she couldn’t deny it. “I don’t think I’ve got one person who has a motive to harm Jackie. His complaints and lawsuits are annoying, but he runs a nice place and serves good food. Oscar’s family speaks highly of him, and Mona told me that Jackie thought Oscar was the best employee they’d ever had. You don’t seem to be the kind of person who would go to the trouble of breaking in to get back at Jackie. I figure you’d have other methods if you wanted revenge.”

He seemed to have no idea what Andi was talking about and she didn’t push it. Bringing up how easy it was to change a story by reporting the facts without context would just give her heartburn.

"Money, trophies… Did you find out if there was anything else in the safe that might have been the target?"

Andi shook her head. This wasn't her information to spread, especially not to the newspaper editor. Mona's child might be old news, but she still wouldn't like to see it on the front page. Mark studied her face for a moment. He was about to speak when Andi said, "And there's Wanda, but I can't imagine anything would drive her to revenge."

Andi shrugged and shivered at the light breeze across her arms. "Jackie's given me a list which includes almost every person who's ever been into the diner, but neither Mona nor my Gram thought he'd identified any real suspects. Interviewing them all could take forever, but I have this feeling it's personal. Someone wanted to hit Jackie where it hurt. Why else would they take the trophies?"

Andi leaned back as Reanne placed a large pizza between them. It was piled high with a little bit of everything. She gave Mark two small plates with silverware rolled in paper napkins stacked on top.

"Can I get y'all anything else?" she asked with a very perky smile.

"No, we're set here," Mark answered.

When she left, Andi asked, "So, do you have any ideas?"

After he piled a slice on each plate and handed one to Andi, he leaned back in his chair. "Two. First, if you think the thief has a vendetta against Jackie, maybe you should start with the most recent dispute. Seems logical it would be someone who's still mad."

"I like it," she said. "Got any idea who that could be?"

"I might know something about that." Mark wore his usual little smirk right before he took a huge bite of pizza.

"Are you going to share?" Andi had to admire his technique. He'd turned the tables on her and he was pretty cute while he did it, even if she would never tell him that.

"What's it worth? A second date maybe?"

Andi laughed quietly. "Maybe. Although some people might hesitate to blackmail the sheriff."

Mark nodded. Andi watched him as he chewed. He made sure to take his time, leaving her poised on the edge of her seat. Literally.

"I seem to recall that Howard King over at the hardware store went a round or two with Jackie this summer. Maybe start there."

Andi remembered seeing his name on the list but couldn't remember how high Jackie had ranked him.

"And for my second trick, I'd like to suggest another motive." Mark wiped his mouth before he asked, "What if Jackie wasn't the target?"

Andi puzzled over his question. "You mean Jackie's trophies and cash were stolen to hurt someone else? Like Mona or Oscar or…" She looked across the table to meet his stare. "Or me?"

He shrugged and took another bite before he answered. "It's just a thought, but the election is coming. One of the biggest loudmouths in town was robbed—someone who's sure to let everyone know about the sheriff's failure to recover his stolen property."

His theory made some sense. And that made

her mad. If Ray Evans was behind the theft, he was really leaving nothing to chance.

Finally Andi shook her head. "I hate elections. I do. I never wanted to be sheriff. If Ray had hired me when I came to town, he'd be running unopposed. Of course, I get the feeling I'm just going through the motions with this campaign. Ray Evans was born to be a sheriff."

"You ought to think about what you want to do if you lose. Can I suggest going on dates with a handsome gentleman and not caring what people will think?" Mark picked up a second slice of pizza. "So, what would you do if you weren't sheriff?"

It was an impossible question. "I guess I'd have to move away from Tall Pines."

He made the "continue" motion with his fork.

"I mean..." It was going to be hard to explain no matter what she said, so Andi decided to stick with the truth. "I like being in law enforcement. You know about my dad, my history here. Everyone does. My job gives me a chance to show I'm different. I can work hard and serve the town. But there are too many memories here. If it wasn't for Gram, I might never have come back." She looked around and absolutely no one was paying attention to them. Still.

Mark frowned. "So you're happy here, even with the memories, because of your job?"

Andi shook her head. "Maybe I mean working in law enforcement *made* me happy. Being sheriff isn't exactly what I thought it would be. I expected people to be impressed with my training so I could make changes, all the while watching over Gram. But…"

"It hasn't happened that way. I'm guessing you realized things worked pretty well without your changes, people were less happy to see you than you thought, and there's been very little saving the world and a whole lot of meetings."

To steady herself, Andi took another drink of her beautiful sweet tea. He was pretty close to the truth and that made her nervous. Most days *she* didn't understand why she felt the way she did.

He narrowed his eyes. "Let me guess. You were a good student and determined to get a scholarship. You always did your homework, aced tests, volunteered for projects and generally annoyed your classmates."

Andi shrugged. "Maybe."

His lips twitched. He knew very well how close he was. "Why law enforcement? You could have been anything, right?"

"Well, Doctor, you see..."

Mark nodded thoughtfully, pushed his imaginary glasses up his nose and pretended to lick an invisible pen. And she felt a little of the tension ease out of her shoulders. "I think I wanted something that made me feel in control. My dad left when I was nine. My mom got sick and died of breast cancer when I was in high school, and everything was so chaotic. Rules. Laws. Procedures. They made sense, and I knew what was expected. I could measure myself against them and excel, but I didn't want to be a police officer. I wanted to be a federal agent. I wanted to make a *big* difference."

He tilted his head to one side. "Seems a stretch for a girl from Tall Pines."

Andi laughed. "Yeah, it really does. You ought to try flipping it, being ex-FBI back here. Throw one Chinese word into conversation or correct someone about Afghanistan's geography and people look at you like you've just sprouted wings or said you voted Democrat." She wadded up the corner of her napkin. "Do you remember that show, the one with the female FBI agent who solved crimes with the profiler? Her name was Agent Shenandoah Steele and she wore black boots and a gun holster and solved impossible crimes. She gave me the idea."

Mark choked a little on his pizza. When he finally got his voice back, he said, "Warn me before you hit me with truths like that, Andi."

"Not exactly what you expected?" She laughed. "I liked her. Agent Steele worked hard and was proven right every single time. People respected her work. She was the best at what she did. That's all I wanted. The fact that perfection is impossible to achieve in real life has been a disappointment, let me tell you."

He shook his head and tangled his fingers with hers while time stopped. The sounds of the restaurant disappeared, and there was nothing except him, the warmth in his eyes and the small smile on his lips. She couldn't breathe, but she didn't want anything to shatter the moment.

When Reanne dropped a stack of napkins on the table, they both straightened and Andi took a deep breath. She slowly slid her hand back across the table and regretted it instantly.

She licked her lips. "When I told Gram I was going to be an FBI agent someday, she didn't laugh. It made perfect sense to her. We went to the library and researched how you become one. I picked a college and two majors to get the education required. And I did it."

"Could you go back?" Mark asked. "I mean, things have settled down here. Would they hire you?"

"Yeah, but that scare… When I thought I might lose Gram, it was like I woke up. I've only made it home once a year since I graduated college. We talked on the phone almost every day and she was fine. It never occurred to me that something could happen to her." She shook her head. "I can't be that far away again. She needs me too much."

Mark sighed. "You know something bad could happen to Gram even with you living around the corner, right? Even as the sheriff of this town, something bad—something you can't control—could happen to her."

Andi felt the sting of tears and took a soothing drink of her tea. "I know, but I hate it."

He nodded. "Yeah. No matter how hard you try, you'll never be in control."

Andi didn't answer for a moment. "Gram tells me to go, but I can't leave her. I guess if I lose the election, I can try the state police or maybe another county. I could drive up on the weekends to see her..."

"I'm going to say one more thing before I take off my psychiatrist's hat, step down from my soapbox and ask about your favorite movie—as is only right for our first date..."

Andi braced herself.

"You deserve to build a life that makes you happy, and you can't if all you do is what people expect." He shrugged. "And that's true whether you live here, in beautiful Tall Pines—home of your grandmother and some of the area's finest yarn—or someplace else. Don't give up any of that happiness for a job. I bet your grandmother would say the same."

For minutes or hours, neither of them spoke.

His eyes were locked with hers and it was okay. He didn't say that she'd made the wrong choices, that she should have taken better care of her grandmother or that she was crazy for getting her life's direction from a television show. He understood her unwinnable war to be in control. The look on his face said he admired her no matter what.

And that admiration was so different and new it was impossible to ignore.

Finally he smiled. "Now tell me your favorite movie."

Andi laughed. "Well, I don't know if it's my absolute favorite, but I can quote huge chunks of *Sleepless in Seattle*. That's probably a sign of my misspent youth."

He looked a little horrified so she reached over to pat his hand. "It's okay. If you don't know it, I have a copy that I'd be happy to show you." He shook his head slowly. "Or I could run through as much as I remember."

He coughed and pretended to motion for the check, and then they laughed together. It was nice. He and Andi traded favorites and flirty jabs until there were two slices of pizza left and she'd had enough sweet tea to feel the buzz again. The deck emptied and by the time they paid the check, the restaurant was deserted, too.

Mark handed over the bill and cash to cover it. “Are we closing the place down?”

John chuckled as he counted out change from the drawer. “I think you guys are it.” He whistled as he looked from Mark to Andi and back. “I’d say that’s a pretty good sign for a first date.”

Mark pocketed the change, then grabbed Andi’s hand. As he opened the door, he waved at John. “Me, too. Thanks for letting us hang out.” John waved back and came around the counter to lock the door behind them.

“It takes some getting used to,” Mark said, “this dating with the whole town watching, doesn’t it?” Out on the sidewalk, they could hear faint strains of music on the square.

Andi tangled her fingers in his. Without talking about it, they both walked in that direction. Andi hoped it meant neither of them wanted the night to be over.

When Mark began pulling her across the street toward the crowd on the courthouse lawn, Andi dug in her heels.

When he looked back, she pointed to the corner. “There are crosswalks painted on the street for a reason, Mr. Taylor.”

Mark hung his head for a minute before he rolled his shoulders. Then he very obviously looked left and right at the empty street and back at her.

Andi tugged her hand from his. “What can I say? It’s a pet peeve. It’s a simple enough rule to obey.” She marched down to the corner and waited for him.

When he rejoined her, she threaded her fingers through his and pulled him off the curb into the crosswalk. The crowd in the town square was a decent size considering the heat they’d been having. There was a group on the stage playing a decent version of “Stand by Me” and dancers circled to the side. A soft breeze cooled things off and Andi and Mark sat along the brick wall to listen to a song or two. Every now and then his fingers would squeeze hers or his thumb would trace over the top of Andi’s wrist. It was weird. And nice.

And that’s when Jackie, Mona, Miss Margaret and Edna strolled by. Andi tightened her grip on Mark's hand to get his attention, then she smiled at Mona. She seemed to be the friendliest of the group.

Jackie fired the first shot. "Nice to see you've got plenty of time to enjoy yourself, Sheriff."

Mark flashed a smile that showed all of his teeth and nothing else. "Nice to see you aren't letting your losses ruin your weekend, Jackie."

Jackie pursed his lips and shot a glare at both of them before he stomped off. "Mona, I'll be in the car."

Miss Margaret and Edna *hmmed* in unison before Edna said, "And now I understand why you were so all-fired ready to defend Maylene, Sheriff. Thinking you might need breathing room yourself?"

Andi shook her head. "Well, now, Edna, I hope I've always wanted to keep my nose out of other people's business. It's only the right thing to do, after all. I can hardly wait to hear the news you'll be spreading tomorrow."

One of her eyebrows twitched and Andi could tell Edna wanted to let her have it with both barrels, but instead she moved her lips in a poor imitation of a smile and said, "Nice to see y'all."

Miss Margaret watched her walk away and then turned back. "I guess I should go with her. She's my ride home." She patted Andi's hand in Mark's and smiled as she left. Andi was shocked when Miss Margaret turned around to mouth, *Way to go!* Now, she might have been impressed with Andi's shutting down Edna or her snagging a date with Mark Taylor. Andi preferred to think the two thumbs up meant she was impressed with both.

Mark looked at Andi, then smiled at Mona. "Sorry, Mona. We're good at clearing a room, I guess."

She chuckled. "That's a handy talent to have." She started to walk toward the car where Jackie sat, no doubt steaming up the windows with his ire.

"Hey, Mona, I wanted to ask…" When she paused, Andi lowered her voice. "I didn't see Ray Evans's name on the list Jackie made. Has there been any trouble between the two of them?"

She peered off for a moment to think. "I

know they wrangled a bit when he was sheriff over some slight. Jackie always thinks people ought to do more than they do, but they've been friends a long time." She shrugged. "I guess it's hard to imagine Ray wanting to steal from Jackie."

Andi nodded. "Okay. Thanks. Y'all have a good night."

When she walked away, Mark looked at Andi. "So you think the ex-sheriff might have a motive?"

Andi moved closer. "You have a disturbing lack of concern for the rules that keep our society whole and you're too charming by half, but I think you're more than just a pretty face."

There could have been a flush on his cheeks but it was too dark to tell. He rested his forehead against hers, and his breath tickled Andi's cheek when he said, "Don't tell anyone, okay? You'll ruin my reputation."

CHAPTER NINE

WHEN ANDI SCREECHED to a stop in front of Shady Pines on Sunday morning, her phone beeped to let her know she'd gotten a text message. After a quick glance at the clock to see exactly how late she was, Andi decided against digging the phone out of her purse to check. Gram got antsy when they were running behind schedule, but when they were late for church, her grandmother went straight for atomic meltdown. She'd leave nothing behind but rubble if Andi didn't get her to her seat before the music started. Andi hadn't even unbuckled her seat belt, and Gram was rolling across the threshold and shutting her door with a slam.

Her grandmother's mouth was tight when she snapped, "I guess you overslept, then?"

Andi jumped out to help her get in the car. She shoved Gram's chair in the trunk and hopped back in. Breathlessly, she said, "Yes, ma'am. I'll drop you at the door and find a place to park. I hope you won't miss much."

"I should start riding with Nettie. That woman's never late." Gram huffed once and loudly, then it looked like she was trying to calm herself. Finally, she turned to ask Andi in a much more civil tone, "So, did you have a good time last night?"

She had, but the memory of holding his hand as they listened to music on the square brought her warm pleasure and scared her to death. She wasn't ready to talk to anybody about that, so she said, "It was a fun time."

"Going out again?" Gram leaned forward to urge the car to go faster. "On a real date this time?"

Andi wasn't sure how to answer that. Mark hadn't asked and if he did, she didn't know what she'd say. They were still working on Jackie's case, so dinner might come up again, but there was no good reason for a real date. She was leaving. Eventually. Besides, she would never be able to trust him. Would she? Andi shrugged.

Gram tsked. "Use your words, Andi."

Andi took a deep, calming breath as she

made the last turn to get Gram to church. "We haven't made any plans." Getting Gram's hopes up and then disappointing her would be just another thing to lose sleep over. "We'll see. He had some good ideas. Mark's smarter than I expected."

Gram was quiet for a second before rough chuckles spilled out between her lips. "I'm not sure that's the most glowing praise, Andi."

When they reached the drop-off area, Andi threw the car in Park and ran around to get her grandmother's chair and help her out of the car.

One of the ushers hurried over. "Morning, Ms. Jackson." He acknowledged Andi with a nod. "Let me help you inside. The music's about to start." Gram shot Andi a glare over her shoulder before she smiled sweetly up at Bob Randall. "Why, yes, Bob, I know. We got a later start than normal today."

Andi rolled her head on her shoulders after she slid behind the wheel. She hated the thought of walking in late, but at least Gram could enjoy the singing. That was her favorite part. If they'd missed all that just to arrive in time for the sermon, lunch would have been spent in tense silence.

As she parked in one of the handicapped spots, Andi pulled out her cell phone to turn off the ringer. One ring in the middle of church, and Gram would probably never speak to her again. She noticed the text message again before dropping the phone into her purse.

The first blare of organ music hit her full in the face when the single remaining usher opened the door. She hunched her shoulders a bit as she speed-walked down the aisle to slide in beside Gram. All through the service, Andi wondered about the text, but she knew pulling out her phone in church would not be well received. If she'd gotten up on time and been early to pick her grandmother up, Andi might have chanced it, but as it was, she told herself it could wait.

She wasn't on duty this weekend and if there was an emergency, her staff knew to call and keep calling. Plus, chances were good that someone else in the sanctuary could let her know if something happened long before anybody gave her a call.

Andi tried to pay attention to the sermon and the songs and the announcements, but she was pretty sure she had a stupid grin on her face too often, betraying the fact that her mind was not on the here and now. She was thinking about pizza and a man who was smart enough to see things about her that she didn't show anyone…and also hadn't given her a real kiss good-night…or tried to tease one out of her. She wanted to make excuses for him, but part of her was convinced he was only in this for the information. Didn't that prove she should keep everything strictly business? What might it be like to have more?

When Gram patted Andi's thigh, she realized the service was over. And it looked like it had been over for some time. She must have gone through the motions, because nobody but Gram seemed to think anything about her behavior. Her grandmother was amused by it, so Andi had high hopes she was over her disgruntlement. "Gram, are you ready to go?"

She tilted her head. "Honey, I've been ready for ten minutes now. We'll be the last ones out of the parking lot."

Gram muttered something about how fitting that was since they were the last ones in, but Andi wanted to let that go, so she pretended not to hear.

They were quiet on the short drive back to Shady Pines. The noon meal on Sunday was a big family event, and Gram and Andi always ate there after church. It was nice to see her trading barbs with her cronies and watch how the staff treated the residents. It was a good place. Andi would rather have her at home, but Gram was happy. And if the meal left something to be desired, mainly salt and any kind of fat, that was fine.

Sitting at the lunch table at Shady Pines was like being stuck in a chair at the Hair Port. The conversation meandered here and there, and most of it was centered around what somebody heard from so-and-so, who'd picked it up from the girl at the grocery store. Andi was on pins and needles throughout the meal because there were too many potential missiles to hurl her way. Eventually she dropped her guard and was enjoying her chocolate cake when disaster struck.

Edna's sister Rose was one of Gram's card buddies. She leaned around her granddaughter and said, "So, Andi, I heard you were out on the town with the newspaper man last night. Edna said you looked really…flashy." She leaned back to watch the fireworks.

Gram opened her mouth, but Andi stopped her with one look. "That's right, Rose. We did go out. We ate dinner, we listened to the music and then we went home. And you'll have to get more info on my outfit from Gram over cards. She's the one who picked it out. Please make sure you get all the details right when you relay Gram's answer to Edna because I'd hate for it to get distorted before it even makes the rounds."

One quick glance around the table showed that everyone was waiting with bated breath for Rose's response. Rose looked a little shocked. An apology was trembling on the tip of Andi's tongue. She'd apparently developed a zero-tolerance policy on gossip and was scorching earth left and right, even against less-frequent offenders. She shot a look at her grandmother. Gram was calmly folding her napkin, but when she met Andi's gaze, she tilted her chin up and straightened her shoulders. And Andi smiled.

Rose pursed her lips. “Well, now, Andi, I’ll be sure to do that.” And everyone else at the table was very interested in their own plates.

Andi squished all her cake crumbs with a fork and licked it clean before she stacked her empty plate on top of Gram’s. She wasn’t going to apologize, and she was going to get over her embarrassment at being the topic of conversation. Her worry over what people thought of her was not a problem confined to Tall Pines. Whether she was here or in Atlanta, she had to find a way to handle it.

Andi smiled. “I knew I could count on you. That’s one of the things I love about living in Tall Pines. Everyone is so helpful and caring, just like one big, happy, dysfunctional family.” She patted Rose’s hand.

Andi hoped she hadn’t made it too difficult for her grandmother to show up for her Monday morning card game. She followed Gram back to her unit. There was an interrogation coming.

Before she’d fully cleared the doorway to her unit, Gram asked, “Why’d you oversleep, young lady?”

Andi wondered what she thought the possibilities were. Had she slept in because she'd been too busy with her new live-in lover to hear the alarm? Or maybe she was in an alcohol-induced haze and needed buckets of black coffee to get it together? The coffee part was right, but Andi was only in her normal haze.

Andi dropped onto her grandmother's sofa. "I couldn't sleep last night after I got in. Too keyed up, I guess.

Gram picked up her yarn. "So you had a good time, then?"

Andi didn't want to get her grandmother's hopes up. She really didn't. "We went to Fat John's for pizza and we talked about the case a while."

Gram was looking at Andi over the rims of her glasses and slowly shaking her head.

"Just a little. Mark had a good question. What if the motive for stealing the recipes and the trophies wasn't to hurt Jackie but to cause me trouble?" Andi raised her eyebrows.

Gram added a few double crochets to her dishcloth before nodding her head. "So maybe Ray sees a way to discredit you in front of the town?" She looked out the window for a minute before she asked, "Do you think Jackie would be in on the plan, then?"

"No way." Jackie would never have risked Mona's unhappiness.

Gram watched her hands work the hook and yarn. Andi didn't know why. Her grandmother had crocheted without looking for years.

"Well, I don't think Ray would want to tangle with Jackie for no reason."

Gram had a good point. There were easier ways to get her. Of course, Ray couldn't have known what was in the safe. It would have seemed easy enough—a little prank maybe—to break in and take the trophies. Stealing from the safe would make it look legitimate. Andi wanted Ray to be guilty, too.

That might be a problem, something that clouded her judgment. Darn it.

"What else did you talk about?"

This was dangerous territory. Andi usually glossed over anything that might cause her grandmother pain or worry.

"Oh, you know, the usual. A little bit about growing up in Tall Pines, the FBI, what I'd do if I weren't sheriff. He had some good insight there, too."

This was something else she was going to have to come to terms with. Acting as if her father didn't exist or pretending she hadn't been hurt when he left or after her mother died—or even when people said unkind things about her—didn't work. And escape was starting to seem more and more unlikely. Gram was here. Tammy was here. She had a good job. It was a beautiful place. And then there was Mark. Maybe. Andi had a lot of incentives to stay in Tall Pines.

Andi shook her head. "I really hope I didn't say too much. Maybe the amount of baggage I have is more than he'd like to carry. Or maybe he got exactly the information he was looking for, and we'll see it on the front page next week." Her stomach clenched at the thought of how easily he'd talked her out of her reserve. He'd been a good sounding board. Was he going to make her pay for her honesty and vulnerability?

Gram watched her closely. "Was what you said true?"

Andi bit her tongue and stifled the urge

to get into what "true" meant again. What she'd said had been both factually correct and true. "Yes, but that doesn't mean it needs to be said. And even if I might say it to you, I don't want it in print for the whole town." If Gram knew how she felt about staying here and what she wanted, their arguments would start up again, but if it went out in the paper, Andi would lose this election.

Gram patted her hand. "Andi, honey, think about Mark, not Ray and what he'd do to win. Do you really think you're just another story?"

Andi took a deep breath. She thought about the look in his eyes when he was frozen on her front porch. And the warmth in his voice when he said she deserved to be happy. And the comfort in having his hand wrapped around hers.

As her heartbeat slowed, she said, "Thanks, Gram."

Gram completed the round she was working on then changed yarn colors. Very little seemed to rattle her. Except maybe being late for church.

"How do you do it, Gram?" Andi asked.

"How do you stay here in Tall Pines after all that's happened? Doesn't it bother you?"

Gram peered over her glasses. "Honestly, Andi?" She shook her head. "The only thing that really bothers me is that it bothers you."

She rubbed her right hand with her left before flexing her fingers. "I had a hard time when John left town. I still don't really understand how he could desert his family like that…

"But the truth is that I couldn't make decisions for him. You couldn't either. He did what he did on his own. I hate that he left and that he's the kind of man who could abandon his family for his own selfish gain—mainly because of what it did to you and your mama. Money only gets a person so far. You needed your daddy."

Gram picked up her crochet hook. "They were his decisions. Not yours. And they had absolutely nothing to do with you, who you are or how lovable you are. Never doubt that."

Andi swallowed and forced herself to ask the question she was afraid of. "Gram, did you think I'd abandoned you? I mean, I hardly ever came home. Not until it was almost too late. What if I'm just like him?" *What if Edna had been right?* Her accusation had stung, but it was hard to ignore the similarities between her father's escape and her own.

Gram frowned. "Girl, you know better. Of course I don't think that. You were living your life."

Andi twisted a loose thread on the throw pillow. She couldn't look at Gram. She could feel the burn of impending tears in her eyes, but she willed them away. "But I could have—"

"And you would have. If I'd called and said I needed you to come home because I had a paper cut, what would you have done?"

Andi shook her head. "You already know. I would've come right away and given you lots and lots of grief."

Gram snorted. "Yeah, you're pretty good at harassment when you want to be." She patted Andi's leg. "You came when I needed you. You will always come when I need you. Because you understand that's what families do."

Andi put her hand over Gram's. "Because I love you, Gram."

"And I love you, whether you're down the road or hundreds of miles away." She smoothed out the dishcloth and admired her work. "But if you'd stopped carrying too much guilt over things you can't change, or if you didn't ask so much of yourself, these last two years would have been completely different. You're good at your job. You're a good person. But you care too much what other people think. You were going to apologize to Rose at lunch, weren't you?"

Andi shrugged. "It's a reflex. I almost had to bite my tongue off to keep the words inside, but I think I realized then that the only person I need to worry about pleasing is you, Gram. I'll never be able to make everyone else happy, so I need to concentrate on the most important person. As long as you're happy, who cares what everyone else thinks?"

Gram shook her head mournfully. "For such a smart girl, Andi, you surprise me sometimes."

Andi had no idea what she was talking about, and she had a pretty good feeling it showed on her face.

Gram tapped Andi on the arm with her

crochet hook. “I’m not the most important one. You are. You’re the person you need to please. And if that means heading back to Atlanta, you need to go. If that means calling Mark Taylor and demanding a second date, then you better do it. That’d be *my* choice. The clock’s ticking, Andi.”

She picked up the yarn again. “You asked me how I stay here. The truth is that I have a lot of family in Tall Pines. If you go back to Atlanta, Tammy’s still here. So is Margaret. And Mona. Edna and Rose. And we’re family whether we’re fighting like cats and dogs or giggling over cards. Always will be. So stop worrying about me and figure out what you want.”

Andi wasn’t surprised at her grandmother’s words. She’d heard parts of this speech in the early days when they were still fighting over Shady Pines and where Andi should live. And she knew Gram was right. She had a family here in Tall Pines who would take care of her. It was that kind of place. Everybody knew everybody and interfered way too much in their business but that was the way family worked best, when it was close.

Andi was too tired to figure it all out right then. She rested her head against the back of the couch and closed her eyes. As she lay there, she remembered so many Saturday afternoons spent at her grandmother's house, doing the same while she listened to her grandparents talk and laugh and argue. How nice it had been to know she was safe with them, and because things never seemed to change, she'd thought they never would. Change had always surprised her. She didn't know what it was like to make a decision that forced a change.

Maybe now was the time to try.

"Gram, do you think it's too late to make a change?"

Her grandmother snorted. "Andi, I don't even know who or what you're talking about, but the answer is no. It's never too late." Andi twisted her head to see that her grandmother was very serious and a little annoyed at the question.

"Look at me. I moved here to Shady Pines, something I once said was the same as giving up, and I've never regretted it for a minute. Card games, lunch with my friends, shopping and so little housework I can't even remember how to turn on the vacuum cleaner. I made a decision, made a change, and am happier for it." She looked over her glasses. "Does this have anything to do with the newspaper editor?"

"Maybe a little, but it's just…I feel stuck. And I don't think it's all about Tall Pines. I might feel the same in Atlanta."

Gram went back to crocheting. "The thing about change is it's scary. It's always scary, whether you make the decision or it happens to you. But that's when things get interesting."

Andi looked up at the ceiling. "I wish I knew what Mark was thinking. Are we working or is it…"

"Maybe forget about him and figure out what you're thinking. Is it work or is it more?"

"I'd know the answer to that if he'd kissed me, Gram. Think that means anything?" Even the thought that she might want something more made her heart pound. It was the old familiar feeling of anxiety that had accompanied most of the changes she'd been through, but the zing of restless anticipation was new.

Gram laughed. “Give it some time. When your grandpa dropped me off at the door after our first date, he shook my hand, and even that looked like it was done against his better judgment. It took him a while to build up steam but once he had it, he never lost it.”

“Sheesh, Gram.” It was an old routine of theirs. Andi pretended to be embarrassed and Gram pretended to care. Andi pulled her cell phone out of her purse. She had forgotten the text in the excitement of tuna casserole and chocolate cake.

First Andi turned the ringer back on and touched the message icon. The text she'd been trying to read all morning was from Mark.

Good morning, beautiful sheriff. I hope you slept well. When can we go out again? Lunch plans?

And Andi regretted her near panic attack. But she was happy. And sorry she'd overslept, missed his message and his offer.

She texted back. Sorry. Just read your

message. Overslept and had to rush to get Gram to church. Lunch: Shady Pines tuna casserole. You? She couldn't resist typing another message. Have a flash of crime-solving inspiration overnight?

Gram was watching Andi closely. After a quick glance at her tapping foot, her grandmother asked, "Did he send you an email?"

Andi nodded. "A text. He wanted to go for lunch, so I answered that I missed it because I was late for church." She clutched the phone to her chest. "He called me 'beautiful sheriff.'" Of course he did. He was a dyed-in-the-wool flirt.

Gram's brow wrinkled before she shrugged. "Well, it's not a bad thing but you'd expect something better from a writer, wouldn't you?"

It was perfect. She was beginning to think Mark Taylor would always say the right thing to her. Andi straightened up. "But look, he spelled out all the words!"

Andi hated text abbreviations. She hoped he did, too. When her phone dinged again, Andi shushed Gram as if she couldn't read while her grandmother spoke.

His answer: Sorry I missed that. Hate tuna casserole but would've liked to eat with Gram. Can't do dinner, Mom's here. Catch you tomorrow?

When Andi read his answer, she was disappointed. There was no other word for it. And then she felt like an idiot. It was one date. One *working* date.

Andi texted back: Yes, definitely. I'll drop by tomorrow night to talk Jackie's case? Strictly OFF THE RECORD. Andi hit Send before she could talk herself out of it.

"Well, what did he say?" Gram asked.

"He can't go to dinner because his mother's in town." Andi looked up as her phone beeped again. "So I'll see him tomorrow, find out if he has any new leads, and it'll be good." She smiled nonchalantly. Or tried to.

His answering text was one word: And?

Andi didn't know how to pass along rolling eyes in a text so she sent back, And what? Andi could picture his smirk when he got her message.

And you'll miss me until then, right? Andi snorted. Gram raised her eyebrows, but Andi didn't explain. She texted back, Not nearly as much as you'll miss me.

She dropped the phone on the couch cushion, satisfied that she'd gotten the last word in. When it beeped again, Andi shook her head. She liked that he texted. She liked that he spelled out words fully instead of relying on stupid strings of consonants. But he might be too smart. She'd probably never get the last word in.

When she read his answer, Andi decided she didn't care so much this time.

I'm afraid you may be absolutely right.

Andi had to wrap her arms tightly around her abdomen to contain the laugh of joy that wanted to escape. He missed her. He made her smile. And she had a sinking feeling that she was in serious, serious trouble with him. Her heart was in danger and that was one thing she never messed around with.

CHAPTER TEN

On Monday morning, Lori greeted Andi with her customary shark-toothed smile. Andi much preferred Nettie's "Good morning, Sheriff, hon" but she'd started taking Mondays off to join the gang over at Shady Pines for a game of…whatever it was they played. Gram was pretty vague when Andi asked so she took that to mean it was a game of high-stakes something or other, and it was better the sheriff knew nothing about it.

Andi kept expecting Nettie, Edna and Miss Margaret to move into units over at Shady Pines. At that point, they'd have to change the name to The Sorority House because shenanigans would ensue. There'd probably be brawls in the street, too, so Andi didn't encourage Nettie to consider it.

Andi filled a mug with coffee and leaned against the counter to try making civil small talk with Lori. “Mornin’, Lori. Have a good weekend?”

Lori blew a big pink bubble and let it pop before she answered. “Not quite as good as yours, as I hear it.” She tilted her head forward as if she were ready to hear Andi’s spilled beans at any time. Andi smiled. It was a fake one and Lori could probably tell, but that was all she was getting.

Finally, Lori shrugged. “I guess it was fine. The kids stayed over at Daddy’s, and Ralph and I took a little trip, just the two of us, to shop and see a movie.” Ralph was her second husband, and he seemed interested in making Lori happy. They hadn’t been married for very long, but he’d lost his job at the hardware store right after the wedding. It was difficult to find good jobs in Tall Pines, so money had to be tight. An overnight trip must have seemed like a nice getaway. Andi didn’t know firsthand, but she imagined twin boys could be a handful.

Andi sipped her coffee and said, “That sounds like fun. Did you see anything good?”

Lori smiled, and this time it held a little more warmth. “We watched that new alien movie, the one with the guy from the soap opera?"

Andi had no idea who she was talking about, but she nodded.

"It was pretty good. Maybe you can get Mark to take you next weekend." The look on her face said she had her doubts that Mark would be taking Andi anywhere as nice as that movie theater. In fact, Lori clearly had no idea why Mark would take her anywhere, ever.

"I'm glad you had a good weekend. The kids enjoy time out at the farm?" Ray lived about ten miles outside of town and had some horses. The boys should have been overjoyed to run wild out there. Andi glanced over Lori's shoulder where two towheaded toddlers dressed as cowboys smiled from a Halloween photo.

Lori waved one hand. "They love it out there. When Ralph finds another job, we'll be able to do a little more traveling, but it doesn't fit the budget right now. I think Daddy loves it more than the boys do when they stay. He doesn't have enough to keep him busy."

There was no doubt in Andi's mind who Lori blamed for that.

Andi patted the counter. "I guess I better get to work."

She could feel Lori's pointy sharp glare right between her shoulder blades as she picked up the weekend reports and walked into her office. Andi spent a lot of time with whoever was working dispatch. She hated when that happened to mean she and Lori were alone. Andi could take her in head-on combat, but Lori had the look of someone who preferred guerilla tactics. To be fair, Andi might have formed that impression because of her father's preference for the ambush.

After a quick read through of reports that included the usual accidents, lost things, found things and conspiracy theories, Andi filed the paperwork and pulled up her report on the Country Kitchen. She made a few notes about all the conversations she'd had that weekend, then leaned back while her chair made an awful racket to contemplate the ceiling tiles.

She didn't see any way around it. She'd

have to talk to Ray Evans sooner or later, and Andi had a feeling she ought to make it sooner.

Doing her best not to exhale a lengthy, put-upon sigh, Andi picked up her tiny notebook and told Lori, "I'm going to head out to talk to your daddy this morning. I'll swing by the high school if I have time. Call me on the radio if you need me."

Lori was surprised and Andi knew she'd lost any advantage an unexpected visit would gain her, but she didn't figure he'd be storing the trophies on his front porch anyway. She drove around the courthouse square to make sure everything looked fine before she took the highway heading out of town.

Andi maintained a nice, lawful speed all the way and blessed the lack of trailers and RVs that normally slowed traffic. When she turned onto the dirt road that led to the little community Ray lived in, Andi slowed down. She managed to brake in time to narrowly avoid a deer darting across the road. After a long, hot summer, they were a hazard on every road at all times, and she should have been paying better attention. The only thing this week was missing was a phone call to the local wildlife officer. He owed her one or a thousand for the various creatures she'd run off in her time as sheriff, but she didn't want to listen to the grief she'd get if she hit Bambi. Thank goodness he'd moved fast.

When Andi turned onto the lane up to Ray's house, she could see him sitting on the porch waiting. He wasn't happy to see her. The cowboy hat riding low enough to cover his eyes, his crossed arms and his grim face told her he wasn't going to make this easy.

When she got out of the car and walked over to the porch, Ray said, "Sheriff, what brings you?"

That was the way with Ray. There was never a "good morning" or a polite "how are you?" because he wanted her to know exactly where she stood. Andi could see his influence on his daughter, and she sort of appreciated it. He didn't like Andi. That part was clear, and she didn't have to wonder why or how to fix it. With Ray, there was no need for that. Still, she was in the mood to make an effort today.

"Morning, Ray. I can see y'all are overrun with deer out this direction, too." She made a halfhearted gesture toward the dirt road, but the intense silence that greeted her first lob and his lack of any attempt at a return volley confirmed her suspicions that polite chatter was a waste of time.

She propped her hands on her hips and did her best not to stare too obviously at the dark, older-model pickup truck parked next to a dusty station wagon.

"I wanted to talk to you about Jackie's missing trophies and recipes."

He shrugged. "Well, this is something. Sheriff Hotshot come to ask for help just as we're getting ready to go back to the voters." He leaned forward and placed his elbows on his knees. "Can't handle it on your own? I was pretty sure *you* thought you knew *everything*."

Lots of people were good at hiding the truth. They could lie to a person's face and make him swallow every word and like it, but Ray had never been that sort of man. If she had to guess, he had no idea why she was standing in front of him to talk about Jackie's case. Her hopes plummeted.

Andi was still feeling the effects of mishandling Ray Evans. She did her best to never make the same mistakes twice, so this time she was going to try honey instead of vinegar.

"I've questioned Jackie's first group of suspects, but I can't find a real strong motive. I thought you—with all your experience with the troublemakers in this town—might be able to shed some light on who I should look to for general pranks involving the Country Kitchen."

Andi crossed her arms over her chest and leaned back against the porch railing. She waited to see if that was enough flattery to pay off. He was inspecting her face carefully.

Finally he nodded. "You know, Andi, I don't have the same training that you do. I didn't make it through the FBI academy and spend years working federal cases, but I do know this town." He straightened his shoulders and tilted his chin up, daring her to argue.

"I'm not stupid, either." He scratched the ears of an old hound dog that came around the corner of the house to stretch at his feet. "I think you're here because I might have stolen those things in order to make you look bad."

He snorted. "And I wish I'd thought of that. I might've tried it."

He patted the dog again and leaned back. "But I didn't. You and I both know I don't need dirty tricks to win this election. And I don't think you're looking for pranksters." He stood. "Now I've done my good deed for the day. I've helped the less fortunate. So if you don't have any more questions, I think you ought to be on your way chasing down the next lead. Good news is you won't have to do this much longer, hon. When I win, you'll be free to find something you're better at than bein' sheriff."

Andi didn't move from her spot on the railing. "The thing is, Ray, I only have your word. Why should I believe you? I know you want to win. And I don't think there's anybody in this town better suited to pull this off without a hitch. You have motive and means." Andi shrugged. "Did you have opportunity?"

She might have seen a gleam of respect in his eyes, but that had to be a trick of light. Andi wouldn't swear to it and he would have denied it if she'd asked, but Ray sat back down.

"Well, now, Andi, I wasn't sure you had it

in you, but I see you won't take no for an answer." He shook his head. "Maybe I should have hired you. Too bad you decided to show off that day. Seemed a little too much like your daddy."

Andi wrangled her eyebrows back to their normal position. They wanted to fly right off her forehead. She contented herself with a small smile and a nod. "And it's too bad you can't let it go. I think we'd have both been happier if you'd hired me, Ray."

Andi would have bet that she saw calculation in his eyes.

"What about now? If I promise to hire you, will you drop out of the race?"

Andi might believe he hadn't stolen Jackie's stuff, but she didn't trust Ray Evans to keep his word, not one bit. She pretended as well as she could. "I'll think about it, Ray."

He nodded once. "Hey, Martha, can you come out here a second?"

His wife appeared in the doorway, and Andi could see how much Lori resembled her mother. Martha walked out of the house with an apron tied around her waist and a dish towel in her hands. She also wore a smile, and

Andi wondered at it. A genuine smile from an Evans? Weird. Somehow Martha Evans had missed the "We All Hate Andi Jackson" memo posted on the refrigerator.

"Morning, Sheriff. Everything all right?"

"Yes, ma'am, everything's fine," Andi assured her.

"Sheriff Jackson needs me to account for my whereabouts on Wednesday night, Martha. Can you tell her where I was?"

She looked from him to Andi, and she had such an honest look of confusion Andi knew this was another dead end. "Well, we went to church and got home about eight. Then we worked on the bunk beds we got for the boys until after ten. Then we went to bed."

Andi wrote down a few useless notes. "And Thursday morning?"

She laughed once. "Well, we got up about our normal time, before six. I made breakfast…and what else, Sheriff?"

Andi smiled at Martha, who was her favorite Evans even if she had destroyed the only plausible lead Andi had. "That's good, Martha. Thanks."

Martha's smile didn't return quickly. "You

don't think Ray broke into the diner, do you? For what possible purpose?" She was confused, and Andi knew her hold on the one positive member of the Evans family was slipping away.

Ray snorted. "She thinks I mighta broken in and taken what I could find to cause her trouble during the election."

Martha looked thoughtful for a minute, then she nodded. She patted him on the shoulder. "I'd say she knows you pretty well then." Her smile was back when she turned to Andi. "But this time he didn't do it, Sheriff. I'll vouch for him. He mighta taken the trophies as a prank, but he wouldn't steal Jackie's money, not even to give you trouble."

She and Andi exchanged nods, and Martha escaped the porch. Ray's face was hard to read, but he finally said, "Good luck with the case, Andi."

"Thanks, Ray." Andi stepped off the porch and hurried to her car.

After another quick glance at the truck, Andi said, "Hey, Ray, I notice your truck's pretty clean. Were y'all using that last week to haul the bunk beds and drive in to church?"

He tilted his head and pulled off his cowboy hat. After a quick swipe of his brow, he pushed it back on and stood. "No, I loaned it to Lori last week. She had some car trouble and hers was in the shop. Ralph washed it for me before they picked up the boys this weekend."

Andi opened the door to the SUV. "All right. Thanks for your time. I do appreciate your help."

Ray held up a hand. "You wanna tell me why you're asking about the truck?"

Andi smiled, shook her head and slid into the driver's seat. She waved once as she backed down the lane. She had to get to the Fall Festival committee meeting at eleven. She'd already attended four other interminable meetings where every possible planning option was discussed—even though they would run everything just like they had for the past twelve years—but she couldn't miss it. She had to make sure enough people were in place for crowd control. It was the one weekend a year where the whole department worked and Andi called in all the reservists. When she reached the end of the lane, Andi considered asking Ray if he'd like to be involved but headed to town without stopping. Calling on Ray Evans wouldn't help her get reelected.

When she got back in the office, Andi checked her messages. She'd requested a few state police units to help with the crowds for Saturday's parade and the chili cook-off. Her normal crew could handle the increase in accidents and petty crime, but it made her feel like everyone was more secure to have the state police present along the route. A voice mail confirmed that four units would be in town on Saturday.

Andi also had a panicked message from Tammy regarding the debate. Since she was about to see her friend at the planning meeting, she deleted it. The last message was from her old boss in Atlanta. As always, Marcus Hightower was direct. "Call me back, Jackson." One voice mail, four words, and he was probably already annoyed at her delay. She'd have to call him later. She was late. After a disappointing check of her cell for any texts, she walked out.

"Hey, Lori, I'm headed over to city hall

for a Fall Festival meeting. Should be back around lunchtime."

Lori blew a bubble. That was about all Andi could hope for.

When she stepped onto the sidewalk, a cool breeze ruffled the bangs that refused to stay corralled in the official ponytail. Andi combed through them with her fingers as she crossed the street.

"Morning, beautiful sheriff." Mark handed her a cup of coffee. "I was waiting for you but you walked right on by."

Andi looked down at the cup in her hand and a stupid grin crossed her face. Apparently her frowning reflex had been replaced by a goofy smiling one. She wasn't sure that was an improvement. She also couldn't imagine not noticing him. Andi realized she'd been unconsciously looking for him ever since they said good-night on Saturday.

"Good morning. Headed to the planning meeting?" Andi wished she had something cute and clever to call him, but she couldn't get the words out of her mouth. Frustrated by the limits of her vocabulary, she took a long, satisfying drink of perfectly prepared coffee.

Of course, it didn't get any simpler than plain black coffee, but she was glad he knew her that well. Probably. She might have been terrified. But it was a beautiful day so she was going to go with glad.

Mark sipped his coffee. "Got to get all the details down so I can put them in this week's paper. I don't expect they'll be much different than last year's, but I can't imagine the fury that would rain down on me if I got them wrong."

Andi laughed. "Not even the full might of the sheriff's department could protect you from that."

"Aww, but you'd try? That's sweet. And a sign of real progress in our relationship."

Andi ducked her head, and he bumped her shoulder with his. He smiled. Andi tried to. He held out his hand, and she twisted her fingers together with his. And they went into city hall. Holding hands. She could pretty much stop trying to convince herself the whole thing was for show. At least on her part anyway.

Tammy was gesturing furiously at Andi when she walked in, and Mark and Andi both went to sit next to her. "Girl, don't you answer your phone anymore? I've been trying to get in touch with you."

Andi shrugged. "I was out at Ray Evans's this morning, and I just got back. What's the problem?"

"I think we've got everything arranged for the debate. We need to start preparing as soon as possible." Her eyes were anxious as she watched Andi for a reaction.

Andi didn't get the panic. She looked at Mark, and he shrugged so she said, "Okay."

And Tammy's eyes nearly bugged out of her head. "I just got all the details set and realized how little time we've got to get you ready."

She was whispering, but it was still loud enough to give Andi a sharp pain in her head. "It'll have to be enough."

Andi honestly didn't see the problem. She wasn't trying to be difficult. Sometimes Andi did try, especially when it came to Tammy's planning, but not this time. She needed to recover Jackie's trophies and papers, but the thought of dealing with this investigation for even a day longer than she absolutely had to filled her with despair.

Andi tried to smile reassuringly. “We’ll be fine. I’m comfortable speaking on the issues, and we’ve got everything lined up. We’ll be ready.”

During the meeting, Mark and Andi made notes about the times and places of the weekend’s events. And Andi was glad to escape the dreary wood-paneled conference room when it was all over. Good or bad, things changed very little in Tall Pines. The parade would start at noon. A deputy would lead the parade and the sheriff would end it. The chili cook-off would be judged at two and the winner announced before the music started at six. East Street would be blocked off for vendors from Friday evening through Sunday afternoon. And the parade route followed the same blocks of Main Street as it did every year. It was good nothing much had changed. Andi had a hard time concentrating on the conversation. She wanted to watch Mark write. And when she figured out that was the problem, Andi wanted to find a flat surface to beat her head against. She had it bad. Who knew what lunacy would overtake her if they actually went out again?

When they made it to the lawn outside city hall, Andi took a deep breath of air that had a slight fall feeling. Mark flapped his notebook and said, “The news never sleeps. I guess it’s back to work.” He smiled down at Andi and gave her a quick kiss on the lips. He met her surprised glance with a wink. In a low tone only she could hear, he said, “Sneak attack works every time. I’ll see you tonight, right?”

Andi swallowed and nodded. When he stepped back and waved at Tammy, Andi gulped for air and shot quick looks over both shoulders. There were plenty of people milling around but no one, with the obvious exception of Tammy, was paying them any attention. She was making obnoxious kissy faces. When Andi thought about how many times she’d restrained a snort when Tammy and Peter got too gross for public consumption, she killed Tammy with her eyes.

When she’d had enough, Tammy laughed. “Fine. I know you’ll be swamped this week with the festival, but I’m going to leave you a list of questions I think may come up. Next week we can talk about how to answer them all in a positive manner."

Andi held up her hands in surrender. "Okay. I'll be prepared."

Before she knew what was happening, Andi was wrapped in a Tammy hug, all squeezing arms and strawberry shampoo. Before she let go, Tammy said, "I'm happy for you! You guys are darn cute together."

"Don't get too excited. We're just working together and, you know, pretending." Weren't they? At least, he was. Wasn't he? Whether they were or not, that's what she wanted Tammy to believe. She smiled awkwardly, patted Tammy's back and stepped away. Awkward was apparently going to be her new normal.

Andi cleared her throat. "Uh, I better get back to work, Tammy. Drop the questions by."

She smiled at a disappointed-but-suspicious Tammy and turned on one heel to hurry away. It was going to be a crazy week. She needed to get everyone scheduled and to talk to the people at the city works department to make sure all the road blocks were planned and ready to go. The sheriff always kept a close eye on the vendors who rolled into town on Friday. If there was going to be any trouble, it was likely to start there. Tents and money were a dangerous mix. And there was still Jackie's case to consider. Before the Fall Festival overwhelmed her, Andi wanted to talk to the principal at the high school and the owner of the hardware store. The sad truth was she had nothing better to go on.

CHAPTER ELEVEN

ANDI KNOCKED ON the door to the newspaper office at ten minutes until eight. And Mark took a deep breath for the first time since he'd left her in front of the courthouse. He'd been sure she'd find some reason to skip this. She was too smart for her own good sometimes. The fact that she'd shown up...well, it should mean she was as anxious to see him as he was to see her. But it might mean she was at the end of her crime-solving rope. He'd been pacing in the shadows of the newsroom for at least twenty minutes, plotting his next move in case she stood him up. He'd been so certain she would, he'd run over to Purl's Place right before it closed to get her a gift. Then he'd have an excellent reason to track her down. He'd been glad to see that Tammy was absent. Nicole, a very nice eleventh-grader, had helped him pick out a skein. It was his newest ace in the battle to win over the sheriff.

Even before he opened the door he could tell it had been a long day for Andi. She looked tired. Really tired. The kind of exhausted he'd moved to Tall Pines to escape.

Mark opened the door and took her hand as she walked in. "Hey, beautiful sheriff, tough day?" The office was dark, as he liked it. It was peaceful to sit there, surrounded by his newspaper, and watch the quiet Main Street. She stopped him as he reached over to turn on the lights.

"No, dark is good," she muttered. "I'm certain I look like roadkill tonight. I am more tired than I ever was in Atlanta. Monitoring conversations of suspected terrorists and war criminals was so much easier than breaking up a fight between two cheerleaders." She twisted her arm to show him her elbow. "And I have girl slap bruises. Tears, hair, hair spray and flying elbows and not a single new lead to show for it."

Mark didn't say anything. He also didn't laugh.

"And Howard King, hardware-store owner, is on vacation. Yes, he and the wife are on a beach in Hawaii right now. The kid running the place either played dumb really well or is actually very dumb. And either way, he was no help. That means I have to talk to Jackie. Again." Her voice said very clearly that the idea was dismaying.

"Ray Evans was clearly not involved, even if he is the proud owner of one dark pickup truck. His lovely wife vouches for him. It's just been a long, disappointing day, you know?"

He eased his hands to her shoulders and guided her to a chair in front of the window with a perfect view of the deserted Main Street. "Sit. Relax. I have just the thing to improve your mood."

The newspaper offices were prime real estate, perched squarely in front of the courthouse on Main Street. From her seat, she could clearly see the Country Kitchen as well as the Smokehouse, Hair Port and her office. He knew that for a fact. He spent a whole lot of time in that very spot.

Mark held up a plate. "I have a piece of chocolate pie with your name on it and a nice cup of coffee. Want it?"

Andi held up both hands and made "gimme"

motions. She took the first bite and sighed with happiness. "Please don't tell me you can cook chocolate pie, too. That would be almost more than I could handle at this minute, right here, feeling like I do." Then she laughed.

He desperately wanted more details. Feeling like she did? What did that mean? Was she talking about just being tired? Maybe she'd missed him all day yesterday as much as he'd missed her. And if that was the case, they were both doomed.

And why wasn't he scared to death by the idea?

When she glanced at him, he shook his head and motioned up with his fork. "Nope, but my mom can."

She grimaced. "I'm sorry. Too wrapped up in my own junk. I should have asked about her visit. How's it going?"

He licked his fork and set it on his plate before he reached over to give her a mug of coffee. "Good. She's staying for the Fall Festival. She likes it here." When his eyes met hers, his lips twitched. He was pretty sure that she would understand that little admission was a source of both satisfaction and concern to him. He'd been happy with the way things were. Having his mother in town could be a big help or a big pain in the neck and was liable to be both at different times. Still, he loved her. Tall Pines was a great place. It was probably a match made in heaven.

"That's nice." She looked a little unsure about where to go from there. He could understand the dilemma. "Is she staying to see you win the chili cook-off?"

He laughed. "No, I decided not to enter. I was afraid that losing might actually kill Jackie if we don't track down his trophies before then." He took a sip of hot coffee before he added, "But my mom hasn't forgiven him yet, so she's entering and she's pretty sure she's going to win."

He took the chair beside Andi, scooted closer and pointed down the street. The lights in the Country Kitchen had just been turned off. A red convertible whipped to a stop on the street right in front of the door. "That looks like Wanda's car."

"She and Jackie have a little exchange going on," Mark said.

Andi's lips twitched as she watched Jackie

hand Wanda a pie pan. "Pie for money…a tale as old as time."

Mark whistled. "Maybe you haven't solved the case yet, but you are doing some investigating, aren't you? Wanda's secret, unrest over at the high school, travel plans of local business owners and a showdown with your nemesis. You've got to be getting closer."

Andi hummed and finished her pie with her eyes closed. She needed a kiss. Obviously.

His fork clinked on his plate as he set it on the windowsill.

Mark turned his hand over in hers and twisted their fingers together before he rested them on his thigh. "You'll figure it out."

Andi looked up to meet his eyes in the dark. "Thanks for the vote of confidence."

One corner of his mouth quirked up. "Well, *I* am on the case, too."

She smiled back and straightened in her seat. "You've been a big help, Mark. I don't suppose you have any more ideas for me. Now that I've completely cleared my list of suspects, I'll have to do some creative brainstorming tomorrow and I couldn't even stir up a breeze at this point."

He laughed and stood to pull her up out of the chair. “Here’s a thought…maybe it wasn’t Ray, but someone who wanted to help Ray.”

Andi pursed her lips. “So that moves the mayor to the top of the list. Lori would be second. Or maybe the other way around, but something to think about.” She rubbed her forehead. “You’re pretty good at this.”

The words and her tired smile were too much. He clenched his hands to keep from grabbing her and kissing her.

Andi headed to the door. Her face and her walk all said casual ease, but she froze in the doorway. Nonchalance had never really suited her.

And the time was right. He was done waiting. There was no better place or time in the world than this peaceful office after dark, when it felt as if they were the only people left in the world.

He leaned closer and then she asked, “Why didn’t you kiss me good-night?”

When he paused to look at her face in the light from the street, it seemed as if she was holding her breath.

Mark squeezed her hand and stepped closer.

There was a smile on his lips when he said, "How many times have you said '*working* date' to me? That seemed to be going a little too far to sell the story."

He could see doubt and dissatisfaction on her face. Teasing her, watching her frown in annoyance was fun, but maybe here, in the quiet, shadowy office, he should be completely honest. "But I wanted to, Andi. And if you don't leave quick, I'm going to right here. Now."

He held his breath and watched her analyze his answer. Before he could make good on his promise, Andi tilted her head up and touched her mouth to his tentatively. His free hand slid around her waist to pull her even closer, and he tilted his head to fit their mouths together in a sweet kiss of introduction. She fit his arms perfectly and he did his best to memorize her weight against him, the sweet heat of her mouth, and the way her hands gripped his shoulders. Finally he stepped back and loosened his hold.

Andi shook her head. "We're in so much trouble."

Mark bent and pressed another kiss on her

mouth. "We're going to stop calling them 'working' dates, right?"

Andi closed her eyes and took a deep breath. "We shouldn't be doing any dating at all."

An angry answer came quickly to mind but he'd negotiated with her before. He had just the right light, easy answer ready when she surprised him. "But I do need your help." She rolled her eyes. "I hate it, but you've had the best suggestions. And..." She reached up to smooth her hand down his arm and tangle her fingers with his, and Mark did his best not to either slump with relief or shout in victory. "I have no idea how we could ever work, with your history and mine, but...you make Tall Pines better." She closed her eyes for a second. "Or you make me better or you make me feel better here or...something. I don't want to give that up. Not yet."

"Maybe after you solve Jackie's case? Or even after you win the election?" Mark studied her face. They were important questions. "Or when you leave town for sure. Then you'll be okay with giving that up?"

"I think we're past that." She squeezed his

hand. “I think… The things you’ve said to me, they matter, Mark. So…that’s all I know.”

He tried to ignore the flash of satisfaction that surged through him at her words. He’d started this to improve communication with the sheriff. He hadn’t counted on how well they’d connect, but he was glad he wasn’t the only one getting in too deep.

He wrapped his arms around Andi and pulled her close until she rested against him. Instead of pushing him away, Andi put her head on his shoulder and Mark rubbed the tension in her back and massaged her neck until she melted against him, like once she’d let go of all the stress of the day, there wasn’t much left. Anything that might look like an iron backbone had disappeared along with the knife-edge creases in her pants and the starch in her collar. Andi was done. She let out a long, tired sigh, and Mark felt it all the way to his bones.

They stood there quietly for a minute, and he ran his hands up and down her back. He wasn’t sure if she actually fell asleep or just desperately wanted to. Her hands shifted on his back, a slow quest from the small of his back over his shoulder blades. And, if it was possible, she relaxed further into him. Her breath sent a tickle of shock down his neck and he shivered.

Easing back reluctantly, he asked, "Remember when I warned you about killing yourself for a job like this? That there'd always be more to do, more work waiting?" He pulled her closer. "I hate to see you wearing yourself out like this."

"It's the job. You understand that." Andi straightened, stepped back and pointed at the plates stacked in the window. "Um, you aren't going to leave those there, are you?"

Mark looked over at the small stack, then back at her. "What if I am? Is that against all the rules that keep the earth spinning upright on its axis?"

Andi frowned. "Of course not. I think it's a safety issue. You'll have broken dishes if you aren't careful and this is a place of business, so someone could get hurt and then you'll have a real problem on your hands, so…"

He stopped her lecture with another kiss. Her lips were warm, and he could feel the traces of her smile before he stepped back. "I'll pick them up, Sheriff. I solemnly swear."

Andi nodded.

"Should I pass along your compliments to the chef? My mother's upstairs even now, slaving away on her new and improved chili recipe."

"Oh, definitely." Andi swayed toward him before she straightened her shoulders and turned to the door. "I need to get home. Tomorrow's going to be another day like today."

Mark held up one hand. "Well, I bought you a present, but I understand perfectly if you'd rather wait until you can properly appreciate it."

Andi stepped closer and tilted her head. "A present? For me? Why?"

Mark laughed. "You seem to be getting a second wind."

Andi smiled and twisted her hands together in front of her.

"Close your eyes and hold out your hands."

Andi rushed to do both, then fidgeted while she waited. He dropped the skein in her hands and said, "Okay, open your eyes."

Andi looked down and stepped closer to

the window so she could read the label. "Sock yarn." The look on her face said she was impressed. Really. But not quite sure.

She smiled. "Self-striping yarn in tans. This is great. It'll blend right in with my uniform. What a great choice, Mark. Thank you. This is a great end for what started as a pretty rough day." The look on her face said she was trying to be happy with the color, and Mark wanted to laugh out loud at her transparency.

"I love it," she said. "Thank you for thinking of me." She kissed his cheek and gave the skein a squeeze.

He nodded. "Nicole said that one is all it would take to make a pair."

"When I win the election, I'll have some lucky socks."

One corner of his mouth lifted. "Yeah, but…that's not for you. Well, I mean, it is. But it's for you to make for me." He threaded his fingers through hers and walked her to the door. "I'm not scared of some silly knitting superstition. Make me a pair of socks. Let's dare the universe."

Andi froze for a minute and then laughed. "It sounds dire when you say it like that.

Can testing the universe or karma or whatever wait until after the election? I need to be well-rested for something as monumental as all that."

Mark squeezed her hand. "You bet, but I expect to see twelve wooden needles poking out of that yarn the next time I come over to visit Mojo." He muttered under his breath, "For someone who lectures about safety issues, I think you're missing a big one with all those needles."

Andi shook her head. "It's only four needles. They each have two pointy ends, that's all."

Mark raised an eyebrow. "Right. Well, you're the professional. I trust you not to poke your eye out."

Andi stepped slowly onto the sidewalk. "I guess this week is going to be nuts so..." Mark was happy she wanted to spend more time with him, maybe almost as much as he wanted more time with her. But it might do him some good to get a little distance, just to make sure he was comfortable with where this seemed to be headed so quickly.

He leaned a shoulder against the doorjamb.

"Probably so. If you have time, drop in and we'll go to lunch." Sad to let her go, he added, "And we'll text."

Andi waved her yarn skein. "Thanks for the help. And the pie. And the yarn."

He didn't move until she drove by the newspaper office.

After he wandered back inside and locked the door, Mark dodged his mother to set the safety-issue stack of dishes in the kitchen sink. If he forgot them and someone knocked them over and was injured, Andi would never let him live it down. The idea that someone could get hurt was hard to believe, but he didn't want to deal with "I told you so" for the rest of his life.

And as he realized he was thinking in terms of the rest of his life, he froze. He'd started this as a way to get the story and help the sheriff. That was it. Now he was missing her when she wasn't around, plotting how to kiss her next and imagining the long term.

Clearly he should never have answered Jackie's phone call that morning. He could have wasted some time out on the lake and avoided this…whatever it turned out to be. If she left tomorrow, he'd miss her. And if she didn't…he was afraid it would hurt even more when she did go.

His mother had the radio cranked, blasting country music and singing along at the top of her lungs, while she mixed her third pot of chili. She was taking this cook-off seriously.

As he tried to calm his breathing, he was thankful he had no neighbors.

With a slow turn of a knob, she lowered the heat under the pot so it could simmer. After a quick glance at his face, she also turned off the radio.

"Better? You look a little sick." His mother's warm brown eyes were beautiful. He hated that they were also sharp.

He rubbed his stomach and nodded. "Yeah. I'm fine."

His mother tilted her head. "Was it the pie? Did Andi like it?" She looked in the sink. "That's not what made you sick, is it?"

Mark shook his head and reached over to run hot water into the sink. He laughed as he started adding the rest of her discarded utensils to the soapy water. "Nah, nobody's sick. And yes, she loved the pie."

His mother crossed her arms over her chest and leaned against the counter to watch him wash dishes. “Then what’s the problem?”

He shrugged a shoulder as he worked through the stack of dishes, washing and rinsing them before putting them in the drainer. “No problem.”

“Right. Then why are you so pale? You look like you ran into a ghost downstairs.”

There was no way out of it. She would keep asking questions until he either told her the truth or ran to his bedroom and slammed the door. He was too old for slamming doors. Probably.

With a sigh, he turned off the water. He pulled the towel from behind her and dried his hands as he tried to figure out the least inflammatory way to say what he needed to say.

His mother snorted. “You realized she could be the one who might convince you to take another chance on women, dating, love and forever. Right?”

Even hearing his mother say it like that made it impossible to breathe easily. He couldn’t admit that he was farther down the road than his mother knew.

She patted him on the shoulder. “Good. It was bound to happen sooner or later. And I like her. She’d be good for you.”

He shook his head. “I’m not so sure.” When his mother raised an eyebrow, he said, “She’s too serious, she doesn’t trust me and she works too hard. It’s a little like looking the old me in the face sometimes because she never stops thinking, planning, working. And she wants out of here so badly she’s probably got flight schedules memorized.”

As she put away the cups, his mother asked, “What’s the worst that could happen, Mark? What are you afraid of?”

What a good question. And a scary one. He crossed his arms over his chest and forced himself to say, “My heart could be broken again. She could leave. Or worse, I could spend who knows how long with another woman who doesn’t trust me until she leaves *and* breaks my heart.” He nodded. “Yeah, that would be the worst. Or…maybe I’d give up this place that makes me happy to go where she’s happy, get caught up in the race, and mess everything up all over again. That might be the worst.” The fact that he couldn’t rule it out, even after dealing with the sleepless nights and bad memories, bothered him.

"Right. And what's the best that could happen?" his mother asked as she leaned a hip against the counter.

His stomach was a hard knot. "Everything that I've always wanted, the stuff I thought I'd lost, like a family and kids and just…loving someone, it could all come true."

His mother sniffed. "It's going to come true, Mark. If you let it. Maybe it's Andi. Maybe it's not, but you have to try."

That was easy for her to say. She wasn't the one taking the risk. "I've been pretty happy here, but investigating this case with her…it's been just the right thing for me." Mark folded the towel and threw it back on the counter. "Why did I have to pick one who's so hard to work with? She won't make anything easy."

His mother leaned forward. "Easy's boring. Always has been, always will be. Go for exciting. Besides, there's one thing I know about the sheriff. You won't have to worry about her sneaking away if things get too difficult. Or giving up easily on something she really wants."

Mark snorted but he wasn't so sure. She worked hard, didn't give up on her career, but he wasn't sure about people. She'd been happy enough to cross her hometown off the list. "You're probably right. She'd be more likely to strike a mortal wound."

His mother hugged him. "I like a woman who knows how to keep a man in line." When he frowned at her, she laughed. "I guess you better decide whether you like it, too. And if you do, just how much you'd be willing to gamble to make it work."

He scratched his head. "I don't think there's much deciding left to do."

His mother's smile was blinding. "Then maybe you bet on yourself, Mark." She wrapped her arms around his neck and hugged him tight once more. "You're a smart boy. You've already been down the road you're afraid of. You know you've changed. If you hadn't, we'd have killed each other three times by this point of my visit." She patted his shoulder. "This time do it differently. I have no doubt that you'll take your second chance and run with it, whether you do that here or somewhere else. You know what you want now. As long as you keep that in sight, it's going to work out."

Mark wanted to believe he'd learned from his mistakes, but following the story was exhilarating and seeing his words in print was satisfying. One thing was certain. Hiding was no way to test himself. He needed to go for what he wanted, take the bumps that came with failing and enjoy the ride.

His mother reached over to turn the radio back on but kept the volume low. "You know, when I move to Tall Pines, I think I could stay here for a while, just to make sure this town works for me."

"And where am I going to stay?" The apartment was three rooms: bathroom, bedroom, living room/kitchen combo. Two people would never be able to live here. Having his mother stay for two weeks was a test of his nerves and self-control.

She shrugged. "Oh, I don't know. We have a little time to figure that out."

He watched her for a minute, trying to understand what she was saying.

Finally, she patted him on the cheek. "When

the babies start to come, we're all probably going to need bigger spaces."

He started to ask "Whose babies?" but he hadn't lost all his wits. She was already planning on grandchildren. He was still trying to finagle a real date out of her earmarked baby mama. The one who sometimes looked at him like she expected him to disappoint her at any time. And the one who wanted to be anywhere but here, the place he'd quickly decided was his home.

The one whose kiss made him feel strong and alive and a little in love.

He laughed as his mother danced in front of the stove. One thing was for sure: the idea of babies hadn't sent him screaming from the tiny apartment. That had to mean something. Mark had a feeling it meant something big.

On Friday, Andi had just grumbled a good morning to Lori and dropped into her desk chair when she got a text from Mark. He'd been true to his word and they'd texted back and forth while she juggled the nightmare that was the Fall Festival. This would probably be the worst day yet, but Andi could still feel the stupid grin on her face when she read, Good morning, beautiful sheriff. Looks like you're on top of things. Any progress on the case?

Andi looked over the stacked-up reports, loose messages from the reservists who would be partnered with her full-time deputies, the blinking light on her phone and her email in-box, which contained thirty-seven emails that had come in overnight.

Finally, she texted back, Not much. It's all Fall Festival, all the time right now.

Andi halfheartedly clicked on the first email message while she picked up the phone to listen to her voice mail. Lori had responded to Andi's plans for Saturday's parade. Last year, Lori and Dan had ridden in the front to toss out candy and Nettie rode shotgun with Andi. This year, Andi had switched it up, and Lori would ride with her. She was going to make Lori like her if it killed her. Or maybe Lori. Lori's answer to this was one word: Fine.

The first voice mail was from Marcus Hightower. "All right, Jackson. Call me. I mean it. I have an empty desk. I want to fill it." She could see him sitting in his leather office chair in his spotless office in Atlanta. His frown would be impressive.

But she didn't have time today. Besides, she had no idea what to say.

When her phone dinged again, Andi picked it up to read Mark's answer. *Here, too. Mom's pretty hot and spicy. And so is her chili. She'll give J a run for his money.*

Before she could answer, another message came in. *You're doing a great job, beautiful sheriff. I hope you have an easy day. xMark*

Andi had wanted to put her head on her desk and cry before this, but now there were actual tears burning in her eyes. And this was when Lori knocked on the door.

"Hey, Sheriff..." She paused, probably wondering if Andi was getting ready to snap under the strain. "I wanted to let you know we've got the candy ready for the parade. Nettie and I'll split it up in the morning."

Andi nodded. "Thanks, Lori."

She turned to go but paused in the doorway. "Everything okay, Sheriff?"

"Yep," Andi said. "Just a couple more days, right?"

Lori smiled, blew a bubble and popped it before she disappeared. And Andi knew exactly how that piece of gum felt: stretched out and losing its flavor.

ANDI WAS SO BUSY on Saturday she didn't have time to catch her breath until she and Lori were riding in the parade. Lori was wearing her dispatch uniform and tossing handfuls of chocolate to kids along the parade route. Andi had wondered once if she'd ever seen a real smile on Lori's face, but today she had one. And when Lori saw her two boys standing on the sidelines with her husband, Ralph, she clapped and waved and generally acted like a person who loved the world. It was nice to see. Unusual but nice.

As Andi turned off the parade route, Lori leaned back against her seat with a happy sigh. "I've always loved riding in this parade." She looked over at Andi then quickly glanced out the side window. "When I rode with Daddy, I almost felt like a princess. I wish the boys had a chance to ride with their grandfather now that they could remember it, but…"

Andi was tired. Her brain function had shrunk down to survival mode, so she was able to focus on getting from one place to another in time to meet this obligation or that one. She hadn't figured out a tactful way to question Lori about the truck and where she'd been when someone broke into Jackie's. Under other circumstances, tact was pretty low on her list of concerns, but with an employee who probably had an Andi doll with pins in painful places, she didn't want to make things worse.

Andi parked the car next to one of the barricades around the courthouse, and they both got out and headed to the chili cook-off. Andi couldn't help but smile as Lori's boys squealed and tackled her legs. Andi might have trouble with the whole family, but the happiness of two identical little rascals was nice to see.

Mark wrapped an arm around her waist and gave her a quick peck on the lips before he gestured at the sophisticated woman next to him. Her smile seemed genuine and one small slice of Andi's tension slid away. "Beautiful sheriff, you remember my mother, right?"

Andi was embarrassed and pleased at the same time, but she held out her hand and greeted Mark's mother. "Of course, Mrs. Taylor, it's nice to see you again and under happier circumstances."

Mark's mother shot a look at Jackie, who was watching the whole conversation closely. "For now, but when I win this cook-off, you may have to prove my innocence." Clearly, Mark's mother held a grudge. Andi appreciated that in a woman.

Andi nodded over at Jackie. "Going to win again this year, Jackie?"

He snorted and made an ugly face. "You sure don't seem to be making much progress in finding the other trophies so I guess I'll have to replace them the hard way."

Andi gritted her teeth in what she hoped would appear to be a smile. "Well, I have a new lead that I'll look into after the festival. And for now, I'll wish you good luck."

Mark raised an eyebrow, and she nodded once before she was distracted by Ralph, who had entered the contest. Ralph had worked in one of the hardware stores in town, but maybe he loved to cook.

"Jackie, has Ralph ever entered the cook-off before?" If anyone would know, it was Jackie. He probably had a dartboard with every competitor's face.

He stirred and snorted again. "Naw, he doesn't stand a chance, either. I expect the newspaper man's mama is my only real competition."

Andi stepped back as the judges made their way down the line. She made silent bets on the winners. The judges stayed longer at Jackie's table, Mrs. Taylor's and Ralph's. Lori's boys were ecstatic when the judging was over. Andi heard one of them say, "Hey, Ralph, I bet you're going to get another trophy!"

Ralph shot a quick look around to make sure no one was nearby and shushed the boys. Mark tilted his head down then looked at Andi. She nodded once to show that she'd heard it then said to his mother, "Mrs. Taylor, could I get a sample of your chili? Mark says you've been working hard on it."

Jackie straightened and rounded his table. "Good idea, Sheriff. Me, too."

Mrs. Taylor smiled graciously. "Well, since *one* of you asked so nicely..." She handed them both small cups of chili, and Andi was amused to see the look of unease slide across Jackie's face as he took the first bite.

He narrowed one eye at Mark's mother. "Is that brown sugar?"

Mrs. Taylor just shrugged. Jackie sniffed. He turned sharply and said, "Now yours, Ralph. I want a taste."

Ralph shook his head. "No way. Can't be giving away the trade secret, now can I?" Andi watched his face go from a nice tan color to a bright red.

Lori patted his arm. "Oh, come on. We all want a taste."

Ralph looked around the crowd, which included Ray and his wife, Martha. He cleared his throat and started handing out samples, leaving Jackie last. While everyone murmured over how good the chili was and Lori beamed with pride over his accomplishment, Andi watched Jackie. The minute the second bite touched his lips, he jabbed one pointy finger and said, "My recipe. That's *my* recipe!" He whirled to advance on Andi. "Arrest him. He's using my recipe…and…" He whirled again. "You! You broke into my place! That recipe was locked up in the safe!"

Everyone froze. Ralph shook his head feebly. "You weren't supposed to taste it. I just…"

Andi glanced around the courthouse square. The crowds were clustered in front of the small stage, so they didn't have much in the way of an audience. But Jackie was just getting wound up.

Andi stepped between the two men. "All right. Here's what we're going to do. You're all going to go over to the office and wait in the conference room so I can sort this out. Now." Jackie opened his mouth to blast her with…Andi wasn't quite sure, but Mona stepped forward to put a hand on his arm and he settled. With an angry nod, he marched off.

"Ray, will you take Ralph and Lori over?" Andi tried to smile reassuringly at the twins while she waited for him to agree.

He clapped a hand on Ralph's shoulder. "Martha, you okay with the kids?"

Martha Evans blinked back tears and then clapped her hands. "You bet. We're going shopping!" With noisy celebration, the twins forgot the tension in the air and all three headed for the vendors.

"I'm going to grab Mr. Brown," Andi said. "Be right there." She propped her hands on her hips and watched Ralph and Ray head toward the sheriff's department.

"What can I do to help?" Mark asked. Andi was glad to see he didn't have his little notebook out. Obviously he knew better. His mother just looked shocked. Andi couldn't blame her.

"Nothing for now. I'll see you tonight when they announce the winners?"

He smiled and gave her a quick kiss. "I wouldn't miss it."

He pulled her against him and they stood like that for a long moment before Andi forced herself to talk to the high school principal who was also the head judge. After a heated exchange, she convinced him to withdraw Ralph's entry. As she headed back across the grass in front of the courtyard, she tried to convince herself that justice was all that mattered here. She'd done what she could to keep the cook-off fair, and now…she had to figure out what to do about Ralph.

CHAPTER TWELVE

RALPH PORTER HAD probably just handed Andi the election. The biggest case she'd had in months would be solved and the thorn in her side would be neutralized, maybe forever. She didn't understand why she didn't feel happier.

When she thought about the embarrassment they would all go through when this came out, Andi felt sick. Ray and Lori had made her life difficult, but Lori loved her father and he had been a good sheriff. He'd been hardheaded, too, but Andi might have a predisposition to that herself.

When Andi entered the sheriff's office, Brenda Lawrence was working dispatch. She greeted Andi with a smile.

"Hey, Brenda, we're going to use the conference room for a minute. Don't let anybody back until we're out, okay?"

She nodded once. "Sure thing, Sheriff." A strong gust of wind might knock her over, but

Brenda had served the office for more than twenty years. Andi had a lot of faith in her abilities. And her smiles were genuine, not grimaces with teeth like Lori's.

Andi turned to look at the pictures plastered over the wall next to the desk. Happy faces stared back at her. There were the boys in their Halloween costumes. Ray Evans holding two bundled newborns, one in each arm, in the hospital. Martha Evans smiling up from a pile of Christmas presents, two little boys wrapped in her arms. There was the first day of school and birthdays and swimming in the lake and a beautiful wedding photo of the whole family.

And when the news came out, because it would, Ray Evans and his family would probably be fine. There'd be some talk and laughter and that might never end, but she wasn't sure about Lori and Ralph. Lori was proud of her father. Instead of helping him, Ralph had seriously damaged Ray's position.

Andi squeezed into the conference room and shut the door behind her.

After she carefully sat down at the head

of the table, she wondered how to get this thing started.

Ray beat her to the punch. He had a stern look on his face as he turned to Lori, and Andi suddenly pitied his daughter. “What did you do with the trophies?”

Everyone in the room was silent for a beat. Then Lori turned to Ralph. He looked absolutely miserable.

Ralph rubbed his forehead so hard that his fingers left pink marks behind. He looked lost. “They’re out in the shed. Safe and sound.”

Andi sighed with relief. She’d been afraid he might have destroyed the evidence to cover up what he’d done. After all, why would anyone hold on to trophies? Andi was glad Ralph lacked the mind of a supervillain or even a good criminal. Of course, now he had some pretty juicy information, too. Andi wondered what his plans were for that.

He wiped his sweaty brow. “I took them. I broke into the safe. It seemed like…” He trailed off and wiped his forehead. “I wanted to get even with Jackie. Because of him, I lost my job at the store. We needed money, and

Lori deserves…so much. I figured I could take the money and get the trophies, a little middle finger for Jackie." He cleared his throat. "Thought it might help Ray, too."

Lori was devastated. There were tears in her eyes. Somehow, the idea that she might cry upset Andi more than Ralph's distress. She'd been a worthy adversary for a long time. She didn't deserve to be defeated in this way.

"So Lori didn't know anything about it? Or Ray?" Andi found it hard to believe but she wanted to.

He shook his head. "No, ma'am. I did it on my own, but the boys found the trophies last night when we were out there looking for rakes. I thought I'd hidden them well enough, but it's hard to keep Alexander and Andrew out of stuff."

"And you used Jackie's recipe for the chili you entered in the contest?" The whole world had stopped spinning while they waited for his answer.

Finally he swallowed. "Yes, ma'am." He glanced at a furious Jackie, who was only seated because Mona was leaning hard on his shoulder. "Just another way to show him up and take the prize money, too. With that money, Lori and I could…well, I just wanted to take her someplace nice. She deserves it."

Everybody at the table had a grasp on the danger of the situation. Lori gave out a little cry, and Ray made fists with both hands.

Jackie jabbed a finger across the table. "That recipe…that means you went through my private papers! All the rest of this stuff's just…" He trailed off but there was murder in his eyes.

Ralph raked a hand through his hair. "I didn't mean to. I didn't know what I had, Jackie. You have to believe me. Getting fired made me…just so angry. Still does when I think about what I can't give Lori or the boys but…if I'd known, I'd have left it all there. I've been trying to figure out a way to get it back to you, but I wanted to wait until after the election. Just in case." There was an apology in his eyes as he glanced from Mona to Andi.

Lori and Ray were confused. Mona was crying silently, and Jackie was slowly deflating. He wrapped a hand around Mona's and looked ten years older in a second.

"Ralph, what happened at the hardware store?" This was one of those times when Andi had to take a look at the context. Ralph was a man who loved his wife. There were two little boys in the mix, as well. She wanted to understand why he'd done what he did.

Ralph shrugged and started to answer but Jackie interrupted him. "King fired him because I threatened to sue. Ralph made a delivery to the diner and broke the glass in the trophy case. I wanted someone to pay for it."

Ralph held up both hands. "And I would have, but I never got a chance. We didn't have that much extra, but I could have paid it off eventually. Like I promised I would."

Jackie heaved a sigh. "Yeah, I went to talk to King, told him he better pay for it, but he wasn't prepared to do it. We argued to beat the band and I...well, he didn't agree with me." He glanced up at Mona before he said, "I didn't find out he'd fired you for a couple of weeks and then I told him...well, I told him I didn't care for your replacement. Kid's not bright. King wasn't going to let me win there, either. So…I'm sorry. I guess. But breaking in…"

"I know. It was really dumb. But at the time, it felt inspired. I just… I wanted to get some of my pride back. I wanted to make Lori proud and happy." Ralph leaned forward. "You gotta believe me, Jackie. That other stuff…the papers in the safe, I was going to give it back. And I've been real upset over the unhappiness I figured it was causing you and Mona but…"

Lori and Ray were both in the dark, but they were smart enough to keep their mouths shut.

Finally Andi said, "Okay, well, now we know what happened. What are we going to do about it?"

The black-and-white rule follower in her knew Ralph should get what he deserved for breaking the law. Did it matter that no one really got hurt? Or that he'd done it out of love for his wife? The answer should be no. She should arrest him and let the consequences fall out as they would.

Mona's voice was unsteady when she said, "No harm's been done. Let's all just…get back to normal. I want my things by the end of the day. Then we just…go on."

Jackie shook his head angrily but stopped when he met his wife's stare. They communicated quickly and silently and Jackie said, "That's not right. Gotta be some justice in the world, Mona." He turned to look at Andi. "But I don't think we need the law involved. Not anymore."

Andi wanted to clear out her ears. Jackie wasn't demanding his pound of flesh. Her surprise must have shown on her face.

Jackie looked at Andi and shrugged. "I guess I don't care for the way he went about it, but I can understand trying to keep the wife happy. And the situation with his job… it's been bothering me, so let's just…can't we move on?"

Ralph still looked miserable. He was shaking his head slowly, as if he wanted the answer to be yes but he couldn't quite say it. Lori looked hopeful. Andi sighed. "Well, I have a proposal to make. I *am* the sheriff. I like justice almost as much as Jackie."

Nobody looked happy, but everybody was focused on her.

"Jackie, I know this whole thing has been upsetting, but you're such an understanding man that I'm sure you want to save this family pain." Andi took a calming breath and swallowed back the laugh that desperately wanted out. She'd meant to butter him up, but she believed what she'd said, too. And she wouldn't have guessed that.

"Ralph is going to return everything in the morning when the diner opens." Andi waited for Ralph's nod. "And then he's going to put on an apron and help with whatever you need help with—cooking, cleaning, whatever—every day for a solid week."

Ralph nodded again at her prompting. Lori looked a little bit like her old self. There was a gleam of speculation in her eyes and a bit of color in her cheeks. Ray was an enigma wrapped in a riddle and covered in pure deadpan.

Jackie leaned forward and Andi could see the dollar signs in his eyes. "For free?"

Andi leaned forward, too. "For free. For a week. And then, if you think he's doing a good job, you're going to consider hiring him on."

Jackie stared at her as he processed the last of her words. They might not have tasted good when he got through, but he agreed. "Well, all right then. We'll see. Gonna move that darn override key someplace safe, though."

He shot evil looks around the table and stood to exit in a huff. Andi decided to push her luck. "And Jackie, one more thing. If you can, try not to talk about what's happened, okay?"

His mouth swung open and closed like a fish without a hook. Andi shrugged. "There's no harm done here and I'd hate for little Alexander and Andrew to deal with the talk forever. Right?"

Andi smiled at him. "Guess you'll have another secret or two to use when you need it most."

The calculating gleam was back when his eyes met hers. Andi thought she saw respect, too, but it might have been a trick of the light. And then he was stomping out through the office. Mona followed but she paused to hug Andi's neck and whisper, "Thank you."

When Andi looked around the table, both Ralph and Lori wore shaky smiles. Lori spoke for them both. "Thank you, Sheriff, for handling it this way."

"You owe Jackie your thanks. You must have caught him on a good day." Andi looked at Ralph. "He's tough but seems fair. Do a good job and maybe it'll turn into something."

He nodded. "I enjoyed making that pot of chili. Maybe that's a sign."

"All right," Ray said. "You better go rescue Martha from the boys." He motioned them out and they stood to leave. Lori surprised everyone by stopping to hug Andi. Andi awkwardly patted her on the back, and they waved as they left.

Ray rested his elbows on the table. "And now you have one of those secrets over me, too. I guess you'll want me to drop out of the race?"

Andi shook her head. "No, I didn't do this for any other reason than to help Lori and the boys. You've been no friend of mine, but I won't use dirty laundry to kick you out of the race." One corner of her mouth quirked up. "I've had an opponent who politicked that way and it got old fast."

He leaned back. "So you aren't going to say anything about this?"

"Nope." Andi shrugged. "I'll either win or I'll lose and that'll be that, but I'm not going to hurt your family just because I can. Secrets are next to impossible to keep, but let's give it a try."

He shook his head as if he couldn't believe how dumb she was.

Andi stood and opened the door. "I wish I'd handled myself differently when I came home. I understand why you didn't hire me on. But that doesn't mean I'm not going to try to win the election. I'll see you at the debate."

She spent the rest of the afternoon putting out fires, answering calls and generally running from one situation to the next. That evening, when Andi dropped down next to Mark in front of the stage, she was ready to cancel the Fall Festival forever. Mark wrapped his hand around the nape of her neck and squeezed the tired muscles there. "Did you get everything worked out?"

Andi gave a tired nod. "Yep, barely."

He looked thoughtful, but the emcee interrupted whatever he was about to say. When

Mark's mother won second place, everyone celebrated with high fives and a group hug, and when Jackie won first place, Andi sighed with relief. That was the missing piece.

When Mark took out his notebook, Andi's stomach churned. She wanted to beg him not to put Ralph's name in the paper. She wanted to call on whatever connection they had to make this story fade away. But it was a good story. The town would want to know. He needed to print it. Maybe. And she just…she wasn't sure what his answer would be. They hadn't known each other long. It should still be easy to choose the news over her feelings. And if she asked and he published it anyway, she wasn't sure she'd recover.

The smile slid off his face as he looked at her. "What's wrong?"

She pointed at the notebook. "I'm just worried about what…how you're going to report this story."

His face was serious as he watched her. The clamor of the Fall Festival disappeared as she waited for his reply. "I guess you'll have to trust me." He smiled, but it didn't quite reach his eyes. He didn't do anything else to pull back, but she could feel the distance between them. Andi stayed a bit to listen to the musicians but the long day caught up with her. Finally she said, "Good night, Mrs. Taylor, and congratulations again."

Andi kissed Mark quickly. "Gotta go. I'm on deck in the morning."

He stopped her scramble to stand with one hand and wrapped the other around her nape. His kiss was slow and meaningful. When he leaned back, Andi wanted to follow him. A sharp twang of feedback from the speakers snapped her out of her daze.

Andi was uneasy as she stood, like maybe something had shifted in their relationship. As she made her way through the crowd and back to her car, Andi tried not to think about how tired she was and how many different pieces of her body ached. She should be proud of herself for resolving Jackie's case so neatly, but mostly she wanted to go to bed. And she wondered about Mark, his response and what she should do about it. One thing was certain. All those questions would have to wait until the Fall Festival was over.

THE FESTIVAL started early on Sunday morning. Andi made a few quick trips around the various parking areas to make sure everything looked fine then got out to walk the vendors' area on foot. About lunchtime, her cell phone dinged with a text. Meet me near the Smokehouse. Let's do lunch. xMark

Andi glanced at her watch and the content crowd around her. She thought it might be worth a try so she headed that direction. It was an absolutely beautiful day, one that should be enjoyed to the fullest.

When she got to the Smokehouse, Andi found Mark with his mother and her grandmother.

"There she is, the beautiful sheriff," Mark said.

Gram's face lit up when she saw Andi. She kissed Gram on the cheek. Mrs. Taylor opened her arms for a hug, so Andi did what people do and returned it. And then she gave Mark a quick kiss and a small poke to the abdomen. He grabbed her hand and smiled. "Let's eat."

Once they were seated, Andi asked Gram about the church service. Nettie had picked her up and they'd managed to make it with time to spare. Gram mentioned how happy she was to join them for lunch, thanks to an invitation from Mark. She hated to miss all of the festival.

Andi looked at Mark and he shrugged innocently. And that was it. Andi was done for. He'd brought Gram to lunch as a surprise for both of them and Andi would now follow him almost anywhere.

She just had to decide whether that included Tall Pines *after* she lost the election.

Andi was so thankful that her input was not required for the lunch conversation. Mark and Andi were both quiet, and sometime right after everyone ordered, he clutched Andi's hand under the table. And Andi knew she was going to survive. The Fall Festival had been a challenge, but she was going to live. Andi hated to leave them but as the waitress cleared the plates away, her radio scratched out a call for an accident at one of the overflow parking lots near the edge of town. Andi was the closest and answered that she was on her way.

"Gram, you'll be okay?"

Gram rolled her eyes. "I'm in good hands."

"Yes, you are," Andi said. "Maybe I'll catch up with you guys later." She waved, leaned down and pecked Mark's lips. Then she whispered, "Thank you," and hustled for the door.

Andi meant to track them down, but by the time the festival stragglers left the courthouse square, she was dead on her feet. She poured herself behind the wheel of the SUV and headed for home. Before she got out to face Mojo's wrath for missing dinnertime, Andi pulled out her phone and texted Mark. *Made it home. Thanks for bringing Gram out. I miss you.* And she sent it before she could second-guess the last part.

His answer was quick. *Get some rest. I miss you, too. Mom's staying another week, just for the debate, but maybe dinner sometime? We need to talk.*

The last sentence immediately worried her, but she was too tired to think about it then. She answered, *Maybe, let's talk when I have both eyes open, possibly after a gallon of coffee.*

Andi swung the door open and was convincing herself to stand when her phone dinged. She smiled when she read his message.

Good idea. Good night, beautiful sheriff.

THAT SMILE WAS long gone when Andi made it into the office the next morning. She'd dodged the street crew all the way in. Picking up the litter and cleaning up the barricades and tents would take a few days, but by next weekend the town would probably be back to normal. It would definitely take longer for Andi to recover.

Lori's smile was smaller than normal, but it was a real smile.

"Good morning, Lori."

Lori nodded. "Sheriff. I made the coffee. Thought you might want some."

Andi forced herself to stop and pasted on a smile. "Thanks."

She went to the kitchen and filled the biggest mug she could find before she creaked into her office. Her desk was still covered in reports, but the phone wasn't blinking. Andi had only ten emails, and they were all positive comments. That was a new experience, so she leaned back to savor it and her first sip of the steaming hot coffee.

Lori peeked around the corner and waved an envelope at her. "Tammy left this for you." The phone rang and Lori dropped the envelope on Andi's desk before she ran to answer it.

That sinking feeling in the pit of her stomach was back. Andi opened the envelope and pulled out two pages of topics that could come up in the debate. Tammy and Jackie had gone to the same school for list making. Andi nearly sobbed aloud when her phone dinged.

Good morning, Andi. Doing okay so far?

Andi wanted to text back a loud wail. Instead she wrote, Fine, until I opened my list of possible debate topics, delivered before I even made it to work this morning.

Andi stared at the phone until his answer came back. I can't help much with that, wouldn't be ethical. Could rub your shoulders or your neck if that would help. The winky emoticon made Andi laugh. She hoped that was the idea.

Andi didn't think there was an emoticon to cover her feelings so she answered, *rolling eyes* Thanks. I'll let you know.

His answer was quick. You do that. Hope it's a good day.

Andi texted back, Thank you. You, too.

And then Andi put the phone back in her pocket, where it should have been all along.

She'd put off returning Marcus Hightower's phone call long enough and she'd run out of excuses. As she dialed and listened to the phone ring, she silently willed him to be in a meeting or on vacation or late to work or just anywhere except behind his desk.

"Hightower."

"Sir, it's Andi Jackson. Returning your phone call."

Marcus Hightower cleared his throat then said in a gruff voice, "About time, Jackson. I was beginning to think you were giving me the brush-off."

Andi didn't know what to say to that. While she frantically flipped through polite responses, he said, "Got an open desk. Are you ready to get back to work?"

The idea that he would contact her about a

job was…so nice. That morning she needed the ego boost. But she had no clue what the answer was. "Well, sir, as you know, I'm serving as sheriff now. And my grandmother… I'm not sure she's ready for me to—"

"Up for reelection, aren't you?" Hightower interrupted. "How's that going?"

Andi sighed. "About like you might expect. I could very well be ready for a new job in a month or so."

"Jackson, you get back here to Atlanta. We'll talk terms. You've got three weeks and then we're filling it. Understand?"

Andi fiddled with her pen and made a note on her calendar. Not that she'd need the reminder. "Yes, sir. Thank you for keeping me in mind. I'll be in touch."

"Three weeks, Jackson," he reiterated, and then he hung up.

A man of *very* few words.

Andi turned over her cell phone and thought about calling Gram to talk over the possibilities. She knew what Gram would say. Go. She almost texted Mark to beg him to meet her for lunch. Why she wanted his opinion, she had no idea. But if he said stay…that would be something to think about.

The reasons to go hadn't changed much. She'd been so good at her job. Every day she'd felt she was making a difference. She worked with people who might not really like her, but they respected her abilities. And she was free of her past in Atlanta. No one knew. And if they did, they wouldn't care.

She leaned back in her squeaky chair to stare at the ceiling. She could quit. She could go back just like everyone expected her to. And it would be easy. Here…she would always be her father's daughter. People would remember her mistakes for a long time. But there would also be Gram. And Tammy. And the deputies she worked with, even Jackie and Mona and Edna and people who were family. When she'd left, she hadn't understood that, but now that she was back and she was…different, she couldn't ignore that connection.

She could probably lay the blame for that at Mark's feet.

The truth of the matter was that she didn't have to make a decision yet. She picked up the phone and called Tammy. They made a date to meet at Purl's Place to talk debate answers. The positive yarn vibes might give her the strength she needed to make it through this week.

CHAPTER THIRTEEN

"SHERIFF, I THINK you need to see this."

Andi looked up to see Lori in the doorway, her eyes a red swollen mess and a folded newspaper in her hand. "Looks like your boyfriend got a good story after all." She tossed the paper in front of Andi and walked out.

Andi unfolded the paper and saw a picture of Jackie reunited with his trophies. She read the story quickly and saw that Mark had printed it all. Every fact was there in black and white. She felt the crushing weight of disappointment. Ralph's name and his motive were covered, but nothing about what was in Jackie's safe—other than an unspecified amount of cash—made it into the story.

She put one hand over her aching stomach and tried to catch her breath. Finally she stood up slowly and straightened her shoulders. Lori refused to meet her eyes when she stopped in front of the dispatcher's desk. "Lori, none of that information came from me. He must have gotten it from Jackie…or…I don't know, but I worked hard to try to…" Andi didn't know what to say. She looked at Lori's family pictures. "Listen to me. I know what the talk can do. And you and I, we've had some trouble, but I wouldn't do this."

Lori sniffed and wiped away a smudge of mascara. "I think I believe you, Sheriff. It's just with the election and your…relationship, it seemed…but I understand." Lori straightened her shoulders. "It's just a little talk. The news will be on everyone's lips for half a minute and then they'll be on to something else. What difference does that make anyway?"

Andi knew exactly what difference it made, but Lori had the right attitude so she smiled. Then she walked to the Country Kitchen.

She was happy to see the diner was empty except for Jackie. "How could you give him the information when I asked you not to?" There was no other way for Mark to have all the details. Jackie had broken his promise.

She didn't even want to pretend to make polite conversation. She was as mad as Jackie normally looked.

He dropped a towel onto the counter and said, "I didn't, Sheriff. I'm a man of my word."

The swinging door opened and Ralph walked out. "Sheriff, I talked to the paper guy."

Andi was shocked. "Why would you do that? I had it all worked out. Everything was under control. Jackie agreed. Why?"

Ralph rolled his shoulders. "I just couldn't… I didn't want to live with the secret."

"What about Lori? And the boys? Didn't you think about how this would affect them?" Andi's voice was getting louder. Even Jackie looked concerned.

"They didn't have anything to do with it. And if it's too much for her, I'll understand." Ralph shook his head. "Wouldn't blame her anyway. I did a stupid thing."

Ralph twisted the towel he was holding. "But I gave my word to Jackie and Miss Mona that I won't ever talk about what I mighta seen in the safe. Not even to Lori. That's a promise I won't break."

Andi believed him. She had no idea why. He was a thief, but maybe the same understanding that made Jackie ready to make amends had convinced Ralph to keep Mona and Jackie's secret.

"It takes a man to own up to his mistakes," Jackie said. "Why don't you go talk to your wife? A little explaining can sometimes go a long way." He spoke like a man who'd had plenty of opportunities to learn that lesson the hard way.

Ralph glanced at the clock. "Got two more hours today, Jackie."

Jackie waved a hand. "Get back before the dinner rush. Go now."

Ralph untied his apron and folded it on the counter. Then he said, "Sheriff, I appreciate everything you did." She believed him, but she was so disappointed in the way everything had turned out after all her investigating and her perfect solution.

Andi slid onto a stool, and Jackie poured a glass of tea in front of her. "Helluva thing. I'm not too sure about him, but I gotta respect wanting to tell the truth."

Andi snorted and picked up the glass. "Weren't you the one so determined to keep

Wanda's secret for leverage and to protect Mona's secret?"

Jackie propped his hands on his hips. "Ralph's admitted where he was wrong. I can, too."

Andi nearly strangled on the tea, but she coughed a few times and set the glass down.

He pointed a finger at her. "Don't go telling anybody."

Andi shook her head and stood up. She felt as if she'd run a marathon—every movement was hard work.

"Going to talk to the newspaper man?" Jackie asked. "I think he's sitting on my bench."

Andi looked out the window. Mark Taylor was waiting for her apparently.

"Sheriff, you should know…he came by to interview me and Ralph approached him, not the other way around. Taylor…he might have let it go after I said no comment. Impossible to know now, but…I thought you might need to hear that."

Jackie seemed concerned. Andi couldn't imagine how devastated she must look to have softened Jackie's heart, but she appreciated the effort.

When she stepped onto the sidewalk, Mark turned but he didn't smile. "On a scale of one to ten, how bad is it? Twenty?" Mark Taylor without a smile and good humor shining in his eyes was rare. He looked tired. And grimly determined.

Andi paced in front of him and tried to figure out what to say. Nothing would come. "Ralph told me he's your source."

Mark nodded.

"I guess I can't say anything to that." She waved her hand. She hated feeling helpless. And tired. And disappointed. "Oh, except I think you knew how I'd feel. I had it all worked out. Jackie was happy. Ralph was sorry and ready to make amends. But…now."

Mark leaned forward to brace his arms on his knees. "But now the story's out. Everyone knows it. And they know the truth. Not just the facts, but the whole truth. The whys and the hows—they're all out at once."

"And Lori's crying and Ralph thinks his wife is going to leave and doesn't blame her and there are two little boys who won't understand a thing about that. Ray Evans will be on the warpath, and all I wanted to do was…" She stopped and propped her hands on her hips while she tried to figure out what she really wanted to say.

"All you wanted was to make it all perfect again. For everyone. Ralph understands there will be consequences. Next week Jackie's going to do a follow-up story about the cook-off, what it means to have everything back and how Ralph's helping in the restaurant. There's the whole story. I mean, Andi, I understand you. I know what you want. You want perfection, mostly from yourself. You want everything tied up in neat bows, but not even Tall Pines is like that. It doesn't mean you haven't done a great job or that Ralph and Lori and their boys can't be happy now. The truth is out. Why talk about it anymore? Jackie's made it clear he's satisfied. Thanks to you, Ralph has a job and it's the perfect way to show the whole town who he is. I did my job. You did yours. Justice. Truth. They're tied together."

He meant every word. Andi shook her head. "But…you knew how I felt. You did something you knew would hurt me and you didn't even warn me. What am I supposed to think about that?"

Mark was serious as he stood and took her hands in his. "I didn't do it to hurt you. If you think I did it lightly, you're wrong. But it was the right thing. And if you think I'm going to be afraid to do the right thing because it ruffles feathers, even if they're yours, you don't know me. You wouldn't like me, either, if that's who I was."

Andi pulled her hands from his and looked up at him. He had a point but that didn't make her feel better. There was an ache in her chest, and she could feel the sting of unshed tears. She didn't want to walk away from him. "Maybe you're right. But I just don't know if I can trust you with me, if I can live with the threat of the front page hanging over my head."

"Andi, not one word of that story came from you." He shook his head with a bitter laugh. "I don't know if I can spend time with a woman who thinks I can't tell the difference between what's news and what isn't, what's really important and what isn't."

Andi licked her lips. “I guess, maybe…let’s just hold off on this discussion until after the election, okay? Maybe I just need…”

“Time.” Mark’s voice was hard. “Yeah, me, too.”

Andi nodded and walked back to the sheriff’s office.

WHEN THE NIGHT of the debate rolled around, Andi was too tired to be nervous. Losing had started to feel inevitable, so Andi began looking at other sheriff’s departments in neighboring counties and had even checked out the application procedure for the state police. She spent her time with Tammy or Gram drilling her on crime statistics, where they’d apply grant money in the upcoming year, her plans for improved community outreach, and the new domestic-violence education program she wanted to roll out.

And she did not text Mark. But she’d missed him desperately—missed his face, his smirk, his way of cutting through her reserve. She’d liked having him to bounce ideas off of or just listen. The more she thought about it, the clearer it was that even if she’d never made the decision to trust him, she'd done it anyway. Without a conscious thought. That said a lot about him and it scared her to death. She still wasn't sure what to do about him, about leaving Gram, about a job. It felt like the whole world was balanced on this election.

Just before she stepped up on the stage she heard her phone ding.

Good luck tonight, beautiful sheriff.

Andi looked up to see Mark behind the moderator's table. He smiled and she smiled back. The nervous butterflies in her stomach went wild, but she was nearly sure they had nothing to do with the debate.

With a sharp squeal of feedback from the microphone, Mayor Jones got the attention of the audience, a group of people seated in lawn chairs around the grass. Fall had arrived just in time and everyone was wearing fleece in the hometown colors. Andi was looking at a sea of crimson and black. She hoped that wasn't an omen.

"Ladies and gentlemen, if I can have your

attention, we'll get the debate started. We've allotted thirty minutes for this event and we plan to get the entertainment started right on time."

The crowd quieted down, and Mayor Jones hit Ray with the first question. He and Mark traded back and forth in the beginning, asking questions about statistics and revenue and plans to expand the department. Ray and Andi were a chorus of two. Their answers were nearly identical so she couldn't fault Ray's logic. Tall Pines was a comfortable town with little crime and not a whole lot of revenue to play with. The only improvements that could be made involved updated systems and new hires. Ray and Andi both wanted those things. Andi had no idea why people didn't bail except the musicians were already anxiously lined up along the stage.

"My final question is this." The mayor paused and waited for everyone to quiet down. "We know both of you. Tell us what makes you the best candidate. Ray, why don't you go first?"

Ray cleared his throat. "Well, now, I've got to say I've learned a lot from watching Sheriff Jackson. She's increased our involvement in the schools and in the community in ways I admire and plan to continue and improve. But the honest truth is that Sheriff Jackson has not been transparent with the citizens of Clinton County. I plan to change that. I'd like to believe Sheriff Jackson has other ideas that would benefit Tall Pines. My goal is that she will continue to serve as a part of my staff. She has done a sound job as sheriff. I think she has more to offer and hope she'll do so."

Andi looked over at Ray and he looked away. It was almost an apology, but he'd done it so well that he looked like the bigger man. She glanced at Mark, and he shrugged. She hadn't prepared for this.

"My qualifications and experience make me the best candidate." Andi glanced at her grandmother and added, "I grew up in Tall Pines. I know this town and you all know me. I want to serve here." She wanted their votes because she needed the job. That was the honest answer, but Andi was almost sure that wasn't the winning answer.

"Sheriff, Mr. Evans brought up a valid point. Would you care to address the sheriff's department's communications?" Mark leaned back in his chair and winked at her.

Andi looked out over the crowd. All the girls from the Hair Port were there and so were Miss Margaret and Edna. She could see both Amanda and Sarah from the Smokehouse and Fat John was seated in the crowd. So were all the deputies and Lori and her family. Tammy was there with Gram. And Andi decided she was done hiding. If she was going to stay in Tall Pines, they were supposed to be her family, too.

Finally, Andi took a deep breath. "Ray does bring up a good point about communication, although I don't believe the department was a great deal more transparent under his leadership." She glanced his direction and he tugged on his shirt collar. "The fact of the matter is that I am not sworn to transparency." Andi watched Edna's eyebrows shoot up. "I am not sworn to dispel speculation or to satisfy idle curiosity. I am sworn to protect. That is the first and highest goal of my job and it's the guide for all I do."

A few people in the crowd nodded and Andi felt stronger.

She laughed. “Even when you don’t seem to appreciate it, I try to keep the good of the whole county in mind. I’ve had a conversation with a very smart man about the difference between the facts and the truth and it all boils down to getting the whole story.” She glanced at Gram. “So here’s some truth. I may not be as transparent as you like because I spent a lot of time being the focus of the stories, the center of gossip when I had absolutely nothing to do with the cause and no way to fix it. My father left. He didn’t feel one single minute of the shock or scorn or pity or fascinated judgment my mother and I did. So I am sensitive to the effects of words, and I’ll always do my best to hold on to that. It makes me compassionate, and that’s a good thing to have whether you’re the victim of a crime or the victim of a loved one’s stupid decisions.”

Gram nodded and Andi took another breath. “And I’ve made my own mistakes. I was gone for too long, but I haven’t forgotten the importance of family. Tall Pines is where I need to be. And I’ll admit I’ve probably gone too far—communicating as little as possible through the newspaper and other sources. I was trying to protect myself instead of serving Tall Pines. And that's a mistake."

She looked at Mark but his face was hard to read. "I know everyone remembers the domestic-violence article I was quoted in when I first took office. And I said every one of those things that made you all so angry, but some of what I said didn't make it in. I talked about how the people of Tall Pines look out for their neighbors, care for them, do the right thing even when it's hard. Because we're family. I meant it then, but I understand it better now. I've done a good job. So has Ray Evans. I expect this to be a close election, but you're all going to have to judge me on my record."

And Andi was done. She wanted to drop the mic and walk off stage, but it was attached to the podium so she couldn't move until the whole thing was over. She had to stand up there and stare back at the crowd. Mayor Jones looked at his watch. "Thank you for coming out. We hope tonight will help you make your decision when you go to the polls."

They were whisked off and before Andi's feet touched the grass next to the stage, a fiddle was tuning up.

"You did so good up there." Tammy hugged Andi's neck, and it was impossible to tell what she really thought. Andi decided then that she wasn't going to second-guess what people said anymore. It only wore her out.

"I did, didn't I? And it feels good. Maybe it was enough." Andi shrugged and tried to still the shivers of nervous energy. She wished Mark would wrap his arm around her but he kept his distance. She really wouldn't blame him if he kept his distance permanently. He'd helped her, and she'd reacted like her old self instead of trusting what she knew about him. This time she would have done better to look at the plain black-and-white facts. Mark had printed the story, but he hadn't used their relationship against her.

Gram reached up to take her hand. "You look completely worn-out. Let's get out of here." It was a good suggestion. Andi glanced over her shoulder to see Mark and his mother walking in the direction of the newspaper office. The separation between them made her sad. She did her best not to cry as she helped Gram back to her unit.

"So, you haven't patched things up with

Mark yet?" Gram asked as she moved to her recliner.

Andi rubbed her face with her hands. She was so tired. "I'm not sure how to."

Gram snorted. "Well, you're going to have to forgive him. You did what you thought was right. He did, too. And that's a hard thing to hold against a man."

Andi was afraid she was right, and with every second she waited, it got harder to acknowledge. "I think I've already forgiven him, but asking him to forgive me for…not trusting him, that's harder somehow."

Maybe forgiveness had been her problem all along. And maybe she was the only one holding on to the past, letting it color every single day. Pulling back, shutting down communication with the people in town, that had been a mistake. Was she making another one with Mark?

"Well, now, that's a whole different question. You never have been very good at admitting you were wrong, have you?" Gram's face was serious, but Andi could see the spark in her eyes. Gram wasn't going to tell her what to do about Mark, but she had faith

Andi would figure it all out. Sometimes, Andi wouldn't mind a few step-by-step suggestions. "How about this? Edna was fairly well enraged when she read that story in the newspaper. She'd gotten a few tidbits here and there, but your man flat-out stole her thunder." Gram wrinkled her nose, and the twinkle in her eyes boosted Andi's spirits.

"Somehow that does make me feel better, Gram." Andi laughed as she bent to kiss her cheek. "I'll come by at the normal time in the morning?"

Gram patted her shoulder. "No, you're tired. Nettie's going to pick me up to go grocery shopping and then we'll head over to Purl's Place. Why don't you sleep in?"

Andi felt a twist in her chest at the change of routine. She was the one Gram relied on, but it was as if…she needed Andi's help less and less. She had so many friends, so much to do, that Andi was starting to feel less important.

Gram smiled up at her as she shooed her out. "Get on home. Call me tomorrow, okay?"

"Sure thing, Gram." Andi forced a smile and then carefully locked the door.

As she walked back to her SUV parked on Main Street, Andi couldn't figure out how she felt. She was relieved the debate was over. And in just a few days, she'd know whether she was unemployed. Ray's offer was out there, and she needed to get back to Marcus Hightower. And then there was Mark. She hated seeing him but not being with him. She paused in front of the newspaper office and was not really surprised when the door swung open and he stepped onto the sidewalk.

"Excellent investigative skills, Mr. Taylor." She pointed at the SUV, but then she had the stupid-hands syndrome again and crossed her arms tightly over her chest.

When he wrapped his arms around her, she sighed with relief.

"I wanted to congratulate you and…I don't know. Apologize?" Mark said, "But mostly I want to hold you. I've missed you."

When he didn't continue, Andi tilted her head up to look at him.

Mark's lips tightened before he said in a rush, "I don't know how far we can go if you can't trust me. I can't live like that, not again."

"It's not that I don't trust you."

Mark shook his head.

"Okay, maybe it is a little bit, but I am listening to you. I reread the story after Ralph told me he was the one who'd talked to you and I could see that...your story told the whole truth and not just the facts. I'm sorry I jumped to the wrong conclusion." She rested her head on his shoulder. That was the best she could do for now.

She shivered as a cool breeze moved between them.

"An apology? Is that what I'm hearing? I can hardly believe my ears." Mark kissed her temple and pulled her closer.

"I've just missed you so much. I picked up my phone to text you every twenty minutes." Andi sighed. "Thank you for not giving up. Popping up when I least expect it. Watching out the window for me. Whatever."

Mark rubbed his warm hands up and down her back and Andi took a deep breath. This was comfortable. This was what she'd been missing. She didn't want to move. Ever.

"Okay, but you need to know I can keep

promises. I might work too hard. I might find it impossible to let a puzzle go, but I can keep promises. And I swear I won't print anything I find out because of our relationship without your permission. I'm a man and I…need you to trust me, believe in me."

Andi understood where he was coming from. She didn't know how fast she could get to where he wanted her to be.

"But I understand it takes time. I wanted to… I guess I needed to let you know that it…" Mark broke off and snorted a laugh. "Ugh, it hurt my feelings, okay?"

Andi smiled up at him. "You're such a girl."

He pulled her closer and hugged her to his chest. "I know. I'm sensitive. You'll have to carry my heart with kid gloves or I'll cry."

"And I'll be sure to keep a clean hanky at all times." She looked away and then said in a rush, "Are we talking about your heart? Because I think we might be talking about… mine."

Mark kissed her sweetly. This time she could feel the smile on his lips but there was heat there, too. Standing there, on that sidewalk, on a breezy, cool October night, Andi was more content than she'd ever been. Mark sighed. "I'm afraid so. And it's scary. I wasn't planning on this."

Andi didn't say anything.

"Apparently I don't do slow. I just jump right into things."

Andi snorted. "Oh, really."

She could feel the vibration of his laugh as she rested her head on his shoulder. He squeezed her tighter. "But for both of us, you have to decide where you want to live your life. Win or lose, Ray's made it clear you have a job here. All you have to do now is decide Tall Pines is home."

When Andi forced herself to step back and slowly pull her hands away, she was glad to see he looked even unhappier to let her go. "You're right. But there's something I need to do before I can."

"Well, sure. We all have to cast our votes in the upcoming election, don't we?"

Andi tried to smile, but she was alarmed when the prickle of tears started again. By the look on his face, Mark was alarmed, too. "Don't cry. Win or lose, this election is just another day, you know?"

Andi sniffed. "Right. You're absolutely right. Win or lose, it's just a day. I still need to figure out if this place will ever fit me, if I can ever be who I am here."

Mark sighed. "Andi, you and I both know that being yourself…that's not something you've been great at here or away. But you need to find the place where you can. Ask yourself what's really important? What do you want more than anything?"

There were so many answers to that question. "I want to be happy. That's all."

Mark's eyebrows shot up. "Good answer, Sheriff. Mine's the same. What will make *you* happy? Will going back to Atlanta and helping to save the world do it?"

Andi frowned. "Shouldn't it?"

Mark sighed again, even more loudly. "What's so great about Atlanta, Andi?"

"Do you know what it's like to live where everyone knows your biggest heartbreaks? No, you don't. That's Tall Pines for me. My father, my mother…everyone here watched me live it. In Atlanta, I don't have to be that girl. I can be strong and smart and who I am today." She forced herself to meet his gaze.

He needed to understand. "In Atlanta, I can focus on working hard, making a difference. Here I have to spend too much time getting over the past."

Andi took a deep breath to push back the tears burning her eyes. "But now...I can also say how much I'd hate to leave Tall Pines. I'd miss my family, even Edna. And I can't even believe how much you've come to matter to me in a few weeks. I...appreciate everything you've done. And I'm sorry my head's all over the place. I think...I'm going back to Atlanta after the election, just to...see."

Mark's face was serious as he nodded. "I hope you'll make me the first or second person you call once you decide."

Andi turned to go but decided then and there that she was going to change, ask for more, get what she wanted. He reached out a hand when she turned back, and she stepped into his embrace. With her head on his shoulder again, she said, "You know, they have newspapers in Atlanta. Good ones. Probably."

Mark's arms tightened around her, and she could feel his sudden tension.

"You aren't…I mean, are you suggesting that even if you go back to Atlanta, maybe…"

Andi kissed his cheek. "I have no idea what I'm saying. I'm so tired right now I could be spouting complete nonsense, but there's… I don't want to say goodbye to you, so I just wondered if you'd ever…"

Mark leaned back to look at her.

She shrugged. "I'd be back with the FBI, and you'd be covering more than the elementary school field day. We could make such a difference. Together."

Mark stepped back. "I just pulled myself out of that rat race, Andi. I don't know if I can go back." He rubbed his forehead. "Besides, think about how much happiness we could have here. We have family and friends. I have a job I love and you could, too. Happiness, Andi. Remember what you said you wanted? Maybe…I think the best place to find that is here."

Andi was having a hard time catching her breath. If she went to Atlanta, she'd be on her own. But that was fine. She'd done it before. She could again.

Mark shook his head. "But…maybe I'll give Atlanta some thought, too."

"So you aren't saying no to me, then, just Atlanta."

Mark narrowed his eyes at her. "If you're in Atlanta, I'm not sure I can say no to either, but the job, my work, almost killed me, did kill my relationships."

Doing her best to ignore Mark's weary eyes and the way his smile had vanished, Andi kissed him softly and had to blink back tears.

She slid behind the wheel of her SUV and made the short drive home without looking back.

Two seconds after Mojo descended on his cat food as if he'd been on a diet for days, she fell into bed.

Andi didn't sleep the entire weekend away, but it was a close call. Nettie and Gram made it to church without her on Sunday, and she lazed on the couch with a remote in her hand. About four times every hour she picked up the phone to call Mark and ask him to come over, but each time she put it back down and forced herself to pick up her knitting needles. She'd cast on a spare set with the skein of yarn he'd given her. Maybe she could have a pair finished by Christmas. Maybe they'd still be together at Christmas. Or maybe he'd have something to remember her by.

CHAPTER FOURTEEN

ON THE NIGHT of the election, Mark, Tammy, Peter and Andi were in the family room at Shady Pines with Gram and about a million of her closest cronies. Andi was happy to see Gram teasing her friends, but she still felt like the outsider here. The television was on, and everyone chatted or laughed until election results flashed across the screen. Rose and her sister Edna whispered in the back corner, while Miss Margaret did her best to perform hostess duties with a tray of juice and cookies. Mark held her hand, but they didn't say much.

When her cell rang, Andi knew it had to be the results.

"Hello?"

"Sheriff Jackson, this is Elbert Brown. I'm calling with the results of the election. Ray Evans has won the race by a margin of nearly ten percent. I'd like to confirm these results.

Do you have any concerns over the election or the outcome?"

"No, Mr. Brown, I concede the race."

Andi had no idea what he said after that. She hung up and took a deep breath. And she didn't have to explain anything. Everyone had heard and their faces showed their discomfort. Everyone except Gram.

And all at once, Andi was free. It was the craziest feeling. She hadn't felt free since… the day before her father turned the whole world upside down. She'd been living with the weight of proving herself to Tall Pines since then, and it had taken a vote to convince her that she had all the approval she needed. Gram had a big smile on her face. Mark winked when Andi laughed out loud, and Tammy collapsed against the couch and said, "I'm glad this one's over."

Now she had to choose her own direction. She'd decide what sort of change she wanted to make. It was amazing to have that freedom. And scary.

Mark scooted off the couch to stand in front of Andi. "Congratulations, beautiful Andi, on losing the race. I'll be heading over to ask Ray Evans if he's got anything to say for tomorrow's paper." He squeezed her hand. "Did you want to make a statement?"

She needed to think about it. "I'll email you?"

He smiled. "Sure, but I need it fast. I'll be working late to get it to the printer tonight." Andi nodded and he waved at the rest of the election party and left.

Tammy and Peter hugged her and made a quick getaway. The room slowly emptied as a few people stopped to give Andi their condolences. Edna and Rose were the first out the door. Andi imagined their telephone lines would be glowing red like stove-top burners.

When everyone was gone, Gram sighed and patted Andi's hand. "Okay?"

She was. She had no idea what she'd do, but it was going to be okay. "Yes, ma'am. I'm going home to think about a gracious way to say 'thank you for not voting for me,' and tomorrow I'll pack for a quick trip to Atlanta."

Gram patted her hand again. "That's a solid plan."

Andi walked her grandmother to her unit and as soon as she rolled through the doorway, Gram turned and said, "Go on home and get some sleep. Don't forget to lock up."

Andi raised her eyebrow at that reminder and snorted. She kissed her grandmother's cheek and said, "Got it, Gram."

They were both smiling when she turned the lock on the knob, stepped out and pulled the door shut behind her. She walked over to the sheriff's SUV and slid behind the wheel to drive herself home.

When she made it in, Andi quieted Mojo's yowls with a nice bowl of premium cat food and went to sit in front of her computer. She was so tired, but she knew her mind would turn over and over until she wrote something. She opened her laptop and clicked to create a new message. She addressed it to Mark and filled in the subject line with Concession Speech, then she tapped her fingers against the desk. There was no point in doing anything but sticking with the high road.

Finally she wrote, I'd like to congratulate Ray Evans. The voters have chosen an honorable man who will serve the town and the county well.

She hit Send, and then on impulse entered

Mark's name in the web search. When she scanned the list of results, she saw that most of them were articles with the state paper. She clicked the first and read an in-depth report about corruption in the state capital. The next one was about voter fraud in the last presidential election. As she quickly opened and scanned each article, she saw stories on political races large and small, investigations of fraud and corruption, and a few cold-case mystery investigations. The second page of results turned up three awards for journalism, one from the state newspaper association and two from national committees.

Nobody accomplished this without a whole lot of work and care. And she could understand why he needed a change. Tall Pines meant a whole new life, his own chance to be happy instead of being the best. He was going to stay right here. She needed to find out if she was ready to do the same. She sent off another quick email to Marcus Hightower, requesting a meeting. It was time to make a decision and the only way to do that was to head back to Atlanta.

AFTER TWO DAYS of dodging Mark and accepting well-meaning condolences every time she stuck her head out of her office, Andi was glad to be back in Atlanta. She'd taken Marcus Hightower's first available appointment and booked an expensive direct flight. As soon as she'd dropped her bags in the standard room of a business-class hotel, she went out for her favorite Thai food and then fell into bed.

The next morning, she blamed the nagging feeling that nothing was quite as good as she remembered on her lingering travel anxiety. And she wished she'd had someone to share her pad Thai with.

Andi watched the cabdriver bang out a drum solo and decided she was ready to take on the day. She'd slept better than she thought she might. Andi had expected all her worries about Gram to plague her the minute her plane had taken off, but she'd left Gram at Purl's Place in Tammy's capable hands the day before.

She glanced out the window at the parking lot that was the freeway and realized she'd either forgotten or blocked out how bad the traffic was around Atlanta. Andi glanced at her phone to check the time and tried to calm her nerves. She still had plenty of time.

"First trip to Atlanta?" the driver asked.

"Oh, no, I lived here, but it's been a while since I've been back. Traffic's worse than I remembered, though."

The driver waved his hand. "No doubt, miss. Always count on that." He went back to tapping and inched toward their exit as Andi's phone rang.

"Morning, Gram."

"Miss FBI, I just wanted to wish you all the luck in the world with your interview."

"Thank you." She hadn't told Gram yet that she was pretty sure the job was hers. Gram would tell her to take it. And then…she'd have to face the fact that Gram had never been what was holding her in Tall Pines.

"Nettie's on her way and we're planning to fleece Rose and Edna out of all their spending money with a stiff game of Texas Hold 'Em, but I didn't want to miss the chance to say how proud I am of you."

Andi felt the sting of tears as she stared out the window. "Gram, you never really needed me at all, did you? I just… I guess I wanted to think you did."

Andi heard Gram laugh. "Oh, honey, I do need you, and if it made you happy to live five minutes away, I'd be so pleased, but more than I need visits, I need you to be happy. Your whole life that's all I wanted and it's the only thing you don't see. Forget about what other people think. Do what you want. You had a dream. You made it come true. Not everybody can say that. And you deserve it. So go ace that interview. Get that job. And we'll celebrate when you get back."

Andi watched the tall buildings pass as she tried to figure out how to ask her next question. "Gram, what if…" Her heart was pounding as if she were running a race. "What if my dream is different now?"

Gram didn't answer immediately. "Well, then, I'd say…go after your new dream. I mean, you've done it once. You can do it again and I'll help. So will Tammy. And Mark…" Gram sniffed. "Is this about Mark?"

Andi wasn't sure how to answer. "Yes and no."

Gram chuckled. "Gotta say, I love that answer, Miss FBI. Means he's important, but he isn't the only thing. And that's exactly how it should be."

Andi laughed. "Think he'd be as happy to hear it?"

"Well, now, I don't know. I'll ask him at dinner tonight."

The cab pulled up in front of the FBI field office, and Andi fumbled with her wallet to pull out cash while she clutched her phone in the other hand. She paid the driver with a smile and said, "Keep the change."

As she straightened her favorite pantsuit, she asked, "You're having dinner with Mark?"

"He asked right before I called you. And I said yes." Andi could picture the twinkle in Gram's eye. "The boy's darn persistent in a way I gotta admire, you know?"

Andi shook her head. She really did know.

"Do you have a message you'd like me to pass on?" Andi could hear the metallic clink of her grandmother's doorbell.

"Sounds like Nettie's there." Andi smoothed a loose strand of hair behind her ear. "Gram, I love you. I'll see you tomorrow. And just tell

Mark… I don't know. Maybe tell him why I'm such a good catch."

Gram laughed. "I will most certainly do that, Andrea Louise Jackson. I've got that speech memorized. Good luck now."

"Thanks, Gram." Andi ended the call and took three deep breaths as she stared at the doors. She'd spent a lot of time in this building. It shouldn't feel so…intimidating.

She straightened her shoulders, pasted on her best poker face and kept it firmly in place as she talked to the receptionist and made it through security.

Marcus Hightower himself met her at the elevator. "Jackson, I'm happy you finally made it." He held out his hand and she shook it. Then he turned sharply and led her back to his office. As they wended through the halls and desks, Andi noticed very few familiar faces and no one gave her more than a cursory glance. After a couple years of being under constant scrutiny, it was nice…until she realized she didn't know these people, they didn't know her and they probably never would.

When she'd started in Atlanta, the anonymity had been such a blessing. She didn't have to worry so much about missteps or even what people would say about her choices. But now that she was back, the building was cold and it wasn't just the stark furnishings and institutional-gray color scheme. She paused in front of her old desk. It was bare but set up like someone could pull the chair out, have a seat and get right to work. When she'd worked there, she hadn't added much to the space. Now the idea of sliding into that perfectly quiet desk chair and working the hours she had before felt more like…a job instead of a mission.

"Have a seat."

Andi perched on the edge of the leather chair opposite her former boss. She'd never been quite comfortable in his office. Or in his presence. He was the picture of a company man with his dark suits and ties, conservative haircut and stern face.

But he'd given her a chance. And she was certain he appreciated the work she did.

"Lost the election, did you? How soon can you start? I need somebody with your focus, drive."

Andi smoothed sweaty palms down her pants leg. "Sir, thank you for taking time out to meet with me. I wasn't sure what my plan was until I sat down in your chair."

He tapped one finger on his desk twice. That was his only reaction.

"But I think… I think the time I spent as sheriff showed me that—while I loved my work here—my home…it's in Tall Pines." She almost couldn't believe how easily the words rolled off her tongue or the feeling of rightness she got in the pit of her stomach.

"You had to come all the way here to make the decision?"

Andi nodded. "Yes, sir, and I do appreciate your time, but…until I came back, I couldn't really decide between the now Tall Pines and the now Atlanta. Before I went home, I thought Tall Pines would always stay the same, but it's changed so much. I needed to know if Atlanta had changed, too."

"Has it?"

Andi shook her head. "Not at all. But the way I feel about it…yes."

Marcus Hightower huffed out a breath. "So you're saying you've changed."

Andi smiled. “Yes, sir, I absolutely have.”

One corner of his mouth quirked up. “Nothing I can do to change your mind? New desk? Need help getting your husband a new job? Kids…” He frowned. “Do you have kids?” Then he shook his head as if he realized how ridiculous the question was.

And that was enough. The person who knew her best in Atlanta had just asked if she and her imaginary husband had kids. Andi stood and held out her hand. “No, sir, and I won’t waste any more of your time.”

He shook her hand. “Anything changes, you call me, Jackson.”

“Thank you, sir.” Instead of a poker face, Andi fought to contain a relieved smile as she left the building. When she slid into the cab, she thought about calling Gram or Mark or both of them, but she decided against it. She still had a little thinking to do.

“Where to?”

Andi had an early flight home but she could get a lot done with the rest of the day. “Lenox Square Mall.”

If she was headed back to Tall Pines, now

was a good time for some retail therapy and a nice restaurant meal or two. Andi leaned back against her seat and tried to figure out just what she was going to say to Mark.

She pulled out her phone to text him.

I heard you're stepping out with another woman tonight. Should I be worried?

She stared at the phone until he answered.

Heard you'd left town. Should I be worried?

So maybe this wasn't going to be as easy as she'd hoped.

Just doing a little shopping. I'll be home tomorrow. Lunch at Jackie's?

The cab was rolling to a stop when she saw his answer.

Meet you there at 1. But are you supposed to be shopping without Gram?

Andi smiled. No, and don't tell her! As soon as she hit Send, she wished she'd added…

I've missed you. Looking forward to lunch tomorrow. xMark

Mark had beaten her to it. Andi handed cash to the cabdriver and slid out before she answered.

Not as much as I've missed you. I hope you're ready to see a whole lot more of me.

She froze on the sidewalk while she waited for his answer.

When she read it, she laughed out loud.

Now THAT sounds promising. Get here. Try another skirt. Wear your hair down. I am so ready to see more of you.

She shook her head. Might as well go for it.

I'm on it, handsome newspaper editor. xAndi

For the first time in so long, Andi was happy. Not content. Or even just satisfied with her work, but hold-on-to-your-stomach-giggle-out-loud happy. She'd left Tall Pines a long time ago, desperate for her own escape. Now she couldn't wait to get home.

CHAPTER FIFTEEN

"GOOD AFTERNOON, beautiful sheriff."

When Andi walked over to her usual table, Mark Taylor was sitting in her spot—the one that allowed her to keep an eye out for the unexpected. Since she was a short-timer now with so much less to fear from surprise visits by the mayor or Ray Evans, she slid into the booth across from him.

"Hey, good afternoon—" she lowered her voice after a quick glance around the diner "—handsome newspaper editor."

Mark batted his eyelashes. "Now that is music to my ears." He dropped a folded paper in front of her as Jackie walked over with two glasses of sweet tea.

"Good to see you, Sheriff. Y'all want your usual?"

"Yeah, thanks, Jackie," Mark said.

Andi picked up the folded paper. She was too nervous to meet his stare so she scanned the front page. All the election results were listed as well as her concession speech and Ray's.

"Not so hot off the press," he said as she flipped it open. "Seems you were hard to track down. I mean, even before you hopped a plane and left the state." Andi looked up for a moment. He didn't seem angry exactly, but his face wasn't nearly as warm as she'd hoped. To buy time, she reread her concession speech. If she'd written any more, she might have stepped off the high road and down into the gutter. She hadn't been willing to do that to win the race. It made zero sense to do it now, even if she was tired of Ray and his inscrutable face.

Underneath her short speech was a longer note from Ray Evans. Andi studied his photo and decided he looked like a sheriff should. He didn't have to worry about the effect bangs would have on his ability to be taken seriously. Lucky dog.

"I'D LIKE TO thank you for voting me back into the sheriff's office. I've learned a great deal the last two years and I think I will do

a better job for it. Sheriff Jackson has done an outstanding job of keeping us all safe and has recently shown me personally the value of both fairness and grace. It is my hope that she will stay on as a deputy for the department, but I understand completely that a law officer of her experience and talents has many choices. I thank her for choosing to serve here and hope that she will continue to contribute her expertise to my office."

THE WHOLE RESTAURANT was watching her read Ray's note. She carefully folded the paper into as small a pile as she could make. When she looked at her hands, Andi noticed the ink smudges and held them up to show Mark.

The smile slid off her face at the look on his.

All he said was "Wow," but Andi whipped her head around to see if anyone had heard him say it. Most everyone was pretending to go about their business. Except for Jackie. He was snickering and shaking his head. Andi blushed and shoved the paper across the table.

She leaned forward. "Would you focus on something other than the awe-inspiring sight of newspaper ink, you weirdo?" She wet her hands on her sweaty glass and wiped the ink off on a napkin as Ralph slid two plates in front of them.

"Sheriff, Mark, I hope you enjoy your lunches." He stepped back. "Can I get you anything else for now?"

Ralph's trial service must have worked out. Mark smiled up at him. "Hey, Ralph, I'm going to bring my camera back and get a picture for next week's story, all right?"

Ralph smiled. "You bet. The boys are looking forward to seeing the paper next week."

"What kind of story?" Andi asked.

"Mark wants to write about what it's like to live and work in Tall Pines when you're a newcomer. Jackie gave us the okay to take a shot at the grill. And Lori…well, she smiled like she hasn't in a while when I mentioned it to her." He wiped his hands in his apron. "Sheriff, I know not everything worked out like you intended, but I owe you sincere thanks for getting me this job. Things are looking really good now."

"You're off to a great start, Ralph. Keep up the hard work." As Ralph walked away, Andi thought he seemed taller. She'd made a huge difference in his life with one inspired suggestion. Maybe Mark had been right all along. She could change Tall Pines for the better. When she turned around to face Mark, one corner of his mouth was tilted up. "So, Sheriff, tell me about this shopping trip."

Andi sipped her tea. "Well, it's like this. I went to try on my old life for size, but it didn't fit me anymore."

Mark nodded. "It had changed, huh?"

Andi shrugged a shoulder. "I think I changed. Atlanta seemed just as crowded and busy and full of good things and bad things all at once, but for some reason, it bothered me to think I could work there every day for years and still not know more than two or three of my coworkers. No one there can bring me my usual drink or sandwich. I can't run into the teacher who set me on the path to everything I've always wanted."

Mark reached for her hand. "But you can wear a short skirt without explaining yourself to the nosy ladies in the beauty shop. Or kiss a handsome newspaper editor on the street in front of everybody without causing a stir." He stroked his thumb across her knuckles and Andi felt the spark. "Those are pretty nice perks."

Andi turned her hand over and threaded her fingers through his. "Even better, I realized I can do all those things here. With a handsome man to hold my hand. And my grandmother to back down the critics. And my history and my skills and my experience and my plans to make this place better."

Mark groaned. "Losing the election didn't convince you to take it easy?"

Andi laughed. "Maybe a little, but I also have a list of things to talk to the new sheriff about. Grants I want to go after for new programs at the high school."

His forehead wrinkled as if he was imagining all that work. "But…you're going to do that as part of Ray Evans's department, right? You aren't about to take on the mayor or something? Because I'm not sure either of us is up for another election." He held up a finger. "Scratch that. I know I'm not."

Andi paused. "Mayor… I could be good as mayor." She hadn't even thought of that. She pictured Ray Evans's frown if she ran and won and decided maybe it was something to consider. Andi shrugged and took a bite out of her club. “Yes. Probably. I mean, yes to working for Ray, but it bugs me, you know? He didn’t even ask, really. And this public request is nice, I guess. People are going to think he’s a magnanimous winner when it took all this to make him see I could do a good job no matter where I lived for the past ten years. Why would I want to work for him?”

Mark put both elbows on the table. “Maybe you forget about what Ray Evans wants or what the people of Tall Pines think about it—” he smiled slowly “—and do what you want to do.”

Andi took a deep breath. She knew he was right. Part of her wanted to shove Ray’s offer/order in his face, but she knew the department would be fine without her so the only person that would hurt was her. And as far as Tall Pines went, she understood exactly what Mark had tried to tell her. It wasn’t a jail. She was free to come and go as she wished. It was home. There were people here who loved her and whom she loved.

While she went in circles on the hamster wheel of her mind, Oscar silently approached to refill her glass. Instead of disappearing when he was done, he cleared his throat. There might have been a smile on his face but it was hard to tell. "Sheriff, I voted for you."

And then he was gone. Andi choked on her sandwich and looked to Mark for help. He laughed. "I think that was Oscar's attempt at encouragement. Maybe he wants you to stay, too."

Andi rolled her eyes. That could very well be, but who would know that besides Oscar? Jackie clapped him on the back when he went around the counter.

Miss Margaret and Edna appeared beside the table without any advance warning, and Andi shot Mark a glare of doom. If she'd been in his seat, she'd have been ready. Instead, Andi had a fry hanging out of her mouth when Edna muttered, "We thought you did a good job, Andi. I hope you'll stay on. The county needs good officers." And then she spun on her heel and marched across the diner to slide into a booth.

Andi chewed and swallowed the fry as Miss Margaret patted her on the shoulder.

When she left, Andi looked back at Mark. He smiled. "I think you're going to have to figure out what to do quickly, Andi."

She fidgeted with the collar of the sweater she'd chosen to go with her short skirt. Which he hadn't even remarked on. "So, say I stay… I mean, I've been knitting away on the perfect Christmas gift, working to overcome the boy-friend curse, risking life and limb with too many double-pointed needles—" she licked her lips "—I wouldn't do that for just any-one."

Mark nodded thoughtfully. "I could always use another pair of socks."

Andi snorted. "You haven't even compli-mented my skirt, the one I bought for you in a very nice shop in Atlanta and wore at your request." Andi reached up to twirl her finger in her loose curls and blew out a sigh that ruffled her bangs.

Mark reached over to clutch her hands in his. Then he leaned forward and winked. "Maybe I was a little preoccupied with the results of your trip. And a little annoyed with how you took it. But now—" he squeezed her hands "—I will say I like the look. A lot."

Andi felt the blush heating her cheeks. "I'm sorry, Mark. I just wasn't sure what to say before I left, but I promise not to do that again. I'm not going to run away. I was really worried. Maybe you'd think I was too much trouble. Too wishy-washy. I get that, so no matter what, I'm coming home. I want to spend time with you but I understand if you...maybe don't."

Mark pursed his lips. "Well, let me ask you this...are you willing to give up sheriffing forever?"

Andi raised her eyebrows. "Forever? I mean, forever is a really long time."

Mark's lips twitched. "Sure, but you're going to have to ask yourself if you can live with being Sheriff Andi Taylor."

Andi groaned at the idea of sharing a name with television's favorite sheriff and then she realized what he was saying. Marriage. At some point. To him. And she wasn't sure what to say. Mark's eyes were warm when he sighed. "Just letting you know what's on my mind. I want to think about the future but only with you."

Andi answered him with a jerky nod and a tentative smile. Now it was safe to tell him what she really felt. "Maybe I love law enforcement and someday I'll probably love Tall Pines as much, but I'm always going to love you more. Besides, if I happen to be Andi Taylor and lose my mind and run for public office again, there's always mayor."

Mark groaned but squeezed her hand. She had nothing else to say so they finished their lunches.

"I don't want to move from this booth." Mark said, sighing, "but I need to get back to it."

Andi shook her head sadly. "The news never sleeps."

He tangled his fingers with hers to pull her over to the cash register. Jackie was perched on what had to be a very high stool, and he wore his usual frown, but he looked less angry and more pleased than anything. It was unnerving.

While Mark pulled out cash to cover the bill, Andi wandered over to stand in front of the trophy case. Jackie had given everything a nice polish so the shine was nearly blinding. He'd added a second lock to make sure everything stayed exactly where it was.

"Looks nice, doesn't it, Sheriff?"

Andi nodded. "I know you're glad to have everything back, Jackie." She pointed at the tallest and shiniest trophy that was front and center. "And a new one to boot."

He sniffed. "Yeah, the newspaperman's mama got close, but not close enough." He shot a narrow-eyed glance Mark's way. It looked like he was telling Mark not to get any funny ideas about entering next year. And from the look on Mark's face, Andi thought he might be doing just that. She was doubly glad the Fall Festival and cook-off were going to be another sheriff's problem. And the idea that it was Ray Evans who'd be navigating those choppy waters pleased her twice over.

Jackie handed over Mark's change and said, "Can't thank you enough for working things out, Sheriff. Your solution was inspired."

Andi wanted to ask Jackie to say it all over again. Mark was shaking his head, which gave her the idea that it would be poor form.

"You're welcome, Jackie. You'll need the

help. I hear Mrs. Taylor's moving to town. She'll be stiff competition next year." Jackie's face puckered as if he was choking on a lemon, and Andi smiled benevolently and followed Mark out to the sidewalk. Ray Evans was leaning against her SUV at the end of the block.

Andi turned back to Mark and heaved a put-upon sigh. "One public apology and sincere request is supposed to fix everything?"

Mark scratched his forehead but did not call her on the irony. Her single apology had been all it took to bring Ray around. Mark cleared his throat with what sounded like a laugh, and asked, "So what are you going to tell him?"

Andi shot Ray an evil glare over her shoulder before she flashed a small grin at Mark. "I'm going to take the job, but not for a while yet. He needs to sweat."

Andi could feel his lips twitch as he gave her a quick kiss there on the sidewalk in front of Ray Evans, Jackie and all the diners in the Country Kitchen, and whoever might be watching in the town of Tall Pines. They were right back where they'd started, but everything was different now and so much better.

When he leaned back, he said in a low voice, "You are a mean woman with evil tendencies." He held both of her hands firmly.

Andi smiled up at him. "And that's why you love me?"

He nodded. "And that's exactly why I love you."

* * * * *